THE INHERITANCE OF AMAYA MONTGOMERY

Geletta Shavers

Geletta Shavers

Copyright © 2024 by Geletta Shavers

All rights reserved. No portion of this book may be reproduced in any form without written permission from the publisher or author, except as permitted by U.S. copyright law.

The protagonist, Amaya, in this book is loosely based on the personality and quirks of the author, Geletta Shavers. The names, characters, events, business, and incidents in this book are fictitious or inspired by the author's imagination. None of the characters in this book is based on an actual person. Any resemblance to persons living or dead is entirely coincidental and unintentional.

www.gelettashavers.com

ISBN: 979-8-9907482-1-7 Paperback printing: July 2024

ISBN: 979-8-3347927-0-8   Hardback printing: July 2024

ISBN: 979-8-9907482-0-0 Audiobook: July 2024

LCCN 2024912944 (print)

Printed in the United States.

To all the readers who have taken the time to pick up my book, I want to express my heartfelt gratitude. Thank you for giving my story a chance.

I would also like to dedicate this novel to my three beautiful children, Raven, Diamond, and Anthony (A.J.)

My grandparents, Robert and Genevia Jackson, who raised me from the time I was an infant until I turned thirteen.

My biological mother, Carolyn Jackson, is the person who brought me into this world and instilled in me the value of independence.

My biological father, Phillip Guess Jr., whom I never had the opportunity to meet in person, still loved me dearly.

Judge Williams, the father who raised me, and Ozella Williams, the mother who chose me.

My sister, Princess Couch for her support.

In 2022, I had the pleasure of connecting with my paternal family, the Guess family, who warmly embraced me with love and acceptance, welcoming me into their fold.

Donyale Pulliam and Brooke Kersey have been my friends for over twenty years. They encouraged me to write a novel based on my life experiences. After much contemplation, I decided to write about the strained relationship I've had with my birth mother, as well as my struggles with anxiety, awkwardness, and the constant battle to feel like I fit in with others.

CONTENTS

Content Warnings	XI
The Beginning	XII
Aurora Illinois, 2019	
1. Amaya	1
Present day	
2. Quentin	12
3. The Surprise Guest	15
4. Josh	24
The account	
5. Amaya	31
6. Quentin	34
7. Bree	40
8. Mystery Man	43
9. The Therapy Session	46
10. Amaya	56
11. Amaya's Diary	59
12. Sandra	63

13.	Quentin Mike Amber	68
14.	The Guest House	74
15.	Amaya Jeff Kathy	83
16.	Quentin	86
17.	The Therapy Session	88
18.	Bree	93
19.	Amber	96
20.	Amaya The voices	98
21.	The Gala	102
22.	Amber	111
23.	Quentin	116
24.	The funeral	123
25.	Sandra	129
26.	Amber Drug Court	132
27.	Amaya	135
28.	Josh Elevations Nightclub	138
29.	Quentin Removing an Obstacle	142
30.	Sandra	146
31.	Josh	151
32.	Amaya Miami	154

33. Quentin	159
34. Amaya 　　Homecoming	161
35. Quentin	165
36. Amaya 　　The therapist	168
37. Josh	170
38. Amaya 　　The Hologram	173
39. Amaya 　　Sandra's Repast	177
40. Josh 　　Amaya's Thirtieth Birthday Celebration	181
41. Amaya	192
42. Quentin	197
43. Amaya	200
44. Josh	205
45. Amaya	209
46. Bree	211
47. Amaya 　　The Reckoning	213
48. Hospital Room 334	223
49. Amber	229
50. Bree	234
51. Amaya	237

52. Amber	239
53. Amaya	242
Additional Chapter	246
Acknowledgements	248
About the author Geletta Shavers, LCSW	250
Charities	252
Chapter	253
Chapter	254
Chapter	255
Chapter	256

CONTENT WARNINGS

This psychological thriller includes themes of domestic violence, gaslighting, child-related trauma, adult language, drug use, drug overdose, and violence.

THE BEGINNING
Aurora Illinois, 2019

The night sky hangs above like an oppressive cloak, its inky darkness suffocating any hint of light. Not a single star flickers, leaving the vast expanse above utterly motionless. His body shivering in the frigid weather, he makes his way down the lengthy path towards the back entrance of what he calls "The House of Constraints." Navigating through the shadows of the night feels like walking in a world devoid of light.

The sound of the hellish wind blowing through the trees, and the annoyance of the leaves whisking across his face, reassures him that tonight is the ideal time for a visit.

Upon reaching the wooden back door housed between two narrow, vertical windows, he peers through at his mother. He salivates, overcome with a sweet aroma, while watching her make her nightly hot cocoa and pull a sheet of warm chocolate chip cookies from the oven.

Entering with a casual demeanor, his mother turns around, clutching her imaginary pearls that would've gone well with her favorite purple bat-wing sleeve moo-moo.

"Whew, you scared me, son! Why not enter through the front door?" she asks, her voice filled with jitters and a hint of curiosity.

He doesn't answer.

"Come on over and have a seat at the table with me."

Miffed and detached, he ambles over and sits across from her.

"Mom, I know you overheard my conversation today with-"

"I did, son. How could such cruelty even cross your mind?" she interrupts.

"Cruelty?" He rubs his temples and exhales loudly. "I guess you would know cruelty. I am permanently damaged from growing up in this house."

"I just can't let you do this to Amaya. Help me understand the reason the two of you want to hurt her. I'm going to warn her," she says.

"Why were you lurking about and listening to my conversation earlier, anyway?" he asks.

"Well, it's a good thing that I did. Someone needs to save you from yourself."

He laughs sarcastically. "You have quite a sense of humor. I must say, you can stop trying to be a mother now. Too late. Growing up, you were never there for me, you were emotionally unavailable, and you let dad subject me to abuse and oppression."

"I'm having lunch with Amaya tomorrow, and if you don't abandon this insane plan of yours, I will tell her everything."

"I know. Why do you think I'm here?" he asks, pulling out a small gun from his right pocket and aiming it directly at her.

"What in the hell are you doing?" she shouts, abruptly jumping up from her chair.

"I'm doing what it takes to stop you from ruining everything." He growls loudly and nostrils flaring in rage.

"You wouldn't shoot your own mother!" she cries with tears trailing down her face. "Son, I have always loved you," she expresses, trying to diffuse the situation and calm him down. "Let's talk about this. I won't tell Amaya anything. Your secret is safe with me. I promise. You don't have to do this!"

"The hell I wouldn't shoot you! I loved you, but you could only think of yourself. How could you not protect me from Dad? What happened to my loving mother from my earlier years? I'm scarred for life because of you and that so-called father of mine who you put first," he scolds, slowly moving toward her. "It would be in your best interest not to beg or run, as my plan to silence you is happening tonight."

With sheer terror coursing through her, she takes several wide steps back to distance herself from the gun pointing at her chest. However, she's not fast enough. Four deafening shots ring out and the scent of gunpowder intermingles with the aroma of the freshly baked cookies just out of the oven. He stands over her with a satisfied smile as the blood oozes out of her body, coating the white vinyl floor. *Damn, that woman can bake. Gonna miss that,* he thinks to himself.

Staring at him as she struggles for breath, coughing up blood, she utters desperate pleas for help. Instead, he elects to help himself to a warm cookie. He slowly chews, savoring the sweet vanilla and rich chocolate that titillates his taste buds while patiently waiting for the woman who gave birth to him finish bleeding out on the floor.

He reaches over for the now lukewarm cocoa to wash down the treat as he watches her take her last breath. Then it hits him, "I need to get out of here." Wrapping three more of the delicious cookies in a napkin, he hurries out the back door.

With a haziness clouding his mind, he's unsure if his blurry vision is from his eyes adjusting to the surrounding darkness, or because he just murdered his mother in cold blood and left her lifeless body to decay in his childhood home.

While trying to quickly and quietly escape through the backyard, he clumsily trips and falls over the large brown ceramic planter that had lived in that same spot for over a decade. Even in the darkest of nights, he should've known it was there. Jumping up, with a sharp pain in his left knee, he hobbles back down the lengthy path to his car.

Chapter One

Amaya

Present Day

Amaya, twenty-nine years old, holds the position of chief executive officer of Montgomery Innovations. In her spacious executive office, she sits in her comfortable chair at her large antique brown finish work desk, which features hickory veneers. Sunlight pours through the windows, adding to the chic office decor. She tucks the left side of her brown hair with auburn highlights behind her ear. Her long, full, natural hair shines brighter when sunlight streams through her office windows, accenting the richness of her hair color, which perfectly complements her flawless medium-brown skin.

It's 5:15 p.m., on the third Thursday of the month, when she volunteers to distribute much-needed items to the homeless. At this moment, Amaya is lost in thought, as she and her husband have been trying to start a family for several years. Still, unfortunately, they have faced fertility challenges. Despite their success in their professional lives, Amaya feels a deep void in her heart, longing to experience the joy of raising a child. Staring at her computer screen, browsing through the Bethany Adoption Services website, she can't help but imagine the possibilities and the happiness that adopting a child would bring to their lives. The tears from the depths of her soul and coursing down her blushed cheeks are a mixture of longing, hope, and the overwhelming emotions that come with the heartfelt desire to be a mother. Being the owner of the largest resource management company in the state has given Amaya the financial stability and flexibility to provide a loving home for a child. She knows that parenthood is a meaningful journey full of difficulties. Still, she is ready to embrace all the challenges and joys that come with it alongside her supportive husband.

Three years ago, a doctor diagnosed Amaya with deeply infiltrating endometriosis. The gynecologist told Amaya and her husband they would never have natural children together. The jaw-dropping news broke her spirit, causing devastation, heartbreak, and feeling less of a woman daily. Looking through the website, she feels intense grief for all the children without their forever homes, causing her to feel more anguish because her heart desires a baby right now. As she reads the children's stories, her cries intensify. She stomps her feet underneath her desk and looks up to the ceiling, asking, "Why me? I deserve to be a mother! God, why me?"

There is a gentle knock at the door, causing Amaya's heart to jump in her chair. She takes a deep breath, composes herself, and delicately wipes away the tears that glisten in her big brown eyes; with a graceful gesture, she beckons the person on the other side to enter. A burst of warm, familiar affection fills her heart as the door creeps open. It's Kathy, her top executive, and her close friend. Kathy's vibrant personality is evident by her assertiveness, self-confidence, and her stylishly tousled hairstyle, reminiscent of Rachel Green's iconic shag/bob from the 90s.

Kathy's adoration for the sitcom Friends is palpable through more than just her hairstyle. She effortlessly mimics Rachel's quirky and lovable character, bringing a touch of lightheartedness to the moment. Amaya finds comfort in Kathy's uniqueness, and sometimes, she wishes she was born with Kathy's personality. She confides in Kathy about her marriage and feelings of inadequacy.

"Amaya, do you realize what time it is?"

"Oh, no! I'm going to be late. I got lost in something. Let me get out of here."

"Is something wrong?" asks Kathy.

"I'm fine. I just let time get past me." She takes her heels off, reaches for her New Balance tennis shoes, and grabs her brown parka jacket.

Kathy quickly grabs a chair and walks around Amaya's desk, sitting beside her boss and friend. "Girl, you can't fool me. What is wrong? Your eyes are bloodshot red, and you can't lie worth shit. We're not leaving this office until you tell me what's wrong, and we may not leave then if it's serious."

"I, um, just give me a minute. I'm trying, but it's hard to explain," she sighs, her fingers intertwined with strands of her hair as she grasps them from the root. "You will think I'm being neurotic or something."

"I have all evening. Take your time, girl. I'm trying to figure out how to cancel tonight's dinner date with this man my cousin introduced me to. The man burped so loud in my ear while on the phone, not once, but twice. No excuse me, and when he laughs, I can't help but stare at that one Cheetos-looking yellow tooth in the front of his mouth."

Amaya giggles. "I needed to hear that story. Why does your cousin continue to set you up with these men? I remember one man didn't believe in brushing his teeth because most ancient people didn't practice oral hygiene. He said they never had cavities."

"Don't remind me, especially since I dated him for three months. He was a great lover; we just never kissed," she chuckles. Okay, spill it. What's wrong?"

Amaya bellows, "I'm freaking sterile, barren, fruitless, and useless! I have everything I could ever ask for except a beautiful baby. And my husband doesn't want to adopt. He has this unrealistic hope that a miracle will happen one day when we least expect it and refuses to discuss adoption. I try my best to explain how I feel about adoption, and he tells me to pray, which is funny because I've never seen him even say grace over a meal."

"You will make an exceptional mother when the time is right. Didn't he say you guys will discuss adoption when you're thirty? That's in a year and a half. You can't adopt a child without him, you know that, right? You have a fine and loving husband. Try to enjoy the couple's time and do the do every night. You won't have that when a baby comes. My mother once said, after having her hysterectomy, 'Take the baby bed out and put the playpen in.' That's how she handled knowing my baby brother was her last child. You never know; miracles happen every day. Regardless, you will have a child, maybe two, one day. I can promise you that."

Amaya reaches over and gives Kathy a bear hug. "Thank you so much for listening and lifting my spirits. I need to get going. I'm running late."

"I will see you tomorrow. Have a good evening. I will text the dude and tell him I'm working late. Call me when you get home."

"Hey, remember I'll be in late tomorrow. I'm having breakfast with the hubby. We're going to try MoRae's Restaurant," Amaya shares in an upbeat voice.

"Girl, I heard that was a great breakfast spot. I hope you two enjoy yourselves. Don't worry about anything. You know I will hold things down. Now get out of here and don't speed."

"I'll see you tomorrow and tell you how our breakfast went."

That evening, Amaya hurries to her brown Nissan Altima. She never drives her silver Lexus LS 500 on the third Thursday of the month when she goes to feed and give essentials to people experiencing homelessness. She drives with a slight disregard for the speed limit; making it on time, she joins her group at Hurd Island - a short distance from downtown Aurora. Amaya volunteers with the New Community Homeless Coalition. Her company donates socks, blankets, Bibles, hats, first aid kits, sleeping bags, and nonperishable foods every month. She does not just donate money and items; she donates her time. Six people, including Amaya, are volunteering tonight in twenty-nine-degree weather.

The group looks around at the displaced people's living conditions. People of different races, creeds, and genders live together on Hurd Island. Alcohol bottles and needles litter the streets. Grocery carts and duffle bags hold all their possessions. The overwhelming amount of trash underscores the scarcity of resources for unhoused individuals. Some people choose to live this way. Most people here have no alternative.

Amaya doesn't drive her Lexus or wear fancy clothes or jewelry when visiting people without housing. Optics are important to her because the goal is to create a comfortable, non-hierarchical environment for homeless people. The purpose is to dress in regular, comfortable clothing while helping the less fortunate. She doesn't volunteer to be recognized for her outfits, as the focus is not on showcasing fashion. Her motivation is to help the people down and out at this time in the best way she can.

They divide into pairs, and Amaya pairs with Sylvia Perez, Jorge Perez's wife and bank manager of One National Bank in Aurora. She compares herself to Sylvia, which makes her feel unattractive. Self-esteem is something Amaya is addressing in therapy. Sylvia's hair is sable-brown and flows over her shoulders. She shows off her shapely figure, which includes large breasts and a curvy derriere, by wearing a fitted coat. Amaya catches Tom Flannery eyeing Sylvia. Amaya wonders why she can't be flawless - like Sylvia. She's such a beautiful lady with a captivating smile.

Amaya hates having difficulty understanding social cues and feels awkward around strangers. She's addressing that in therapy. She knows Sylvia, but not on a personal level. Sylvia starts a conversation with Amaya. Amaya's palms become clammy as she feels an intense fear gripping her. "What if I say the wrong thing?" feeling paralyzed with anxiety. She takes a minute to challenge her negative thoughts and does her deep breathing exercises. The smell of urine and regurgitation in the air sickens her stomach after completing the breathing exercises. Amaya's heart rate and racing thoughts ease, and she adopts a more tranquil demeanor before distributing necessary items to the homeless with her partner.

"How have you been?" Sylvia asks.

"Oh, you know, busy. Lots of things have been going on. How are you and Jorge?"

"The bank keeps him busy, even during our vacation in Paris last week. His work phone remained on, causing me to feel agitated as he took work calls and answered emails throughout the day. I couldn't help but think I might as well have gone to Paris alone, as I probably would have had a more enjoyable time."

"We get caught up in our work sometimes. I hope you two can spend some quality time together soon."

"Me too," whispers Sylvia.

"Let's talk to the man on the park bench by the bridge, and we can work our way back," says Amaya.

"That sounds good to me. Now, the lady on your left just rolled her eyes at us. We should give her the bag and go. I am not trying to get cussed out tonight. It's too cold for all that."

Amaya giggles and says, "I'm glad I'm paired with you tonight. I had a rough day, and your humor is helping me forget about earlier."

The ladies notice a woman crying underneath the green awning of an empty store. An old sign hanging from one string says, "Closing. Everything must go."

"I'm going to check on her," says Amaya.

"Okay, I'll be giving away the bags."

Amaya moves towards the weeping lady, smiles, and gives her a bag. The lady glances inside the bag she just received and says, "Thank you. I need these items."

"You're most welcome. Is there anything else I can do to help?"

"You already did. These things you all are giving us are what we need. I have been out here for fifteen days. I've had nothing to eat in three days. The nearby restaurant will give me water, and sometimes a friendly soul will buy me a sandwich."

"I'm glad that we can help. I wish there were more we could do."

"What is your name?" asks the lady.

"Amaya."

"Amaya, what?"

"Amaya Montgomery."

"Amaya Montgomery, are you okay? I know I don't know you, but you seem sad. I feel people's energy."

"I'm not sad at all. I feel good when I come here. You said that you have been out here for fifteen days? Tell me a little about that."

"Yes, I left my substance-abusing boyfriend of seven months two weeks ago. Using meth is not for me anymore. There is so much I can do with my life. I'm twenty-two years old with some college, and I will turn my life around. He didn't want to get clean and didn't like the idea of me getting clean. I decided I wasn't living that life any longer, so he kicked me out. All the shelters were full. Now, here I am. My family doesn't talk to me. They warned me about him, but I wouldn't listen. I was in love, you know?"

"You can't go back home now that you broke things off with him?"

"No, ma'am. I asked. My parents said I have to live with the consequences of not listening to them and using meth."

"Display your sobriety and the personal growth resulting from that negative experience. Your parents may come around."

"Okay."

"You know my name. What's your name?"

"Sandra Reynolds. You can call me Sandy."

"It's nice to meet you, Sandy. You should be proud of yourself. I wish I could be as brave as you. With your determination, you will achieve your life goals."

Sandy pulls a brown hat with the University of Chicago's logo on it from her grocery cart and shows it to Amaya.

"See, I told you I went to college. I'm going back one day soon," as she waves the hat at Amaya.

Sandy's face beams with pride, a broad smile stretching across her lips.

"I believe you, Sandy. I am glad that I could chat with you this evening." Amaya presses her palms together, replying with a huge, joy-filled smile.

A blast of cold air rushes in. Amaya's olfactory sense becomes overwhelmed by the smell of the unbathed young woman. The combination of sweat and dirt has defined Sandy's street existence for days. Sandy coughs several times, prompting Amaya to put on a mask because she is unwilling to experience another bout of COVID-19. Amaya feels relief now because of the coughing; she has a reason to wear a mask and block the odor.

"Why are you putting a mask on?" Sandy frowns and looks confused.

"We wear masks in response to coughs and sneezes. I hope you understand."

"Oh, okay. That makes sense. Will you be coming by again?"

"Yes, ma'am. We come every third Thursday. I hope you'll be in a warm place before then."

"Amaya, can I give you a hug?"

The woman's uncleanliness causes Amaya to hesitate, yet she doesn't want Sandy to feel rejected. She hugs Sandy while holding her breath. To Amaya, the hug feels like it's lasting forever, but she knows she can't hold her breath for much longer. Sandy finally releases their embrace.

"Thank you, Amaya Montgomery, for everything."

Amaya walks away and meets up with Sylvia. "You gave away all the bags? Okay, I see you. Good job! I still have a few left."

"How was your talk with the young lady?"

"Right now, she's going through a tough time. She should be back on her feet soon. Sadly, the homeless shelters fill up so quickly in the winter. I will look into how I can help more than volunteering."

"I hope so," says Sylvia.

The elements are getting to the volunteers. They must cut visiting the unhoused people short because their feet and hands are numb. The group reconvenes at the original meeting spot. Amaya expresses how it warms her heart to witness the smiles and gratitude of the people they helped tonight. Sylvia agrees. Another volunteer, Tonya, asks Sylvia and two other women in the group if they want to get hot coffee to warm up. The ladies respond eagerly, saying, "Yes." Tanya glances over at her while she's talking. Amaya wonders why Tanya dislikes her so much to exclude her from the coffee gathering.

Once again, Amaya experiences feelings of exclusion. She conceals her disappointment over not receiving an invitation: "I thought Sylvia and I developed a great rapport. I'm wrong again, as usual." It's difficult for Amaya to hide her feelings of hurt, especially since Sylvia didn't ask her to join them. *Why do people always disregard me, starting from my childhood to this present time, as if my thoughts and feelings hold no weight or importance?*

Amaya slowly returns to her car, taking her time to bid her farewells to the group. At that moment, a wave of loneliness washes over her, reminiscent of how she felt when she was just seven years old. At that time, none of her classmates wanted to play with her on the playground, leaving her feeling utterly alone.

She vividly remembers sitting on a bench, tears streaming down her face next to a solitary tree. Determined not to dwell on that traumatic memory, she fights against the urge to return to that dark place. She takes a deep breath and climbs into her car, pausing briefly before starting the engine and embarking on her drive home.

As she drives home, she notices her hands gripping the steering wheel. When she lifts her fingers, her fingerprints are visible on the wheel. Tears stream down her face as she wipes them away with the back of her left hand. Feeling overwhelmed, she calls her best friend and cousin, Josh, to discuss what happened. First, he highlights all the good she does for her staff, family, strangers, and even his wife, never failing to acknowledge her kindness.

"Josh, I feel like an outsider in a strange world that refuses to acknowledge my existence."

"I don't understand why you still feel this way after all these years," he says, his voice filled with frustration and a hint of exasperation. "You graduated college at the top of your class, have a successful business, and have me as your cousin and best friend. What happened?"

"I was volunteering tonight, helping the homeless. The coordinator paired me with a lady who I knew in passing. I thought we were working well together. Joke on me. When we were leaving, she and the other two women went for coffee, but not me because no one invited me. I was just standing there feeling invisible."

"Cousin," he says, his voice filled with disappointment, "You should have said, 'Don't forget about me' or something like that."

"I can't endure any more of this evening. It's been awful. I'm just ready to go home and relax."

"Go home, take a warm bath. Maybe Q will rub your feet."

Amaya laughs hysterically.

"You know damn well my husband would never go near anyone's feet. I needed that laugh."

"I thought physical touch was Quentin's love language."

"Yeah, hugging and kissing. Quentin's only going to touch from the ankles up," she said, trying not to have a wreck while driving. She accidentally runs a red light.

"Cuz, I'm going to check on you tomorrow. Your therapist needs to step up her game, for real. You have been in therapy all these years and still feel inadequate."

"Don't talk about Ms. T. She's a great therapist. She gives me the tools. I must do the work. Talking about my past is difficult. I don't want to go back to that place."

"You are Amaya 'freaking' Montgomery, the heiress of the Montgomery fortune," he exclaims with irritation in his voice. "You can do this!"

"Okay, I'm home. I get it. You're trying to help me because you care. I need you to understand therapy can be a slow process for people like me. I love you. Talk to you later."

"Not everyone can be like you, Amaya. Goodnight."

Amaya arrives home to her stone-built residence, spanning 15,000 square feet and nestled within a sprawling twenty-five-acre lot. With a fully equipped gym and a spacious media room with oversized seating and a state-of-the-art entertainment system, the house boasts six large bedrooms, each exuding elegance, along with five full baths. There is also a charming three-bedroom guest house on the estate.

She pushes the garage door button and closes the garage. She retrieves her items and enters her home through the back entrance. A horrifying sight shocks her in the living room.

Chapter Two

Quentin

Quentin, Amaya's twenty-nine-year-old husband, is busy cooking dinner for three in their spacious kitchen. Standing six feet tall with brown skin, Quentin has one tattoo on each arm. Proudly displayed on his right bicep is a lion tattoo, while his left forearm bears a tattoo of his birth year, 1994. A bald fade haircut showcases a few highlights of gray.

As Quentin works his culinary magic, the kitchen fills with a mouthwatering aroma. The tantalizing scents of beef wellington, grilled asparagus, and creamy mashed potatoes waft through the air. It's a testament to Quentin's creative energy, as he designed the kitchen eight years ago to reflect his unique style. The kitchen boasts an island, marble countertops, white cabinets, a stainless steel oven, and sea-green walls with blue undertones.

Quentin stands over the five-burner cooktop, sporting a solid light brown button-up shirt paired with light brown drawstring waist pants. His hazel brown eyes and chocolate skin tone add depth to his appearance.

Quentin receives a call while draining the mashed potatoes. He cooks mashed potatoes three to four times a week because his wife loves the side dish.

"Who is disturbing me now? My phone has been ringing constantly since I've been home," he wonders, annoyed as he presses answer, taking the call through the speaker.

"Hello."

"Good evening. Is this Mr. Montgomery?"

"No. This is Quentin Johnson."

Amaya, a powerful advocate for preserving her family's legacy, decided not to take her husband's last name. She firmly believes in keeping the Montgomery name alive and honoring her grandparents. Amaya's dedication to her family heritage is essential because she and her mother are the remaining Montgomerys. Amaya feels a profound responsibility to ensure its continuity with no other siblings or close relatives to carry on the name. By retaining her maiden name, she proudly represents the Montgomery lineage. This bothers Quentin. He believes his wife should have her husband's surname.

"I apologize, Mr. Johnson. You are married to Mrs. Amaya Montgomery, aren't you?"

"Amaya is my wife. Ma'am, how can I help you?" He frowns, purses his lips, clenches his jaw, and flares his nostrils.

"Hello, Mr. Johnson. My name is Carolyn Guess. I'm the director of Save the Children Charity in Illinois. Your number was acquired from Mrs. Montgomery's contact list. I wanted to reach out to you first with some exciting news. Mrs. Montgomery has been a generous contributor to our organization for many years. We would be deeply honored if both of you could attend our esteemed 2022 Gala as our special guests. Our organization has chosen Mrs. Montgomery to receive this year's 2022 Philanthropist of the Year Award. We wanted to contact you first about the exciting news."

Quentin has been absentmindedly preparing dinner while only half listening, but now she has his full attention. "Wait, did you just say that my wife and I are receiving this year's Philanthropy Award?"

"Mr. Johnson, your wife will receive the award."

"We are married. That makes us one. We should both be recipients. Any intelligent person would agree with me."

"I understand how you feel. Unfortunately, this is out of my control. Naturally, you're ecstatic about your wife's acknowledgment."

"You've probably never read," he said, his voice filled with tension, "that being married increases the likelihood of donating to charities."

Ms. Guess takes a couple of deep breaths before she responds calmly. He hears her voice as she sighs.

"Mr. Johnson, it is our honor to have you and your wife join us as our distinguished guests."

"We will be there. You can text me the details." With fury in his eyes, he angrily ends the phone call.

Am I just supposed to be her arm candy? How is that woman going to call my phone about the gala and say the award is only for my wife? I am the damn man in this marriage. The head of this house and Amaya. I demand respect. That woman will not spoil my night. Big things will happen at the event. I'm sure of it. I need to call Mike tonight.

With meticulous precision, Quentin carefully arranges every meal element on the Neiman Marcus plates, creating a visually stunning and mouthwatering display of colors. The savory aroma of his freshly cooked food tantalizes his senses and makes his stomach growl in anticipation.

Suddenly, amidst the serene ambiance, the piercing sound of voices raised in a heated argument shatters the tranquility. The loud noise reverberates through the room, jarring Quentin's concentration and shocking him. "What the hell is going on?" he wonders.

He swiftly heads to the living room, his footsteps running into it, intensifying the pressure in the home. The sight that greets his eyes is a scene of chaos, the faces of two women contorted in anger and frustration.

Chapter Three

THE SURPRISE GUEST

Amaya crosses her arms and scowls at the person intruding in her living room, expressing her displeasure. Her plans were simple: come home, take a nice warm bath, and eat dinner with her husband. However, her senses flood with anxiousness, agitation, and an overwhelming feeling of shock as she sees her mother, Amber, standing in her living room, making herself at home.

"Amaya, it's good to see you," says Amber, extending her arms for a hug.

"What are you doing here?" Amaya asks, her voice trembling and knots forming in her stomach.

"I'm here to see you," the mother says.

"I've made it clear, haven't I? I don't want you in my home or anywhere near me. It's been a year, can't you understand that? Just take a good look at yourself. Actually, don't just look; take a whiff of yourself! Your clothes are absolutely filthy, and your hair is a tangled mess. The saggy skin on your face looks like crumpled paper. When was the last time you even took a bath? You reek of vinegar and funk. Look, you made the choice to be homeless and addicted to heroin instead of being with me. I don't think I'll ever recover from that. Amber, why are you here? Tell me the truth this time."

"My son-in-law," she says with a mischievous smirk.

"What do you want, Mom?"

"I could get lost in this enormous house. I have to say you're using my parent's money well."

Amaya stares at her mother, her hands instinctively curling into fists as she asks again, "What do you want, Mom?"

" I guess you don't believe I want to visit you and your husband. I miss you."

"No, I don't believe you. This is my last time asking what you want. I do not want you anywhere near me!"

"Listen, Amaya. I am trying to get an apartment over on Terrace Lake Drive. I need two thousand three hundred dollars to move in."

"And you're here, why?"

"Girl, you're living all fancy and shit on my family's money. I should have inherited everything! You live in this big house with a damn guest house, while me and your daddy live on the street. Why you can put us up in the guest house? You say I stink, well give me a place to wash my butt, it ain't like someone lives there, but you is fine with me and your daddy living on the streets, ain't cha?"

"You're not living in my guest house, Mama. It's a guest house, not a drug house. Where is my daddy?"

"He's in Symetria rehab in Chicago."

"Mama, why didn't you admit yourself to rehab, too?"

"Your daddy was snorting heroin all day and night long. His nose was bleeding all over the place. Just nasty. I done told you all I don't need no rehab. I only snort three or four times a day. Your Mama ain't got no problem."

"You're not getting a cent from me, Mama."

Amber jumps over the cream-colored midsize ottoman with a furious expression, muscles tense with beads of sweat on her forehead, ready to fight. Amaya's eyes widen with fear as she glances around nervously, looking for something to defend herself while her mother charges at her.

"You are going to give me the money for the apartment, you ungrateful mistake! You took everything and left me penniless."

Her voice is intense with fury. Amaya screams at Amber.

"Get out! Get out! You chose this life. Look at yourself. You are disgusting. I can't believe I came from you."

Amber charges at her daughter, overpowering her and slamming her to the ground before landing multiple punches to her face. Amaya tries to fight back, but her mother's punches come fast and brutally. A splinter of glass shatters everywhere from a glass table from Amaya, hitting the small table when her mother knocks her down to the floor. All Amaya can do is scream. Her mother bashes her in the mouth for screaming.

"Shut up! Your screaming is hurting my ears."

Quentin bursts into the living room and pulls Amber off Amaya.

"What is going on in here? I'm in the kitchen, sweating off my Creed Aventus cologne, working hard to make a nice dinner for us."

With a swollen and red face, Amaya confronts her husband, her voice trembling, "Why on earth would you invite this insane woman into our home?"

"Who are you calling insane?" shouts Amber. "Just give me the money, you stingy heifer."

Amaya ignores her. "Babe, I am going to call the police. She has attacked me! You see how my mouth is bleeding?"

"My knuckles are bleeding and bruised. Now we're even," squawks Amber.

"Amber, you're going to have to leave right now. I will not stand here and let you brutalize my wife. Don't even think about calling or coming here again, or you will answer to me." He swiftly points toward the door.

Amber walks to the door to leave and runs back to her daughter, spitting at her. Screaming with venom, Amaya yells at her mother.

"How about reconsidering spitting at people, huh? You may accidentally spit out one of the four teeth left in your mouth," says Amaya.

"Go!" Quentin commands, his voice bellowing with authority.

Amber storms out of the home in a fit of rage, causing a loud crash as she knocks over the blue mirror pedestal and the bronze medal crane statue in the foyer.

The house is now quiet. Amaya tells her husband her plan to disappear upstairs and immerse herself in a long, warm bath, attending to her face and chest, hoping it will erase the memories of this dreadful day. Quentin gently presses his lips against her forehead before heading to the kitchen to tend to their dinner.

She walks up the spiral staircase slowly, stopping halfway, and turns around to go back downstairs to the closet off the living room foyer to get her yellow cashmere throw blanket. She imagines how warm and cozy it will feel as she wraps it around herself and her husband while eating and watching a replay of The Cherri Lamb daytime talk show. Amaya places the blanket on the beige sofa next to two accent pillows stuffed with feathers. Next, she ascends the spiral stairs once more and heads towards the linen closet to retrieve her bath towels.

The bath is amazing. The horrible day becomes a distant memory. As she settles into the warm bath, she feels a comforting sense of peaceful solitude, as if the world outside ceases to exist.

After tidying up the kitchen, Quentin takes the covered warm plates and enters the living room. He sees the yellow blanket on the sofa. Place the dinner plates on the round coffee table crafted from 100% solid teak wood. Folding the blanket, he puts it back in the closet. He grabs a brown plush throw out of the closet and replaces it with the cashmere throw.

He remembers he plans to call Mike, his poker buddy and old friend from college. Mike is the proud owner of his electrician business. Amaya and Quentin provided the capital so that he could start his company, and he's made it successful. Quentin removes the phone from his pocket, meticulously scours his contacts to pursue Mike's number, and then punches in the number.

"Mike, you have a second?"

"Yeah, what's up?"

"The time has come," Quentin says.

"Okay. I'll be over after Amaya leaves and before the housekeeper arrives."

"Sounds good. See you tomorrow. Hey, text when you're on your way."

"Will do."

Quentin ends the call and sits on the couch to wait for Amaya. He grabs the TV remote and looks for the Cherri Lamb show on the DVR. Cherri's boldness and free spirit excite him and his wife. "Did she go to sleep in the bath?" Quentin wonders. "I should go check on her."

Amaya comes down the spiral staircase wearing her black silk nightgown at that moment.

"Oh, there you are. I was thinking you were not coming down after your bath."

Amaya's eyes narrow in confusion, her brows knitting together as she looks at the couch.

"Where is the yellow blanket, babe?"

"Yellow blanket? This brown blanket was on the sofa when I came in here."

"No. No, no," she repeats herself several times, her voice exhibiting frustration. "I put the yellow cashmere blanket here before I took my bath. How did this one get here?" she asks as her eyes dart around the living room.

"Baby, sit down with me. I'm hungry, and you need to eat something."

"Why are these strange things happening to me lately? I did not put this blanket here! I'm sure I put the yellow one on the sofa for us."

"Baby, why are you worrying about a blanket? You're looking all sexy and smelling delicious, almost as delicious as this food we're about to eat."

With a gentle tug, he grabs her hand and leads her to the softness of the sofa. He runs his fingers up her thighs while looking into her brown eyes.

"Are you going to eat with me or keep fixating on a blanket?"

"I'm going to eat with you, babe." She sits on the sofa, scooting closer to him, and places her head on his shoulders. "I'm being foolish because of the crazy day I had. I guess I brought this blanket to the sofa. Forgive me for my over-the-top reaction."

He takes the covers off the plates and passes Amaya her dinner. She smiles and takes a couple of bites.

"Mmm, babe, this food is incredibly delicious, as usual."

"Thank you. You know I'm going to take care of you, girl."

"Q, why did you let my mother into our home? You know I don't want her around me."

"What would you have me to do? She said she wanted to see her daughter, and she was sober. You two have not seen each other in over a year."

"I don't know, but Ms. T. said it's not good to have my parents in my life until they decide to seek help for their addiction."

"Can we forget about all this? You need to relax."

Her mind continues to ponder the mystery of the blanket. Quentin tells her he has something to help relax her. After they finish eating, he brings the plates to the kitchen.

He walks sexily back into the living room, exposing his six-pack chest, ready to relax his wife and relieve some built-up tension of his own. Her sultry body is always captivating for him. He takes her hands, licking all ten fingers, picks her up, and carries her upstairs. He opens the door to their moonlit bedroom. Gently, he lays her on the bed and then selects a playlist of sensual music, creating an ambiance of passion.

He kisses her neck, enjoying the scent of her bath and body lotion. He moves downward, suckling her voluptuous breast. She has both hands on the back of his head. As the music plays, her mind becomes a playground for naughty thoughts. Tenderly, she lowers his lips to the softest place on her body. She moans, and her body trembles from his lips on her clitoris.

Her muscles clench, her eyes rolling in the back of her head. Her body shakes uncontrollably. It's like a balloon filling with air before it pops. Amaya's thighs squeeze his head. Raising her head from the pillow, she screams, "Don't stop!" at the top of her lungs. The ceiling is spinning. Her body explodes with sensation. She falls back onto the pillow, breathless.

The taste of his wife has him aroused. He turns her over, and she finds herself on her knees, the sound of his rapid breathing echoing in her ears.

His warm breath on her back. Kem's "You're on My Mind" love song plays in the background, and he strokes a little faster. His panting echoes through the bedroom. Muffled moans emerge from his face on her back. He's peaking. Holds his breath, savoring the anticipation of a long-lasting sexual moment. He thrusts into her. The euphoric feeling of his throbbing penis. He closes his eyes, panting, and the semen comes. It's an explosion, BANG, the magnitude of lit dynamite. He collapses onto the bed.

Amaya takes his arms to put around her while they fall asleep. After a moment, he removes his arms, leaving her feeling rejected. Amaya kisses the back of his neck, turns over, and falls asleep.

The bedroom fills with a warm, golden glow as the morning sun streams through the window. It's 6:15 am. Amaya places her body on top of her husband and says, "Good morning, babe. Last night was rapturous." He flips her over on her back and gives her a quick peck on the lips. "I need to jump in the shower and meet Josh at the office this morning." They both get out of bed. Amaya puts on her silk robe and follows her husband to the bathroom.

He turns the shower on while talking to his wife, reminding her of his plans with Josh for their essential morning meeting. He steps into the shower. She does not leave the bathroom. Frustrated, she reminds him of their plans earlier this week to eat breakfast at the new MoRae's Restaurant today.

He pulls the shower curtain back and says, "We have not talked about going anywhere for breakfast, sweetheart."

She leaves the room and gets his electronic calendar off the nightstand. She opens the shower curtain and hands him his calendar in the middle of the shower. "Baby, dry your hands and open up your calendar. You will see we scheduled this breakfast date while on the phone Tuesday."

He opens the calendar and shows her the meeting with Josh this morning. She is experiencing fear and confusion. "Am I losing my mind?" she wonders, the uncertainty clouding her thoughts like a thick fog.

Flustered, she takes slow, hesitant steps back into the bedroom. *How did I believe we had a date for breakfast today? I know we planned this, but it's not on his calendar. I need to talk to my therapist. Trauma causes you to forget things. I thought it was things from your past. It's just too much. I don't know how much I can take. I think I'm ready to process my mother and the crap she put me through. Maybe this is the root of it all.*

Quentin's bare feet leave wet footprints on the floor as he walks into the bedroom, towel wrapped around his waist, ready to get dressed. Despite feeling uneasy about the breakfast plans, Amaya's nerves calm as she gazes at her sexy husband. She walks up and takes off the towel. She stares at his naked body. "It's unbelievable how lucky I am to have a husband who is so sexy and loving," she says. He dances for her naked. She feels aroused, but there's no time for sex as he needs to go to work.

Amaya slides back into bed, her eyes tracing every movement as her husband dresses. The aroma of his enticing cologne fills the bedroom.

"Hey, Baby, let's meet for coffee at that cozy cafe downtown after your important meeting with Josh and the potential client this morning. How does that sound, since we aren't doing breakfast?"

"Sure, sweetie. I'll text you when the meeting is over."

"Great! I love you. I know you two will land that client."

"Love you, too."

She sets her phone alarm for an hour to wake up and shower. He collects his wallet, phone, and electronic calendar from the nightstand and heads downstairs. Upon reaching the living room, he directs his attention toward the sofa and smiles as he remembers the events that unfolded last night. He grabs his jacket and heads out the door. A smirk forms on his face as he takes in the untidy foyer from Amber's tantrum last night, thinking, *Now that's a memory I won't soon forget.*

He heads out the door, looks at his electronic calendar, and says to himself, "I'm glad I remembered to delete that damn breakfast date yesterday. I almost screwed the hell up."

Chapter Four

JOSH

The account

At 8:02 a.m. on Friday, the sun casts its golden rays on the parking garage as twenty-eight-year-old Josh eases his sleek, apple red 2022 BMW M2 sports car into a vacant spot. His towering 6'3" frame exudes strength and athleticism. A gentle breeze rustles through the air, carrying with it the scent of breakfast in the building's cafeteria and the distant hum of city traffic. Josh's light brown skin glistens in the morning light while his silky, wavy hair dances in the wind. A perfectly groomed beard and mustache frame his chiseled jawline. Whenever he smiles, the dimple in his chin becomes more prominent.

He gathers his papers from the front seat of his car and places them in his black leather professional backpack. Josh is almost late to the meeting with his partner, Quentin, before a potential client arrives at 9:00 a.m.

He emerges from his sports car. His towering 6'3" frame exudes strength and athleticism as he leaps his way through the lobby to the golden elevators. On his way to the sixth floor where his offices are located, the elevator stops on the fourth floor. When the elevator opens, a woman in a business suit, complete with a short, tight skirt, enters. With each floor the elevator ascends, and the aroma of her fruity, sweet, sparkling spritzer perfumes feels the elevator. Josh becomes interested in her as soon as she looks his way and smiles. Her long legs and short skirt cause him to miss the sixth floor. Josh asks if she works in the building.

"I work as an editor at the Crimson-In-Style magazine, on the tenth floor," she says.

Josh covertly conceals his wedding ring by slipping his left hand into his pocket.

"What's your name?" he asks.

"Elena."

" How about lunch next week, Elena?"

"Hold on, aren't you married? I saw a wedding ring on your finger before you hid it," she says.

The elevator stops on the sixth floor, but Josh doesn't exit. "You caught me. I'm married, but my wife and I have an arrangement."

"Interesting. What's your name?"

"Josh, at your service for anything you need. I'm teasing you. Yes, my name is Joshua Wilson, but everyone calls me Josh. My best friend and I own AQJ investments."

"I know exactly where your office is. Let me think about lunch," she says.

"Don't think long. You don't want a good thing to pass." He nods his head and gives her a wink.

"This is my floor. You have a delightful ride down to your office."

"Hope to see you around," he says.

As Josh arrives at the office, he observes the sound of cheerful employees, including financial advisors, traders, analysts, and many others. The smell of fresh brewed coffee pervades the air. Josh opens his office door and finds Quentin settled in his office chair, with a look of exasperation on his face. There is nothing more irritating than opening your office door to find someone sitting behind your desk. Quentin inquires why he is 15 minutes late, tapping his foot.

Josh shrugs, "I am here now, and ready for work."

Josh sits at his grey circular table and takes files out of his backpack and organizes them meticulously in stacks on the table. He feels Quentin watching his every move. He looks up with discontent in his eyes.

"What... what?" says Josh. "Stop worrying. Everything is all good! I'm ready for this pitch. You just make sure you do your part."

"I always do." Quentin says.

The sound of high heel shoes echoes down the hallway towards Josh's office. It's Debra, the managing executive. Debra is a curvy thirty-one-year-old with a beautiful face and heart.

"Hey guys. I just wanted to say a quick hello."

"Good morning, Debra. Come on in," says Quentin.

"Hey, Deb, I'm glad you're here. I need to ask you a couple of questions regarding today's presentation." Josh says.

"Yes, yes. Let me run to my office and get the figures."

Debra heads out. Josh pulls on his mustache and shakes his head.

"I saw Deb squeezing into her Fiat the other day. All 300 pounds of her. That Fiat was getting a real workout." Josh says, turning in his chair and laughing. "I swear I heard the car saying 'ouch, ouch' going down the street."

Quentin says. "Man, you're such an ass. Debra is one of our most diligent employees. She was at the top of my class. I recruit the best, and she is the best. Come on, man. You can open us up to a harassment lawsuit if she overhears you."

"I'm just saying I wouldn't do her."

"J, you would be the last person she would want to do her," Quentin says with a snicker.

Debra returns and looks from Quentin to Josh. Josh is laughing and Quentin is looking at a file. The energy seems off. She pushes through and begins discussing the figures for the potential client. "Everything sounds perfect," Quentin says, his tone filled with satisfaction. Josh agrees. The clock shows only fifteen minutes left until the meeting. The men are confident in landing the account, their body language exuding assurance.

Quentin gets up from Josh's desk, the scent of coffee still lingering in the air. Josh asks Quentin to get them a couple cups. Josh needs Quentin out of his office before he loses his cool. Quentin attempts to have control over everything and everyone. Despite Quentin's intelligence, he would be no match for Josh in a battle of wits.

With a prideful stride, Quentin makes his way towards the coffee station. His phone rings. He glances at the screen and sees that it's Pamela calling. Frustrated, he declines her call for the fourth time this week. Josh notice Quentin's actions from the window and just shakes his head while putting the final touches on the pitch. With the smooth cups of coffee, delicately spiced with cinnamon, Quentin heads back to Josh's office, the gentle steam rising from the cups.

Josh thanks Quentin for the coffee and then inquires about Amaya's condition following the evening she had spent supporting the homeless. Quentin explains that Amber, Amaya's mother, showed up and their interaction had not gone well.

"I bet it didn't. How is my cousin Amber?"

Quentin says that Amber is still struggling with drug addiction. And that Amaya's father is currently in rehab once again.

"Man, you have your hands full with Amaya and Pamela."

"I'm planning to end the affair with Pamela. She firmly believes that her value to me surpasses being a mere object of sex."

Josh and Quentin have been best friends since high school, despite attending different schools. Their friendship blossomed at a sports camp during the summer before they started high school. During their eleventh-grade year, Josh introduced Quentin to Amaya, who was shy and awkward. Interestingly, Josh is not only Amaya's cousin but also her best friend. He supported her unwaveringly when she faced bullying, especially when Annie, their live-in housekeeper's daughter, started being unkind to her.

Josh made a promise to Amaya that he would be there for her no matter what, and he was, especially during the tragic loss of her grandparents in the car crash.

Amaya invested in AQJ investments, per Josh's request. Josh and Quentin gave her the honor of naming the company. She settled on AQJ for Amaya, Quentin, and Josh investments. Amaya will do anything for Josh because he is her confidant and the person she trusts with all her heart. He saved her from some dark days in her life.

"Q, it's 8:55. Let's get this account. Remember, you start low and I'll come in and charm him into a larger investment plan."

"You know how we do it!" Quentin said with an air of grandeur, his voice booming through the room.

The two men leave the office, adjusting their suits and heading to the conference room. Quentin's phone vibrates in his pocket. Josh looks at him with a firm expression and reminds him to silence his phone. When Quentin turns off the sound, he looks at his message. It's a text from Pamela. She needs to meet. His response to meeting her is blunt and unequivocal "no."

Quentin opens the door to the conference room as Debra is waiting outside. They walk into the conference room. "Good morning, Mr. Patel. Thank you for meeting with us today," says Quentin and he introduces the team to Mr. Patel.

"Glad to be here. I'm looking forward to hearing your presentation."

Quentin begins by explaining the value of the commercial real estate that Mr. Patel is interested in buying. He details the current market rate and explains this is the perfect time to buy. Quentin's presentation pitch is to buy and hold the property, and eventually resell. He explains the floor standards for the underwriting process.

Mr. Patel inquires about the overall return on his investment and asks about the stress test. This is when Josh, the "numbers man," comes in. Josh presents the business model so well that Mr. Patel declares he is ready to sign with them. Josh even talks him into investing in a luxury apartment complex. Quentin is flabbergasted at Josh selling him on another deal in the middle of the pitch for the first deal.

Debra expresses her enthusiasm to Mr. Patel about working with him. She hands him her business card and assures him he can contact her anytime, day or night, if he has questions. Mr. Patel graciously thanks Debra, Quentin, and Josh before taking his leave.

Quentin is doing the football touchdown dance in celebration of the exceptional outcome of the presentation. "What the hell? My brain is spinning. This is the largest account our company has acquired since its inception."

"This is just the beginning. Mr. Patel will bring us other clients. We are going to take this industry by storm," Josh says. He fist bumps Quentin.

At the end of the day, Josh pops his head in Quentin's office.

"Q, it's 5:20. Let's go out and celebrate this account. It's larger than we expected."

"How about Club-C? I can meet you in an hour."

"Okay, man. I will go home and check on the wife and kid."

"How is Bree? Amaya asks about her periodically."

"Bree is Bree. Breaking me with all her shopping sprees. You need to worry about breaking things off with baffling ass Pam. I will see you in an hour, bro."

Josh gives a shout out to the staff on the big account and leaves the office. He pops his head back in and tells Quentin not to be late; he is ready to celebrate.

Quentin puts on his blue suit jacket and praises Debra for their outstanding performance with the projections in securing a big account.

He strides through the glass office doors, making his way towards the elevator, his face beaming with a million-dollar smile. They did it. He enters the elevator and his phone rings. It's Pamela. Quentin ignores the call. He exits the elevator and makes his way to the garage. Josh waves goodbye once more, his hand moving through the air in an exuberant gesture. He hops into his red sports car and revs the engine. The sound rings through the parking garage.

Quentin watches Josh speed out of the garage while he approaches his black BMW and discovers Pamela with her average height and curvaceous body, leaning on his vehicle, crossing her arms.

"We need to talk!" she says, her voice carrying a sense of urgency.

"Oh, shit. What is it now?" he wonders silently, as his eyes scan the garage. He hopes no one else sees them.

Pamela tells him to get in her car. They are going to their special place. Quentin says he will drive his car and meet her there.

"You better show up," she says. She tells him either he takes the time to talk to her or she will talk to the rich, pretty little wife of his. The mere mention of a threat makes Quentin's blood boil. What is so significant that Pamela has shown up and started making threats? Anger? Quentin gets into his car and drives out of the parking garage.

Chapter Five

Amaya

It's 5:32 p.m. Amaya took the day off. Kathy and Jeff can manage all operations in the office. Jeff, who's Josh's estranged brother, works alongside Amaya as the company's COO. Amaya doesn't worry about leaving them in charge. Jeff and Kathy work tirelessly to ensure the company's well-being, day and night. Amaya enjoys her home, her place of solace. It's the ultimate gratification for her. Quentin's presence is what she craves, his touch igniting a sense of completeness within her. Sandra, the housekeeper, is finishing for the day. All that remains is loading the dishwasher. Sandra is a fifty-two-year-old African American woman who is tall and wears a genuine smile and is fearless. Amaya has a lifelong, strong admiration for Sandra.

Sandra walks down the hallway, headed towards her purse when Amaya calls out to her.

"Did my husband apologize for his rudeness the other day?"

"No, Mrs. Amaya. He didn't."

"You know I love you and appreciate all you do in our home. My husband lacks the ability to communicate with others on an adult level." Her laughter bubbles out as she speaks.

With an eye roll, Sandra says, "Mr. Quentin's rudeness has become a familiar part of my daily routine."

The beloved housekeeper often endures Quentin's disrespectful remarks. Quentin's mouth is like a sour fruit, beyond Amaya's control. Amaya's phone rings. Amaya asks her to get the phone. Sandra feels a sense of revulsion when she sees Quentin's name appear on the caller ID. She reaches out and places the cell phone in Amaya's open palm. With a smile, Amaya answers the phone, her voice filled with warmth.

She greets him with a tender, "Hey, my love."

"How's your day, gorgeous?"

"I gave myself permission to do absolutely nothing today. It's wonderful."

"Good for you. I'm calling to let you know I'll be home late tonight. Josh and I are going out to celebrate the momentous account we landed today."

"Congratulations babe. I'll just find something in the fridge to eat for dinner. I love you."

"Love you more with each passing day. I am sorry we could not meet for coffee as planned. I will see you later."

Sandra listens to Amaya's side of the conversation. She is sure Quentin is taking advantage of Amaya's wealth. There's always a lingering sense of mistrust whenever she's around Quentin. After Amaya finishes her call, Sandra assures her she has taken care of all the cleaning tasks and is now ready to depart. She retrieves her purse, dons her cozy coat, and prepares to face the frigid weather outside.

"Be careful," Amaya yells. "I'll see you Monday."

Amaya grabs the remote and searches through the DVR, her anticipation growing as she finds something to watch. She sits back on the sofa, rubbing her neck while sitting Indian style. She settles on her favorite prime-time series, "Will Trent."

"Will is a brilliant and good-looking detective," she blushes.

After she watched for a while, an unsettling sensation washes over her. A chilling breeze floats into the room, causing her to grip the soft, comforting blanket enveloping her. Her eyes move nervously around the living room, a palpable fear permeating her senses. Determined to dismiss her unease as mere imagination, she refocuses her attention on her show. Right then, she witnesses a ghostly white figure floating from one side of the room to the other. In a state of disbelief, she remains motionless on the sofa.

Overwhelmed with fear, she squeezes her eyes closed, trying to shut out the impending danger. Slowly opening one eye, she looks up and feels a sudden wave of relief as the figure vanishes. She chuckles softly, dismissing it as a figment of her imagination. But she looks around one last time, her ears tuned in to any unfamiliar sounds that might show danger or a ghostly presence.

Chapter Six

QUENTIN

While behind the wheel, Quentin brainstorms how to best end his relationship with Pamela. He has XM Radio on and is singing at the top of his lungs, still feeling high from the huge client he landed earlier. Pamela's time has ended. Quentin grows tired of the women he sleeps with after a couple of weeks. Their conversations and physical intimacy becomes mundane. Pamala has lasted three months. "What does she want to tell me?" he asks himself. His nonchalant demeanor remains unchanged. He suspects Pamala wants a weekend getaway. Or money to cover the medical expenses from a nephew's football injury or some trivial matter.

He remembers the flicker of doubt he felt when he'd first met her at the Z-Club. But she'd been worth the time and the little money he'd given her having indulged his sexual fantasies. Oh well, he thinks. Additional ASSets end. He laughs and bangs his hand on the stirring wheel.

As he arrives at Zastodon Lake, a thick blanket of darkness envelops the surroundings, obscuring his vision. The cold air adds to the eerie atmosphere, creating an aura of mystery. A mist akin to death shrouds the trees and surrounding areas. He doesn't see Pamala's black Chevrolet Impala. Then he hears a horn, and the lights are on. He drives forty feet and parks next to her black

Chevrolet Impala. He gets out of his car and proceeds towards her vehicle. As the car door opens, he waits for her to step out.

But she says, "Come in. It's much too cold to talk outside."

Quentin walks around the car and opens the passenger door. He takes a seat, his face void of any emotion. She takes her fingers and wraps them around his chin. She pulls his face towards her, and she seals the moment with a deep, drawn-out kiss. The car is warm, its heater blasting. Quentin takes off his winter coat, blue suit jacket, and sky-blue tie.

"What do you need to tell me?"

"Let me show you, babe."

She pulls out a rectangular gift box. The gold decorative paper shines in the interior light. She gives it to him and tells him to open it. Quentin stares at the box. His eyebrows raise and wrinkles appear on his forehead.

"What is this?" he asks.

"Would you open it all ready?"

In a fit of frustration, he opens the lid, tears away the paper, and pulls out the undesirable gift hidden inside. He lifts out a small white plastic object that looks like a wand.

"It's a pregnancy test. And it's positive. Congratulations! Who's the father?"

"You are."

"I am not the father," he says.

"I haven't been with anyone else."

"If that's accurate, another person peed on this stick. Here, take this thing back."

Pamala insists he's the father. She asks him when he intends to leave his wife for her and their baby. He looked deep into her eyes and says, "I have to go. Have a good life." He grabs his coat, tie, and suit jacket before venturing back into the cold. He gets out of her car.

She jumps out of the car and runs to him. Pamela grabs his right arm. "You can't leave me like this. I love you," she says, pleading with tears streaming down her face. Quentin turns around, takes her hands, wipes her tears and tells her there is no way he is the father of her baby. He offers money to aid her, but this will be their last interaction.

Pamela's tone changes. She adjusts her posture and dries her tears. "I will tell her everything! I have proof of the affair. There is a recording of us making love," she says. Quentin doesn't answer. He surveys the area. The isolated lake reflects the mountains, only the wind blowing through the trees, suggesting no one else is around. He fabricates remorse. She believes he wants to hear her out. He continues to hold her hands to keep them warm. He assures her he will take care of her and the baby. Pamela smiles at Quentin and falls into his arms. She is feeling light-hearted and warmth throughout her body. She feels victorious.

Pamela turns her body around and looks at the shimmering moonlight reflecting on the dark surface of the lake. The light seduces her. She places Quentin's arms around her waist. The lake has captured the attention of them both. She savors Quentin's firm hug, finding sanctuary and stability in his grip.

"I need you to do something for us. Erase the video of us making love. It poses a risk and might create problems for us if it falls into the wrong hands." She agrees. With Quentin watching, she removes her phone from her pocket and deletes the video.

"Where are you going after you leave here?" he asks.

"I have no plans. What do you want to do?"

"Who knew you were meeting me tonight?"

"No one." With a gleam in her eyes, Pamela talks about the future they will build together, discussing their goals, aspirations, and plans for the baby.

Quentin's hands release her waist. He reaches for his tie that hangs loosely around his shoulders. He deftly wraps each end of the tie around his wrist. With a fierce grip, he coils the tie around her neck, his eyes blazing with rage. She tries to scream for help, but the constriction in her throat silences her. She forcefully delivers kicks and punches to him, fighting for her own safety.

Her trembling fingers instinctively find their way between the tie and her throat, a feeble attempt to protect herself from his deadly grip. As she is fighting for her life, one of her shoes flies off from a forceful kick. His grip on the tie slips, causing it to loosen around her neck. He struggles to keep her from escaping. She's strong and resisting more than he'd thought. He's breathing heavily. He tightens his grip.

With a vengeance, she fights him, every strike filled with determination. Quentin did not know that Pamala could be so formidable. With renewed force, he tightens the tie around her neck, cutting off her air supply. Quentin yells at her to stop fighting back. She is growing tired and disoriented. He tells her she made him do it. "Why couldn't you just take the money and leave? You gave me no other choice." His face contorts into a wrathful grimace as he mercilessly strangles the life out of her.

The world around her becomes hazy and indistinct as she loses consciousness. Quentin's eyelids droop with exhaustion, his body aching from the prolonged act of strangulation. She collapses to the ground. He falls with her. They both hit the ground with a thud. He still maintains a tight grip on the tie.

Pamela has lost control of her bodily functions. Just one gruesome detail that accompanies her murder is the sight and odor of urine and feces under her skirt dripping down her legs. Gritting his teeth, Quentin pushes himself up from the frigid ground. His mouth is dry from exhaustion. He reaches into his car and grabs a container of disinfecting wipes. He goes to Pamela's car and wipes away any presence of him being there.

Quentin, with an apathetic heart, returns to the corpse and carefully takes her cell phone. Any evidence that he has been at the lake, he hopes, has vanished without a trace.

It's 6:54 p.m. Quentin arrives at the Z-Club and finds a parking space near the back entrance. He looks in the mirror and puts on his tie, brushes his hair, and straightens his shirt sleeves. He sees Mike, the electrician, getting out of his Range Rover. Mike yells "Hey, I was expecting a call or text from you today about that job." Quentin is not about to yell across a parking lot. How uncouth is that?

Quentin holds up one finger and walks over to Mike. They shake hands and do the bro hug thing.

"What happened to me doing that job today? You just sent a text this morning saying, 'don't come'."

"My wife took off today and stayed home. Come by next weekend. I'm going to talk to Josh about sending the women away for a surprise spa weekend. That will get her out of the house."

"You really think this will work?" asks Mike.

"Yeah, man. If you do it right, it will work. Are you good? If not, say so now."

"I'll handle it," says Mike.

Mike walks into the club first and waves at Josh, who is sitting at the bar. Josh holds up his beer to greet Mike. Mike heads to the DJ stand and talks to him for a while. Quentin walks over to the bar and feels the leather bar stool next to Josh with one hand. He perches on the stool. The sounds of clinking of glasses and the chatter of patrons fill the air.

"What took you so long?" asks Josh.

"Things took an unexpected turn with Pamela. All is well."

"Q, we need to talk about this new account. I...."

Quentin interrupts Josh in mid speech.

"I can't talk about the account now. Let's discuss it later. There's something important I need to talk to you about. I'm sending Amaya away on a spa retreat next weekend. I want you to send Bree too. It'll be good for the girls to go away for the weekend."

"I'll speak to Bree. She will not turn down a weekend of pampering."

"I'll speak to Debra about making the plans for next weekend."

As Quentin orders a gin and tonic, he notices the soft jazz music playing in the background over the noise of the patrons.

In the bar that night, Quentin feels a sense of accomplishment wash over him, easing the noise in his head of what happened with Pamela. Josh is flirting as usual. He's hitting on just about every woman in the bar. He waits until they have a drink in their hand before approaching them. While holding down his head, Quentin laughs at how cheap Josh is.

Quentin notices Pamela's sister, April, entering the bar. He looks away but has an epiphany. He thinks to himself, she would make a perfect alibi. April was aware of the affair, but she keeps her distance from her sister's personal matters. Quentin leaves the bar stool and greets April at the door.

"Hey lady. It's good to see you out," Quentin says.

She hugs his neck and whispers in his ear, "I hope you're staying out of trouble," she asks with a giggle.

He looks at her with his calculating smile and says, "You know me. What do you think?"

"Boy, buy me a drink," she says as she pats him on the shoulder.

Quentin looks around for a table. He spots one, not clean, but it will do. The table is next to the dance floor. As they sit down, they catch the attention of a server to tidy up the table. Noticing Josh in the distance, he signals to their new table with a nod. Quentin leans back in the chair, a smug smile playing on his lips, as he relishes sitting in the bar with Pamela's sister. "I have an airtight alibi," he believes as he thinks he has gotten away with murder.

Chapter Seven

BREE

It's 9:37 p.m. In her green room, the soothing sounds of a small indoor waterfall greet Bree's senses. The green room features snake plants, ZZ plants, philodendrons, and purple orchids. Bree seeks refuge in her greenroom, where the soft lighting and soothing ambiance help her unwind. Bree is a tall lady, with blue eyes which stand out because of her contact lenses. She weighs 115 pounds. Once overweight in her early adulthood from excessive eating, she now rigidly monitors her weight, determined not to exceed 115 pounds. Bree's sisterlocks sways as she moves, the ends grazing the middle of her back.

In her green room, she shuts out the shame, guilt, and regret she feels every day for what she's done.

The sound of Josh's footprints leaving their nine-year-old son's room fills Bree with a sense of edginess. "Damn," she says under her breath, realizing he's already home. Josh enters the green room.

"Hey, Bree Bree. How was everything with you and our little prince?"

The words coming out of his mouth now make her special room feel cold and clammy. He has entered her sacred space. She is not in the mood to see him or make small talk.

"Little J and I had a great day. I saw your text. Congratulations on the new account. We stopped by the office to surprise and congratulate you, but we had just missed you."

"I was waiting for a response. It's nice to know you and the little man were planning on surprising me."

"I'm happy for you. J."

"Can I make love to my wife to celebrate?"

"I'm not in the mood."

"You're my wife. We haven't made love in months."

"Are you missing out on sex? We both know of the women, you see. You know I'm never going to forgive you for..."

"I want to make love to my wife. I have been patient with you. Maybe you should go talk to someone about whatever the hell is going on with you and get some help."

She shrugs her shoulders and turns her attention back to her waterfall. As he continues to talk, she adjusts the water sound to its highest level, drowning his voice.

Bree and Josh have been married for ten years. During their college years, Bree became pregnant with Josh Jr. and they got married when she was seven months along. With the help of Amaya, they managed the rent for an apartment off campus. Despite becoming parents and juggling their academic responsibilities, both Bree and Josh successfully completed their college degrees. However, Bree's accounting degree has remained untouched as she dedicated herself to motherhood. During the initial stages of Quentin and Josh's business venture, Bree provided valuable help. However, encountering Josh both at home and at work was an unpleasant experience for her. As a result, she quit her job.

While her son is at school, Bree fills her days with shopping endeavors and remains an unwaveringly devoted mother at all other times. She is cognizant of her husband's infidelity, but consciously disregards it. She enjoys family time, it's being alone with her husband she dislikes.

Bree was on the cheer team in high school and maintained a 4.2 grade point average. She was a close friend to Amaya, often standing up for Amaya when she was being bullied by the other girls. Bree met Amaya while she and Josh were dating in high school. She was initially unkind to Amaya because of her awkward behavior, but over time recognized her as a sweet and genuine person.

After high school, Bree became quieter and struggled academically in college. Her son and shopping sprees seemed to be the only things that brought her any happiness. She says retail therapy helps her not to withdraw from others and not think she is a terrible person.

Josh turns the waterfall off and apologizes to Bree. He tells her about the spa trip for her and Amaya the following weekend. She sits up at hearing the news. He encourages her to unwind and embrace the spa treatments next weekend. Josh leaves the green room and heads to the shower. Bree reclines in her opulent leather and gold chair, enjoying the sounds and fragrances. She thinks about a wonderful weekend at the spa and distracting herself from her problems.

Chapter Eight

Mystery Man

Quentin makes the call to inform him that the plan has begun. He tells Quentin it's about time. Before initiating the plot on Amaya, they have had ten long years to prepare. Quentin tells him Mike the electrician is coming over next weekend to set up the equipment they need for the plan to work. He asks Quentin if they can trust Mike to be discreet, ensuring their plan remains a secret. Quentin assures him as long as Mike gets his cut, his mouth will remain shut.

After he ends the call with Quentin, he sits back and thinks about all the money Amaya has and will receive on her thirtieth birthday, while he must work hard for his money, and she receives a fortune because she was lucky to be born a Montgomery. There is no hatred in his heart for Amaya, only envy. His feelings stem from Amaya getting what he wants, the recognition and the money. The desire for what she possesses consumes him. He thinks she doesn't appreciate it, so why should she inherit it?

He hopes to himself that Quentin does not screw things up. Should he trust Quentin? It's too late to wonder now. The time has arrived. No turning back. He distracts himself by finding a football game to watch in his man cave. He can't help but wonder if Quentin's insufferable ego will be the downfall of their plan to steal Amaya's money.

As he watches the game, memories of Saturday's family tradition flood his mind—the softness of their comfy sofa, the laughing of Saturday afternoons, and the excitement of watching whatever game was on with his family. Then, at eleven, his world transformed completely. The once cozy sofa morphed into a decrepit old couch. The joyful laughter that once filled the room was now replaced by piercing yells and a torrent of curses.

Getting off the sofa, he paces around the room, his mind filling with agitation. He wonders why did that man he used to call dad have to lose his job? The once vibrant atmosphere of his home turned bleak, like a dark and stormy night. The sounds of his father's footsteps, once a walk with purpose and confidence, changed to a heavy burden. He transformed like the character, Jack Torrance from the movie *The Shining*, his eyes reflecting a haunting emptiness. Everything changed for him then, as if someone trapped him in a chilling nightmare. The loving husband and father he once knew was gone, replaced by a monster.

He and his siblings struggled to focus on their homework amidst the overwhelming list of chores their father imposed upon them. The constant scrubbing, sweeping, and mowing destroyed any chance of academic recognition. Their mother, burdened with the responsibility of cooking meals and satisfying her husband's desires, could offer no reprieve. The scent of her food cooking filled the house, mixed with a sense of tension and doom. Exhaustion weighed heavily on the children as they attempted to do their best in school, aware that any poor grades would cause their father's wrath. The fear of a beating, administered with whatever object was within his reach, hung over them like wearing a heavy hoodie outside in August.

Their mother turned a blind eye to the relentless cruelty her husband inflicted upon their innocent children. The chilling silence that enveloped the house hid their inner screams of anguish. She shielded herself from the physical blows, but willingly allowed her husband to mistreat their vulnerable offspring. Within the suffocating walls of their home, laughter ceased to exist, replaced by a haunting stillness through the empty hallways. The children yearned for the warmth of friendship with their peers, yet were forbidden to have friends outside of school. Dreams of playing sports were crushed under the weight of their parents' tyranny, as they were barred from attending games and practices, forever denied the joy of healthy competition. The scent of alcohol permeated the air, a constant reminder of their father's destructive vice. The unbearable stress it placed upon their mother eventually consumed her, driving her to seek solace in the same poison. In their desperate search for escape, they found no sanctuary within the confines of their own home, dubbing it the "House of Constraints," a prison from which there seemed to be no reprieve.

  He sinks back onto the cold floor, flicks off the game, and immerses himself in silence. After a while, memories of his nightmarish upbringing resurface again, causing him to think about his parents. He tells himself to find something positive in his childhood. He etches one of the best days of his life, when he was fourteen-years-old, in his memory. It was the day his father left and never came home again. His face beams with a smile that could fill a football stadium.

Chapter Nine

THE THERAPY SESSION

It's 9:23 on Saturday morning. Amaya wakes up to soulful music playing throughout the house and the smell of bacon cooking in the kitchen. She steps out of the bed and gives a full body stretch before putting on her silk robe and heading downstairs. She opens the kitchen door and there is a buffet laid out for her. Quentin has prepared bacon, poached eggs, blueberry bagels, strawberries, cinnamon toast, and coffee.

Amaya walks to the sink to wash her hands and sits at the table to indulge in the feast her husband has prepared. After Amaya finishes eating, her stomach is full of the delicious breakfast. She tells Quentin she has an 11:00 appointment with her mental health therapist. She thanks Quentin for breakfast and heads upstairs to shower.

Quentin stops her in the kitchen just as she's about to leave. He reminds her, "You said we needed to talk today. What's up?"

She smiles at her husband and replies, "We'll talk when I come home. Right now, I'm running late for my therapy session." With a playful gesture, she blows him a kiss before heading out.

Amaya drives to her therapist's office. She feels bubbles in her stomach because she intends to use this therapy session to process her past and address the traumatic experiences inflicted upon her by her parents through narration.

Over the past few months of trauma therapy for this target memory, she has processed her thoughts, feelings, problematic behaviors, upsetting events, and triggers of the trauma. To distract herself from her fearful thoughts, she focuses on her plans to talk to her husband about adopting a baby later this afternoon.

Amaya arrives at Ms. T.'s office. Tiffany Heard is the therapist's name. Ms. T., as she prefers to be called by her clients, is in her early forties. She has been working closely with Amaya for a decade, since her grandparents passed away.

"Good morning, Amaya. How have your past two weeks been?"

"It's been up and down. I am still struggling with social anxiety."

"Your anxiety has improved since you started the Lexapro medication."

"I know. There was a situation the other night when I went with a group to feed the homeless."

"Tell me about it."

"Honestly, Ms. T., I am ready to share my story. I've worked on this memory about my childhood. I'm ready to process the next target memory. And a bizarre thing happened since our last session."

"Tell me about it."

"My mother came to my house two nights ago, and it did not go well."

"Amaya, use your breathing techniques and you can pause for a few seconds if you need to."

"Ms. T., I'm ready. After my narration of this memory, I can move to the next trauma. I'll just take off my jacket and get comfy," she says, before stretching out on the therapist's couch and closing her eyes, ready to talk.

The therapist is cognizant of Amaya's level of insight. She is ready to explore painful childhood events. The therapist asks Amaya to take a few deep breaths and think of something that is calming to her and brings a sense of peace. The therapist reminds Amaya that she can stop at any time. Amaya holds a pillow and begins.

```
"A vivid memory from when I was just five years
old is engraved in my mind. I can see it more
```

clearly now, like a picture frozen in time. The sight of my mother lying unconscious on the floor, surrounded by drug paraphernalia, will be something I'm learning to manage with my coping skills. I can smell the acrid scent of drugs from that day. I can feel my rapid heartbeat drowning out everything else as the panic coursed through my tiny body. 'My mommy is dead.' I ran to the neighbor's house, my flip-flops pounding on the pavement, desperately seeking help.

"Shaking like a leaf, I called my grandmother, my small fingers struggling to press the buttons on the phone. The neighbors were no strangers to heroin. They used heroin with my parents. I hated it, Ms.T. This was a haunting presence in my life. It's not anymore, thanks to your help. The neighbors did not seem to care about how frightened I was or about Mama. My grandparents came over and helped my mother. They took me to their house for the weekend while my mother was in the hospital. I felt safe and loved with my mother's parents. My mom and dad never enrolled me in daycare or school. I learned phonics and math from PBS kids, Annie, Sandra, and my grandparents.

"I was always with my parents and their friends, who were often in a drug-induced state. Our house was so nasty. My parents never cleaned. The walls became a playground for roaches during the day, their tiny legs skittering and leaving me repulsed. I was making cereal one morning, and a roach was in the box. I was hungry, so I ate the cereal, anyway. There was nothing else to eat.

"My grandparents begged my parents to allow them to raise me. My mother's animosity towards her mother manifested in using my grandmother's love for me as a weapon to hurt her. Daddy would say to Amber, 'Just let your parents raise her. We don't have the money to take care of her.' She would curse him out and whip me just because she felt like it. She would never hit my daddy, but when he left, she would get her belt and whip me for making her life miserable. She would say. Whew! Narrating this memory with you is so damn painful. It's like feeling the sharp strikes of her belt all over again, each one leaving a distinct mark on my skin. The pain was unbearable. No one was there to hear my screams for help.

"Daddy wasn't as bad. His name is Larry. I can still see his warm smile and hear his goofy voice. He would make sure I ate at least once a day. I remember him playing with me. The sound of us laughing throughout the house made us both happy. But when Mama came home, his focus would shift, and all my father's attention would be on her. In a weird way, my grandparents and I believe he has always loved her and was afraid of her. I had to fend for myself. Washing my clothes in the bathtub. I did not want to stink like my parents. At five-years-old, it was hell trying to wring out my jeans before hanging them over the fence outside.

I remember getting slapped so hard that my body hit the wall and I ricocheted onto the floor. All because I used a bar of Ivory soap to wash my clothes. Every night, tears streamed down my face as I lay on the cold, hard floor pallet. To this day, I can't lie on the floor. The rancid stench of my room filled my nostrils, making it even more insufferable. Ms. T., I can't tell you how I longed to escape from that repulsive and fear-inducing place.

"My daddy took me to my grandparents. He told them to keep me, and he would deal with my mother. I was so happy playing with Annie and our dolls until later that evening. Then there was cursing and banging on the front door. Sandra, the housekeeper, Annie's mom, and my protector, answered the door. We were in the playroom. Annie was three years older than me. She and her mother lived with my grandparents.

"My mother burst through the house, saying vulgarities and demanding to take me with her. I remember my grandmother on her knees begging my mother to let me stay. My grandfather pleaded with her, his voice filled with desperation, warning her to change her destructive lifestyle. I was so scared that I peed my pants. Annie grabbed my hand, and we ran to the third floor and hid in a utility closet.

"My grandparents were afraid to call the police or even child protective services. They thought they could handle my mother with no outside help. They couldn't have been more mistaken. We could hear all the commotion from upstairs. Annie was holding me tight and telling me I was her sister, and she was going to protect me like big sisters do. My grandmother's cries and pleads were too much for me to handle. I stepped out of the closet, Annie's fear-filled voice was blaring in my ears, begging me not to leave the closet. I told her I had to get Amber out of this house. We hugged, and I ran downstairs.

"My mother grabbed my arm so tight, her fingernails were digging into my arm, as she angrily blamed me for Daddy taking me to my grandparents' home. She told my grandparents they would never see me again. I was crying and holding on to the banister for dear life, afraid of what was going to happen to me now. She dragged me outside by my ponytail. My head hurts now, thinking about it. I had concrete burns on my legs from her dragging me to the beat-up brown Impala. My mother threw me into the backseat of the car. I remember looking out the back window with tears in my eyes and pain in my arm and legs. Looking out of the back window, I remember seeing Sandra, my grandmother, and grandfather all crying and holding each other on the porch as we were driving away. I was reaching for them and screaming their names. My mother told me to sit my ass down. I was struggling to catch my breath, gasping for air as if my lungs were being squeezed. My hands anxiously rubbed my legs for some relief.

"When we returned home, with a loving touch, my daddy tended to my legs, making sure no infection set in. He apologized for what happened. We didn't know it, but mama must have packed our bags, leaving both me and daddy oblivious to our impending departure from town that night. I remember them arguing. Amber was telling daddy she was tired of her parents getting in our business. She was the mother, not her parents, and we were leaving town that night. Daddy was refusing to leave. Mama yanked my arm. I can feel the hurtful clutch in my arm right now as I narrate. No, I do not want to stop Ms. T., before you ask. I am okay.

"My father finally gave in. He was not about to let Amber leave with me alone. Daddy helped put the bags in the car. He told me we were going on an adventure. In his peculiar way, he tried to protect me. He would always tell me to go to my room when they got high. I think he was trying to shield me from their illegal indiscretions.

"We drove two and a half hours that night to Whitton, Illinois. Mama had an old boyfriend who lived there. The hippy looking man and his girlfriend said that we could stay with them until we found our own place. Our house was immaculate compared to their squalor.

"My parents slept in the guest room. I cleaned trash from a corner of the living room and laid on the floor crying all night. Their dog slept on the couch, so I had to sleep on the floor. Still, no one ever enrolled me in school. My mother said that she was homeschooling me. We never picked up a book. I learned phonics from the PBS kids' channel and my family.

"We were there for three months. My mother was a little kinder to me. The other lady that lived there helped me. I can't remember her name. I can still smell the smoke on her clothes and breath. They always had parties. I could sleep in Mama and Daddy's room then. No one ever bothered me or tried to hurt me. They were too busy drinking, cursing, having sex, and getting high.

"The man and woman moved out and left us the house to live in. A couple of days later, Mama and Daddy left and didn't come back. Three long days had passed. There was no sign of them returning home. The food was running out. I was so scared. What in the hell were they thinking, Ms. T? Shit, Maybe I need to stop now because I feel like screaming from the top of my lungs. No, I can do this; there's no going back now. Okay, okay, let me get back on track here. Where did I stop? Nevermind, I remember. I did not have a phone to call Grandma and Grandpa. My parents told me to never leave the house. On the sixth day, I had to leave and walk to the corner store. I hadn't eaten in two days.

"I stole chips, candy, Kleenex, and a juice box. The worker could see the items bulging out of my clothes. The worker's stern gaze locked with mine as he stopped me in my tracks, reprimanding me for my act of theft. I broke down and told him everything. The police were called and so was child protective custody. My grandparents were called, and the court granted them temporary custody of me. Finally, I felt a sense of security. Six months later, the authorities found my parents in another state, living on the street.

"At six years old, the court granted my grandparents permanent custody of me. That's the end of my narration. We've been working on this specific memory for months. I rate my disturbance level of this memory a two."

"Amaya, you did well with your narration of the target memory," the therapist says, as she watches Amaya gaze off into the distance. "Amaya. Amaya. Do you hear me?"

"Yes, Ms. T."

"Great work and going from a ten to a two on the level of distress is significant progress. How are you feeling right now?"

"I'm emotionally drained, but I can't deny that I feel an enormous sense of burden leaving my chest. Going through the narration of dealing with my parents today was incredibly cathartic. Right now, I'm experiencing a tremendous sense of relief. The memories are not as frequent and they are not as intense as they were when I first started trauma therapy. During the narration, it felt like I was there living it again, in some parts of my story. I reminded myself that I'm not five years-old anymore and I have a wonderful husband to protect me."

Ms. T goes to the break room to get some ice for Amaya to hold. She returns with two pieces of ice, placing one in each of Amaya's hands. Afterward, she plays one of Amaya's favorite upbeat songs. As a result, Amaya feels calmer and lighter.

"Some of the stress in your daily life stems from the trauma inflicted by your parents. When we talk about things that have a high emotional impact on us, it causes our mind and body to feel physically and emotionally 'exhausted', as you stated. Remember, trauma has helped you to develop strength in-spite of the abuse. You are a survivor. I want you to recognize your strengths. You can still do this without minimizing the abuse. You are in control. We are going to stop here. Your homework is to journal your thoughts and feelings about today's session. Don't forget to write something that you are grateful for at the end of your journaling. When you leave, I want you to do something fun. It's Saturday; go practice some self-care."

"Thank you so much. It was a healing session today."

Amaya decides against talking to her husband about adopting a baby today. She recognizes the need to prioritize the progress made in therapy. "I will go write in my journal and listen to some soothing music, maybe Raheem De-Vaughn."

Chapter Ten

Amaya

Amaya hears the garage door open. Her husband is home. She has been counting down the minutes, anticipating his arrival all day. She wonders if she should tell him about the ghost-like figure she saw in the living room. As she ponders it for a second, she realizes that there's no need to trouble him with her vivid imagination.

As he walks in, he places his backpack on the desk and heads to the living room to greet his wife. When she sees him, a smile automatically brightens her face. She offers him a glass of Marcassin Estate chardonnay to celebrate his new account. He accepts the wine and sits next to her on the sofa. She asks did he enjoy the celebration after work. Quentin's mind goes to Mastodon Lake. The image that flashes through his mind caused him to down the glass of wine faster than usual. Shooting him a look, Amaya laughs.

Amaya offers to refill his glass. He nods and holds his glass towards the bottle. Amaya pours the wine and suggests he sips it, reminding him it's not apple juice. She lends a hand to him as he removes his suit jacket, and he takes off his tie.

"I have a couple of surprises for you, Amaya," says Quentin.

"Really? Tell me. Tell me," she says with enthusiasm in her voice.

"First, put your glass down," he says.

As she puts her glass on the table, she looks at him with a curious expression. He clears his throat and holds his head up high before revealing the surprise.

"The director of Save the Children Charity contacted me yesterday and revealed we are the recipients of the 2023 Philanthropist Award."

"That's great news, babe. But I don't need recognition for giving. My grandparents were incredibly generous people. Why hold on to money you can't even spend in two lifetimes?"

"Baby, we're going to attend this gala and receive the prestigious award. Do you want to hear the second surprise?"

As she hears the news that she'll also be delivering a speech, butterflies flutter in her stomach, and a lump forms in her throat. "Babe, you know I have a fear of speaking in public."

"I know, my love. But I'll be right by your side. You can do it."

She looks down at the floor and admits, "I don't think I can. You're the one who enjoys being in the limelight, not me."

"I'll help you write the speech."

Amaya knows trying to argue is futile. He always wins.

Curious, she asks, "So, what's the second surprise, sweetheart?"

"Babe, Josh and I have arranged for you and Bree to have a weekend getaway at the Peninsula Spa next weekend."

"Baby, I can't go next weekend. I have the board meeting to prepare for."

"Nonsense. Kathy and Jeff can handle things while you're away."

He pulls her close to him, and she can smell the faint scent of women's perfume as they relax on the comfortable sofa. She sits up and asks, "Why do you smell like women's perfume?"

"Man, we were all hugging each other, toasting with our coffee cups in celebration of landing the largest account ever."

"Ah, okay. That makes sense. Debra has great taste in perfumes."

There is silence as she lays back in his arms.

Looking at his tie, he's reminded of Pamela. "I will throw it away in the morning."

Before going to bed, he takes the battery out of Pamela's phone while Amaya is in the bathroom. He'll have to come up with a plan on how to discard the phone.

Quentin's had three glasses of chardonnay. He's relaxed. His eyes are closed, enjoying rubbing his wife's breasts, and she whispers to him.

"Q, we need to talk. It's important, but it can wait until tomorrow."

In an instant, his eyes snap open, and a cold, clammy sweat trickles down his forehead, sending shivers down his spine.

Chapter Eleven

Amaya's Diary

At 11:32 p.m., Amaya and Quentin decide to call it a night after unwinding with wine and watching three recorded episodes of the Cherri Lamb daytime talk show. Amaya quickly falls asleep, while Quentin mindlessly scrolls through Facebook. As he glances over at her nightstand, he notices Amaya's diary. He looks at her. She is dead to the world, with drool trickling from the corner of her mouth. He reaches over her, grabs the diary, and starts reading it.

Saturday, December 4, 2022

Something happened in therapy today, maybe a breakthrough, I'm not sure. While I was in my weekly therapy session, I felt the need to share my early years of neglect growing up with my mama and daddy. At least I know why I'm so screwed up. Thanks Amber and Larry for your wonderful parental skills. Why am I being so sarcastic? Because this is the only safe place I feel comfortable talking and not feeling judged.

Money. Money. Money. I wish Amber understood why granddad and grandmother left the money and assets to me. It's the damn drugs. It's messed up her brain cells. I remember the reading of the will when the lawyer said I would receive a third of the inheritance now and the rest when I'm thirty. The money would be forfeit to St. Jude Hospital and the Trevor Project if I didn't graduate from college and achieve financial stability. I wasn't a bit surprised by my grandparents' wishes. They instilled in me several skills: being innovative, kind, be a leader, honest, and do not be afraid of working toward success. Amber did not learn those skills. I miss them so damn much!

I can still vividly recall the anger etched on my mother's face when she received only some stocks and antiques from her childhood, while our housekeeper and her daughter were each given a million dollars. The reading left her livid. She totally lost it on the lawyer, trying to grab the documents and tear them up, and knocking things off his desk.

In all honesty, the truth is the allure of the money isn't appealing to me. There are more important things I want in life. I don't want money that comes from people losing their livelihoods because of prejudice. My great-great grandparents lost their business and one of their sons in 1921 during the Tulsa Massacre. Maybe I should say the Black Wall Street Massacre. They moved there with the insurance money and started their own black-owned insurance company. Montgomery Mutual Insurance Company. I'm proud of the legacy they left. I'm proud to have the Montgomery name. It's a powerful name. I just wish I was as strong as my last name.

I don't want the money. What I want is my grandparents back. On my sad days, my grandparents had the magical power to stop the rain from falling and send my cloudy days away. I need them to be here with me. It's my fault they died in the car accident. They were on their way to my eighteenth birthday party. I didn't have many friends, but they made sure it was nice. They never came. While I was celebrating, they were dying in their car from a hit-and-run driver. Fuck the person who took them from me. I hope whoever it was is haunted by their actions for the rest of their life. It's been eleven years since the accident and I'm still in this black hole trying to scratch my way out.

I sometimes wonder if I wasn't rich if Quentin would have given me a second look. He's so handsome, but not perfect. Why in the hell does he have to be right all the time? LOL You can't tell him anything. That's just part of his charm. I know he loves me. He put up with my weird ass.

There are a lot of unexplainable things happening to me. Probably from me wanting a baby. Childlessness brings a deep feeling of loneliness. Damn! I wish I had my granddad here to make one of his corny ass jokes and tell me he's going to make everything okay. Maybe being infertile wouldn't be such a punch in the gut if he were here. I've wanted to be a mother since I was twelve. I remember granddad playing with me. He would talk to my baby dolls and tell them they had a good mommy. I just can't get over not having a baby in my home to love. I can't seem to think of anything else.

How can I convince my husband that adopting a baby right now is the right decision for us? Hmm...maybe I will adopt without him? It's important that the Montgomery name doesn't end with me; I want my family name to continue through my children.

I could go to South Korea and adopt a baby. Quentin wouldn't stay mad at me for long. Oh my goodness, he would be such a great daddy to our baby.

Quentin closes the diary, carefully returning it to Amaya's nightstand. After lying in bed for fifteen minutes, he feels the need to pick up the diary once more and continue reading through its entries.

Wednesday, November 2, 2022

I feel like I need more from my husband because although our sex life is great, there is a lack of emotional connection between us now. I've noticed that he has become short-tempered with me lately and it seems like I irritate him sometimes. This behavior is out of character for him, which makes me wonder what's going on. I know he loves me because he is still supportive of me during my moments of constant crying and forgetfulness. I just wish I could help.

Oh, yeah- Josh told me he saw Amber standing outside Woodman's Food Market today. She was clutching a sign, begging for money to buy food. I suspected it was for drugs. It's been so long since I've seen her and daddy. I've made the hard decision that until they choose to live a drug-free life, I cannot have them in my life.

I hear Bae rinsing his mouth after brushing his teeth. That's it for tonight.

"I suppose having a diary should help her feel better or something," he says as he returned the diary to its rightful spot.

Chapter Twelve

SANDRA

It's 8:30 a.m., Monday morning. Sandra, the dutiful housekeeper and Amaya's confidant has arrived to start her workday. She enters through the front door and the first person she sees is Quentin. With hesitation, she greets him, and he greets her back, their voices barely above a whisper. Sandra places her purse and coat on the coat rack. The vibrations of hangers add to the room's atmosphere of unease.

Quentin walks into the home gym to complete his workout for the morning. "Sandra, don't forget to clean and disinfect the whirlpool before you leave," says Quentin as he brags about his body and workout regimen.

Quentin's condescending emphasis causes Sandra's muscles to tighten, and a wave of heat rushes to her face. "I clean the whirlpool every Monday and today will not be any different." She walks away, trying to shake off the frustration of Quentin's tone and his mere existence on earth.

Sandra is kind and protective of Amaya. She has worked for Amaya's family since she was eighteen. Amaya's grandmother hired her as a housekeeper from a local agency when Sandra was five months pregnant and living in a shelter. Sandra's father was a deacon at their church. He and the pastor wanted her to stand in front of the church and request forgiveness for her pregnancy. Her father kicked her out of her house because she refused to do so.

Amaya enters the living room. "Good morning. Is my husband in the gym?" asks Amaya.

"Good morning, sunshine! He's been in the gym for a while now."

"I was just thinking about my grandparents telling me the story of how you came into our lives. You were so brave when you were eighteen. You defended your position. I can hear my grandmother's voice when she told me you told the church in no uncertain terms, 'I have no need for forgiveness from the church. This matter is between me and my God.' And your family kicked you out of the house because you refused to apologize to the church."

"And when your wonderful grandparents heard my story, they asked me to move in as their live-in housekeeper. I never left. It's been thirty-four years now. Your grandparents made me feel like I was one of the family. It's still unbelievable they left Annie and I a million dollars apiece."

"Why not? You're a part of our family. They wanted to make sure you and Annie were financially secure for the rest of your lives. I know you've continued to work for me since the car accident that took their lives, so you could continue to watch over me and take care of me. I'm sure that did not help the strained relationship between you and Annie."

"I'm all you have from your past since your grandparents have gone to heaven. Being a housekeeper is something I love to do, even with my riches in the bank collecting interest. You have always been a second daughter to me. You and Annie were so close once upon a time. I can still see you two dancing and singing to all New Edition's songs. You were in love with Ronny, and Annie loved the bad boy, Mr. Bobby Brown. I took you girls to see them. It was your first concert."

"I remember those days fondly. I remember changing my crush to Johnny Gill. Annie said I wasn't a loyal fan and 'Stick with one member and not hop around'." Amaya tilts her head back, puts her hands over her mouth, and bursts into laughter.

"You two were like sisters. I wish you girls would reconnect."

Sandra is sad because Annie doesn't talk to her regularly because of her envy of Amaya. Sandra loves Amaya like a daughter, but that doesn't diminish the love she has for her own daughter. As Annie entered her teenage years, she couldn't help but notice how her mother seemed to devote more attention to Amaya. The green monster of jealousy reared its ugly head, filling her heart with bitterness towards the person she once cared for like a sister. The sight of her mother's affectionate and constant support towards Amaya over the years caused the two girls to become distant.

"That's true," says Amaya. "She just couldn't understand during our teenage years how I was struggling. She was the social butterfly. I felt invisible when I was being bullied. Annie no longer wanted to be seen with me. I understand how she must have felt, but we're adults now. I'm twenty-nine and she's thirty-two. It's time to let all this go. I reached out to her several times, but she left me on red. She was jealous of me because of the money. I know all about it. I overheard you two talking one evening. You told her, 'One thing a person learns in life is that no amount of money will solve your real-life problems.' That's the gospel."

"Well, Annie lives in a posh neighborhood in Florida with her two elementary school children. She's a single mother who lost her husband to another woman. With all her money- she could not buy happiness. A lesson she has learned the hard way. My daughter will not continue to push me away. I was telling Josh the other day about my plans to fly out and see her soon. I will not tell her because she would make up and excuse not to see me."

"Do what you need to do. Always remember that Annie is family, too. I'm not sure how she will respond if you just show up at her door. It reminds me of the 'Call Your Mother' sitcom, where the mother did the same thing. Sherri, my girl, was her sidekick. It's a shame the show got cancelled. I need to go grab some breakfast and get out of here. This conversation is a great start for my day. I love you so much. Thank you for being the one constant in my life."

"I love you, too, Amaya boo."

Sandra is busy dusting the sculptures when Quentin, sweaty and all, shows up and demands that she iron his white-collared shirt. Sandra tells him she will iron the shirt while he's showering. Amaya overhears the conversation as she comes into the living room with orange juice and wheat toast.

"Baby." she says, "I ironed your shirt. It's hanging on the closet door." He kisses her on the cheek, pats her butt, and then heads to the shower.

Once again, Amaya apologizes for Quentin's obnoxious behavior.

"There's no need for you to take responsibility for your husband's rudeness," says Sandra.

"Sweetheart, before you head to work, did you talk to Mr. Quentin about adoption this past weekend like you planned?"

"No. It's not a good time to talk to him about adoption. There is some good news, though. I completed my second target memory. We did the last part of the intervention, the narration. I shared about Mama and Daddy. Specifically, the time they left me alone for days and grandma and grandad received custody of me."

"How are you? I can't imagine how difficult that was for you," Sandra says, trying not to sound worried.

"I have practiced meditation for the past two days. It's a great way to quiet my mind and slow down the negative thoughts in my head. I can be in the present moment with calmness and peace."

Sandra stands silently, weighing Amaya's meaningful words, feeling elated that Amaya is learning how to show her emotions safely. Now if she can only see her husband for who and what he really is.

"Meditation, huh? I would love to try it with you sometime."

"Whenever you're ready. Hey, I forgot to tell you that Quentin and Josh are sending Bree and I away for the weekend. It's a spa resort. I'm excited. Bree needs to get away. She is always on edge when I am around her, and Josh's cheating on her doesn't help."

"You work so hard too," Sandra says, hearing the exhaustion in Amaya's voice. "The spa getaway will be a rejuvenating experience for both of you."

Sandra glances at Amaya's and Quentin's wedding picture on the mantle and feels a spasm in her back, thinking of the unholy union. Well, holy from Amaya's perspective. She turns from the picture, determined to keep her day free from any negativity. Quentin and Amaya leave for work. Sandra finishes her dusting, sweeping, vacuuming, and emptying the trash. She is ready to take a break. Before she does, she practices her every Monday ritual, searching the web and putting Quentin's name on every spam list she can find.

Chapter Thirteen

Quentin Mike Amber

It's Friday morning, and Amaya and Bree are leaving for their spa weekend. Sandra drives them to the airport and will return to take care of her cleaning duties. Quentin could not drive them. He has more pressing things to do. He has been waiting ten years for this moment.

When Amaya's grandparents passed away, she could only inherit one-third of her inheritance. The probate lawyer will grant the remaining millions to her once she reaches the age of thirty, under the condition that she completes college and establishes a successful life for herself. If she cannot meet these conditions, the probate lawyer will divide the inheritance between her grandparents' favorite charities, the Trevor Project and St. Jude's Hospital.

Quentin drives through the city, scanning the streets for Amber, Amaya's mother. First, he looks for her at Ms. Ryan's place. She supplies alcohol and drugs to people. She has rooms for them to get high for a fee. But Amber isn't there. The faint smell of exhaust lingers in the air as he pulls up to the second location, an old flea market space which has been vacant for a couple of years. Stepping out of his car with determination, his footsteps move with vigor. He spots Amber and a surge of relief washes over him.

He has found her. A smile spreads across her face when she sees him and utters his name in an excited tone. As he talks to her, his voice rises with anticipation of how Amber will help with his plans. A flicker of excitement dances in her eyes when she hears his plan to secure an apartment for her and Larry. Her voice trembles with excitement as she eagerly asks, "When?" Without hesitation, Quentin responds, "Now, let's go."

They soon arrive at the apartment complex.

"All the paperwork is complete, the rent is paid for a year, and your furniture will be delivered within the next two days. Here are the keys to the apartment. I have food in the refrigerator and cleaning supplies. Keep this damn place clean, Amber. You're not living on the streets anymore. The lease is in your name. Just don't mess it up."

"Thanks son-in-law. Ooh, look at this bedroom. Me and my man can do some stuff in here," says Amber as she does the twerking dance.

"TMI Amber. Just enjoy the apartment. Your bed will be here in time for your bedroom rodeo."

"Hey, why you doing this for me? What do I have to do for this? I ain't doing no sexual favors for you," says Amber, laughing and slapping Quentin on the shoulder. "I'm just joking."

Quentin nods, then to stroke her ego, he says-"you have always been smart. I have a proposal for you."

"A proposal? What you want. If I don't do it, I still get the apartment, right?"

"I need your help with Amaya's birthday gift. I want her thirtieth birthday to be memorable."

"Son-in-law, it can't help but to be memorable for her. She is inheriting millions of dollars that belong to me. She's the golden granddaughter. I didn't give birth to a baby. I gave birth to the golden troll who stole my life."

Quentin listens without interruption. Amber looks at him, with tears shimmering like dewdrops on a morning leaf. She tries to portray herself as the victim, her lips trembling. The apartment infuses with a suffocating tension, as she continues to be clueless on how her drug-induced lifestyle caused her to lose everything.

He thinks, "If this damn woman doesn't stop playing the victim all the time." His expression remains composed, as if accepting her chaotic lifestyle is normal. He realizes he must endure this pity party to get what he needs. He smiles and nods his head throughout her venting. This allows him the means to manipulate and distort information about Amaya and her deceased grandparents, weaving his web of lies, deceit, and control.

"Amber, tell me some of the sweet things Mr. and Mrs. Montgomery would say to Amaya. You know, the things that made you furious."

She bombards him with an overwhelming amount of information, her words spinning in a chaotic frenzy. The rapid pace of her storytelling leaves his brain in a dizzying whirlwind, struggling to process it all. He listens carefully, taking mental notes on phrases that he can use later.

Quentin cannot digest anymore of Amber's presence. He tells her, "I need to get to work."

"I'm going to cook you and my baby a good meal. You two can come to dinner next week. How about some fish sticks, canned yams, and some white bread? That sounds good, don't it?"

Quentin warns her, "Amaya would be livid if she found out about the apartment. If you and Larry want to keep it, keep your mouth shut."

"I am keeping my mouth shut," she says, pretending to zip her lips.

As he leaves the apartment, he takes out his phone to send Mike a text.

> Mike, I'm on my way back to the house. What's your ETA?

> I will be there in 20 minutes.

> Do you have everything you need?

> Yes.

> Start in the guest house. The nosey ass housekeeper is there. You can come back to do the bedroom when she leaves on her broomstick.

> Got it, Q.

Quentin arrives at his house before Mike, relieved to hear Sandra cleaning upstairs. Knowing that she always starts downstairs, Quentin stays downstairs to avoid any interaction with her. Sandra questions him frequently, which gets under his skin.

Mike arrives, and Sandra spots him entering the guest house from upstairs. Curiosity piques her interest, or maybe just to be nosey. She quickly dons her coat and heads towards the guest house.

"Hey, Mr. Mike! I am surprised to see you here today. Is there something wrong with the guest house? I clean it once a month, and I've noticed nothing out of the ordinary."

"Good morning, Ms. Sandra. You look as lovely as always. Quentin has requested me to make some upgrades. I'll install remote-controlled ceiling fans, update the outlets, and upgrade the electrical wiring."

"That sounds nice. I'll let you continue with your rewiring. If you're thirsty or need anything, come up to the main house. Have a good day."

"I will."

Sandra leaves and makes her way back to the main house. Mike acknowledges Quentin was right about Sandra. She's incredibly nosy. He calls Quentin and informs him about the encounter with Sandra. He assures Quentin that he handled the situation well. Now, he needs to install remote-operated fans and change the outlets. Mike tells Quentin that it seemed like Sandra was spying on him. Quentin responds, "I told you she was a witch who doesn't know her place.

It's fine. Install the fans and do whatever else you told her. I should have thought of a cover plan for you to be here. I can't believe I didn't think of a cover. Oh well. I'm entitled to make one mistake in my life."

"Umm... Yeah, okay. I'll get it done," says Mike.

It's 5:00 and Sandra's workday is complete. She's looking forward to a relaxing weekend. Amaya is at the spa, so Sandra doesn't have any worries. Quentin notices Sandra leaving and calls Mike to come back and do the electrical work in the main house. His plan is in motion.

Mike returns to complete setting up the house for Quentin's gaslighting plan to succeed. Quentin gives him the run of the house. He sits on the sofa and turns on the DVR and watches his favorite talk show, Cherri Lamb. Quentin goes into the kitchen and grabs a beer. He offers Mike one, but he declines, choosing to be level-headed while working with electricity. Quentin sits back down to watch the show, shaking his head and saying. "That Cherri, know she's fine."

After three hours, Mike informs Quentin that it's finally done. He then hands over the remote control and explains how the hoodwink works. Mike advises him to avoid making mistakes and study the schemes all weekend. Mike mentions he expects to be paid regardless of Quentin's performance.

Quentin makes a call and informs the person on the other end that everything is ready. He has the phrases from the grandparents' conversation with Amaya and VHS recordings, which he needs the person on the phone to give the voice interpreter. "The anguish will begin upon her return," says Quentin.

Quentin's heart races as he remembers he forgot to give Amber the cell phone she needs. Hastily, he bolts out of the house, and the door slams shut behind him. The cold winter air rushes past him, bringing with it a crisp clean smell. Determined, Quentin races towards the apartment, his mind filled with the urgency of catching Amber before she becomes too high on drugs to comprehend his message.

Arriving at the apartment, Quentin knocks on the door, but there's no answer. He attempts to turn the doorknob and discovers that the door is unlocked. Stepping inside, he discovers Amber lying unconscious on the floor. He's too late. Quentin is getting exactly what he is paying for.

Chapter Fourteen

The Guest House

It's 2:52 p.m. on Monday. Bree and Amaya have just returned from their spa weekend. Josh and Quentin are waiting outside the airport pickup area for their wives. The ladies spot their husbands and give them hugs. Bree feels the need to hug her husband to show her gratitude for the spa weekend. Both ladies seem happy and content with life as they laugh and joke while their husbands gather their suitcases.

They all enter Quentin's warm car and ride eighteen minutes home from the airport. "Well," Amaya says, as she searches the Sirus XM Radio stations. "I'd better check in with Jeff and Kathy at the office." Quentin encourages her to enjoy her last day off and touch bases with them when she returns to work.

"Thanks for everything, Quentin and Josh. The trip was amazing and just what we needed. I had the best time catching up with Amaya," says Bree.

Josh softly touches her leg and replies, "You're welcome."

They arrive back at Amaya's and Quentin's home. Stepping out of the car, Amaya adjusts her scarf and coat to keep warm. Everyone hugs outside. "Bree, we better get home. I know you're ready to see Lil Josh," says Josh.

"I am. I need a big hug from my big boy." Bree waves goodbye and takes Josh's hand and they walk to the car. Josh has a puzzled expression on his face. Bree hasn't shown him this much affection in years. Maybe if she had, he wouldn't be a serial cheater. Or he would have still cheated, but perhaps 25% less.

It's now 5:45. The soft golden rays of the setting sun filter through the bedroom curtains. The couple stands in front of their mirrored wardrobe in anticipation of the wonderful evening to come. Amaya gracefully slips into her navy blue long-sleeve side-ruched sequin gown, the sequins shimmering like stars on a clear night. The fabric hugs her figure, accentuating her every curve. Quentin loves her in clothes that show off her body. He's dressed in his black Emporio Armani wool two-piece suit, the smooth texture of the fabric exuding sophistication.

He carefully adjusts his navy blue-tie, not the one he strangled Pamela with, of course. The color contrasts an elegant look against the darkness of the suit. Amaya's perfume fills the bedroom, a rich amber fragrance that lingers. Quentin slips on his sleek black Stacy Adams Cap Toe Oxfords. The polished leather shoes reflect the light from the chandelier above.

Amaya's heart flutters with nerves as they prepare to meet their friends at the symphony that evening. She feels a sense of unease, doubting if she can truly fit in with Quentin's group of friends because of her anxiety. Although the couple they're meeting is nice, they often ignore Amaya's suggestions or contributions to the conversation.

Quentin puts on his Rolex and asks Amaya about the tickets. She says they're in her purse. "Are you hungry?" he asks. Quentin suggests warming up something before they go to the symphony. Amaya declines, saying she's too nervous to eat. However, she's open to getting dinner after the show. Amaya steps into the bathroom to check her makeup before they leave. Quentin lusts for her as she does a 360-turn, showcasing her sexy body in the evening dress. "You look perfect, sweetheart," he says. Amaya blushes, feeling flattered. Quentin's eyes light up with desire, and he whispers, "Oh baby, we might not even make it to the show. You look so tantalizing."

"Come on, baby," she says. "We don't want to keep the Murrays waiting." Downstairs, he gets her coat and assists her in putting it on. Meanwhile, she gathers her gloves and scarf as he dons his own coat. Before they leave, she affectionately plants a gentle kiss on his lips. With her purse containing the tickets in hand, they embark on their way to experience Bruckner Symphony No.8.

The opulent lobby, illuminated by the soft, warm light of elegant chandeliers, greets the Murrays as they enter the grand symphony hall. Dressed in their finest attire, they patiently wait for Amaya and Quentin. The four together ascend the polished escalator, making their way towards the entrance. Approaching the ticket attendant, the Murrays extend their tickets, but Amaya's heart sinks as she opens her purse, only to find no tickets. Panic sets in as she turns to Quentin.

"Baby," says Amaya, her voice trembling with panic, "they're not in here." Her chest tightens, causing heavy breathing, and her hands grow cold and clammy, slick with sweat.

"Honey, you said the tickets were in your purse," says Quentin as he grabs her purse to help her look for the tickets.

Amaya's mind races, defending herself. "I put them in my purse when I got out of the shower," she says.

Quentin's frustration mounts. "You didn't check before we left?" he asks.

Amaya's voice trembles. "No, because I knew they were in my purse."

Quentin attempts to apologize to the Murrays for the inconvenience, but Amaya interrupts, a hint of defiance in her tone. "Don't you dare blame me! You could have checked or reminded me to check for the tickets. I put them in my purse. I'm sure of it." Quentin's face contorts into a sneer, offended by her audacity.

He directs his words to their friends. "We're going to head home. My wife has been forgetful and acting sort of wacky lately. This isn't the first time something like this has happened." Amaya reacts with disgust at Quentin for sharing her memory problems with everyone and now the Murrays. "I don't want to discuss it any further. You have no right to tell anyone about my personal business."

"Enjoy the show. I need to take my wife home to rest."

"It's a shame we can't enjoy this beautiful night together. You two drive home safely," says Stacy Murray.

Angrily, Amaya exclaims, "Let's plan to get together soon, okay? Come on, Q!" Her voice pierces as she storms off.

At home, Quentin berates Amaya about the tickets, and tells her, "I can't continue to live like this. I'm worried about you."

"There is nothing wrong with me. I may forget sometimes, but that comes from stress."

"Are you kidding me? What about when you bought the wrong wine last week? Forgetting your file for that important meeting. Should I go on? I'm worried about your mental health. You should worry, too."

"You are blowing this out of proportion," says Amaya, rolling her eyes.

"Okay, okay. Where's the tickets, huh?" he asks, staring intensely at her.

She searches everywhere for the tickets. She does not understand what could have happened to them.

"I don't know. I guess they fell out of my purse on the way there. Maybe they're in the parking lot."

"Look, I'm going to change clothes and head downstairs to warm up something for us to eat. Stop worrying about the tickets, it's all over. Tonight is a wash."

She's fed up and feeling tired. Without responding to him, she pivots towards her jewelry box and carefully places the pieces she was wearing inside.

After a few minutes, he returns to the bedroom, carrying a plate of reheated roasted chicken that releases a tantalizing aroma of his special herbs and spices. Alongside it is Amaya's favorite food: creamy garlic mashed potatoes, and vibrant green beans. Amaya stands by the open bedroom window, breathing in the chilly breeze rustling the curtains. Amaya's exposure to the cold weather causes a shift in her parasympathetic nervous system. It's a technique called "icing" that helps to relax the body. She learned this from her therapist. Ms. T. taught her other techniques to activate the vagus nervous system and decrease anxiety: taking a cold bath or shower, splashing cold water on her face, drinking ice cold water, and standing outside for five to ten minutes in the cold.

Her eyes narrow as she notices light emanating from the guest house. Confusion etches her face as she turns to Quentin who has put the plates down, and stands near her, the remote control nestled in the pocket of his plush robe. With furrowed brows, she questions him, "Why are there lights on in the guest house?" He walks closer to his wife, the soft carpet beneath his feet absorbing his footsteps. With a gentle touch, he places his hand on her arm, offering false reassurance.

"There is no light on in the guest house," he says, his voice laced with a bogus mix of curiosity and worry.

"What do you mean? You can't tell me you can't see there are lights on in the guest house. Lights are never on. We have not had a guess there in over a year."

"I find it difficult to comprehend the workings of your mind, my delicate wife. Perhaps it is because I'm not burdened by the same brokenness that you carry."

"You can't understand my mind? Are you saying I'm broken? You know, you see the light in the guest house. I don't understand your mind either or your eyesight."

"Who do you think is in the guest house? Tell me."

"Maybe Amber. I don't know," she says, her eyebrows furrowed in confusion, and her eyes fixate on the guest house. A shiver runs down her spine, and a sense of terror grips her when Quentin argues he doesn't see the light in the guest house. With trembling hands, she hastily closes the window, blocking out the eerie howl of the wind. Taking a deep breath, she turns and makes her way towards the untouched plate of food and picks up her fork.

"Put your fork down," Quentin says. "Here's your trench coat. Put it on. It's time to settle this for once and for all. We're going to walk to the guest house so you can face the reality that there is no light on, and the guest house is empty."

"I'll go with you to the guest house," she says, her voice dripping with anger while slipping on her tennis shoes, "so that you can see the lights are on inside. I can't believe we're arguing about lights."

They leave the house and head to the guest house. The night air is frosty with a biting chill that seeps into every corner of their bodies. As they exhale, breath vapors form clouds in the air, a visible testament to the frigid weather. Each puff hangs in the frigid air before dissipating into the darkness. As they get closer, she tells him to look. There are lights on in there; she's sure of it.

She turns to face him to see his expression because she knows she is right. While his hands are in his coat pockets to keep warm, he reaches for the remote and clicks it to turn the lights out. She turns back around, and the guest house is dark. Feeling immobilized, she can hardly process what she's seeing. There are no lights now. Her mind is racing.

"The...the lights were on. I swear they were."

"Amaya, you have been ruining everything lately. You go to weekly therapy appointments, but baby, you're still out of your damn mind. You need to find someone else to talk to. Ms. T. is just taking your money. I'm saying this because I care about you. You have a serious problem, babe, and that is why you only have a few friends. 'I'm so nervous. No one likes me. I don't fit in. I don't deserve all I have, blah, blah, blah.' Would you want to be around such a killjoy?" he says with drooping eyelids and lowered lips, mocking her.

"By the way, I wouldn't go telling that therapist of yours about seeing lights that are not on and failing to remember so many things. She will lock you away. That can't happen. Your company shares will drop and you will lose everything.

I'm telling you all this for your own good. Not to hurt you. All we need is each other. You don't need a therapist. Therapy is a waste of time and money."

Amaya's heart is pounding in her chest as she feels vulnerable and taken aback at Quentin's harsh tone and the hurtful words he just uttered. She cannot comprehend how he could be so savage. His words slash through her like a knife. Amaya runs away as she could not stand to look at her husband after his cruel words to her. But suddenly, she halts, her body trembling from the anger she has inside. She turns around, her finger pointing directly at him, her voice quivering as she musters up the strength to speak her truth.

"You will not talk to me in such a harsh way. I am not your dog. I am your wife, and you will treat me like your wife. You're exasperated with me. Let me tell you something. I am exasperated with your criticism and constant judgment of me. You think I don't pick up on the sarcastic remarks you say to me or about me in front of others? I do. I love you, but this has to stop."

Quentin's heart races as he hears the unexpected sharpness in his wife's voice. Worry grips him as he contemplates his plan to drive her to madness. "What a terrible time for her to standup for herself," he thinks. Unable to find the right words, he stands in stunned silence. The frigid air stings his cheeks as Amaya declares her unwillingness to continue the conversation and retreat into the warmth of the house. Her words stuck in his mind, leaving him fuming. The biting cold seems to seep into his bones as she coldly says, "You can stay out here and freeze to death for all I care."

She enters their home, taking off her coat and rubbing her arms to warm up. Then she heads upstairs to her temperate bedroom. After a quick stop in the bathroom to wash the makeup off her face, she comes out to see Quentin standing in the room. His face fills with resentment as he confronts her. "You owe me an apology," he says.

Brushing off the tension, she calmly replies, "Good night, Quentin. I'm going to bed now." Quentin storms out of the bedroom in anger. Amaya, however, remains composed and thinks to herself, "I know he doesn't expect me to run after him. Whatever."

It's 8:51 p.m. Amaya calls Josh while lying in bed crying, tears falling like raindrops from a cloud.

"Hey, Amaya. What's up cousin?"

"Are you busy? I really need to talk to someone."

"Are you alright?"

"I'm terrified. Lately, I've been so forgetful and disoriented. Quentin isn't making me feel loved or supported at all. In fact, he's acting like an ass. I love him, but I don't know how much more I can take of him."

"What has he done? He's always telling me how much he loves you."

"I know he loves me, but he keeps blaming me for things I know I haven't done. He's said hurtful things to me and then denies ever saying them. Sometimes he even twists things around to gain the upper hand. I just don't feel like myself anymore. It's making me really anxious. I just want to disappear. I would love to wear a magical cloak of invisibility."

"You know how your husband is, cousin. He's been my best friend for fifteen years, but he's definitely an acquired taste. He's a good man, but I won't let him disrespect you. I'm going to talk to him about this."

"No... no, please don't. I just need to talk to my best friend."

"I'll respect your wishes and your marriage. But if this continues, I will speak to him."

"Thank you for always having my back. I love you, cousin."

Josh and Amaya stay on the phone for about forty-five minutes until she eventually drifts off to sleep while talking. Josh hears her snoring and hangs up. Quentin creeps into the bedroom and places the lost tickets in Amaya's everyday purse, then climbs in the bed.

At 6:30 a.m. on Tuesday morning, Quentin's vibrating Fitbit alarms go off, signaling it is time to wake up. He gently nudges Amaya, hoping to wake her up without startling her. As she sits up in bed, he notices dried tears on her face. Quentin asks if he could talk to her for a minute, but she immediately refuses, grabbing her pillow and covering her head with the quilt. Determined to make an obvious disingenuous amends, he expresses his desire to apologize by kneeling on one knee in the bed and giving her the puppy dog look. Amaya sits up once again, listening as he speaks. Quentin says, "I'm sorry for the harsh way I spoke to you last night. I apologize for the hurtful impact my words had on you, but you can't deny the truth. I regret causing you pain, and I promise that I'll never let it happen again. Please trust me and find it in your heart to forgive your husband."

"Last night can't happen again. It feels like I'm losing my mind. This has been going on for months now. I have to talk to my therapist about what's happening to me. I have no one to talk to but my therapist. You continue to tell me not to tell her because of the company. I'm not listening any longer."

Quentin, with bug-eyes and nervous trepidation, fears the therapist will catch on to his scheme, and reminds Amaya that's not an option.

"Sweetheart, you can talk to me. I will help you. You don't want to look weak to the stockholders or your staff. You worry about people judging you. What do you think will happen when she has you admitted to a behavioral mental health hospital?"

"I'll think about it. She really helps me."

"You have me. The person who loves you the most. Talk to me. We can get through this together."

After their early morning conversation, Amaya heads to the shower to prepare for the workday ahead. Meanwhile, Quentin shakes his head with relief, a devious smile creeping across his face as he realizes he still has control over his wife.

Chapter Fifteen

Amaya Jeff Kathy

When Amaya walks into the office's conference room, she notices Kathy and Jeff discussing a project that is of top priority for the company and needs to be finished by a deadline. "Hey guys. I'm back and ready to dive in. Catch me up on everything," Amaya says with a blissful tone, trying to detract herself from the horrible events of the night before.

"Girl, welcome back! Come, sit and tell us all about your weekend," says Kathy as she takes Amaya's hand and guides her to the leather office sofa.

"Cuz, I want to hear all about it. Everyone can't afford to go away for a revitalizing weekend," says Jeff.

"It was a peaceful escape from my daily stress. I was feeling a little guilty for leaving you two to manage the staff with a deadline looming on this project."

"Was it beautiful there?" asks Kathy.

"Oh yes. There was an exquisite inside garden atrium filled with vibrant flowers and lush greenery. When we arrived, we felt like royalty. The servers were so nice and friendly. They presented us with a glass of velvety wine. Bree and I indulged ourselves by basking in the soothing warmth of the mineral pool, treating our skin to rejuvenating facials that have never felt so good, and immersing ourselves in invigorating yoga classes. When she practiced Pilates, I lay next to the therapeutic waterfall, meditating and allowing the gentle mist to caress my skin. It was Heaven."

"One day, my wife and I may go on a couple's spa retreat," says Jeff.

Amaya expresses her intention, saying, "I am actually thinking about taking all the employees and their partners to a spa weekend this summer." Kathy, with laughter in her voice, replies, "Well, since I don't have a partner, just send me to the spa a day early. I won't feel shortchanged since it's only me."

"Alright, alright. Let's buckle down and get to work. It's great to have you back, cousin," says Jeff.

Amaya tells them she will be right back and walks to her office. As she reaches her office, she pauses for a moment, taking a deep breath to prepare herself for the work ahead. Carefully, she hangs up her coat and reaches into her purse in search of a peppermint. A look of bewilderment washes over her face as she discovers the lost tickets are in her purse. Her breath catches in her throat, and more doubts creep. Is she really losing her mind? "Could my husband be right? Is there something seriously wrong with me? Am I incompetent?"

Amaya calls Ms. T. and requests a therapy session tomorrow instead of waiting until Saturday. Ms. T. agrees and tells her to come in at 10:00 a.m. Amaya practices the 5-4-3-2-1 technique Ms. T. taught her. This grounding technique requires a person to be in the present moment without judgmental thoughts, helping to reduce symptoms of anxiety and depression. She begins by looking around the office and naming five things she can see and remaining positive. She provides minor details about each object. Then, she focuses on the next four things she can physically feel. She notices the sensation of her white satin blouse and the softness of her hair. She picks up her personal fan, examining its weight, and finally sits in her office chair, feeling how it contours to her body.

Then, she focuses on three things she can hear. Closing her eyes, she tunes in to the sounds she usually ignores. The printers running outside her door, the humming of the heating system, and the chatter of people become prominent in her awareness. Moving on, she explores two things she can smell. She lifts her candle, allowing the warm vanilla scent to envelop her, creating a comforting ambiance and filling the air with the fragrance of her Parfums De Marly. Lastly, she reaches into her drawer and retrieves a piece of gum. With careful attention, she savors the taste and how the gum feels when she chews.

After finishing the exercise, she takes ten deep breaths, ensuring her mouth remains closed. She inhales as much air as she can into her lungs, holding it at the top of her breath for four seconds, before exhaling through her open mouth. Feeling less anxious, she is now ready to begin her work.

Once skeptical about mindfulness, she now believes in its benefits for well-being and resilience of the practice, and she continues to integrate mindfulness practices into her daily routine.

Chapter Sixteen

QUENTIN

Quentin, sitting at his mahogany desk, engrossed in his work, glances up as his assistant's knuckles tap gently against his office door. The subtle sound interrupts the quiet hum of the Christmas music playing in the background. His assistant, dressed in her burgundy business casual two-piece suit, informs him in a hushed tone that two detectives have arrived to speak with him. Quentin's composed demeanor remains unchanged, but a hint of alarm sparks in his eyes. With a conjured-up warm smile tugging at the corners of his lips, he instructs her to send the detectives into his office.

Exquisite artwork beautifully decorates the office, creating a visually pleasing atmosphere for Quentin's workspace. The detectives admire the decor as the aroma of coffee permeates the air. Quentin kindly offers them a cup, but they politely decline, explaining that they have a few questions to ask him. His assistant leaves the room and returns to her desk.

"You have questions for me?" Quentin asks. "I may not know how to assist you, but I'm willing to try."

Detective Gates, with a stern and commanding voice, looks Quentin straight in the eyes as he asks if he knows a Pamela Hester. Quentin freezes for a moment. No surprise to Quentin that detectives are there to question him about Pamela with the affair and all. Taking a deep breath, Quentin musters the courage to speak the truth, admitting to their three-month affair.

Detective Beal, a tall man with a stoic expression, leans forward and asks Quentin, his voice heavy with curiosity, "When was the last time you saw Ms. Hester?" Quentin, feeling a knot tightening in his stomach, knowing the impending police questioning is unavoidable. He shifts uncomfortably in his chair. The creaking sound of the chair against the floor presents a loud sound in Quentin's head.

With apprehension, he replies, "I ended the affair a mere couple of weeks ago. Despite her persistent texts, I consciously chose not to respond." Quentin's anxious gaze meets Detective Beal's eyes, his body tense as he asks, "Has something happened?"

Detective Gates explains, "We found the victim's body at the lake yesterday. She was strangled to death. As part of our investigation, we have spoken to the victim's sister, April, who is understandably distraught. April mentioned an affair you were having with Pamela. She said she doesn't believe you're responsible for her sister's murder because she saw you at a bar the same night. Mr. Johnson, it is important to note that we are questioning everyone who has been in contact with the victim."

"Any leads? Please reach out to me. I will help in any way I can. This is terrible."

Detective Gates stated, "We haven't found the person yet, but we will. Ms. Hester's murder will not go unpunished, justice will be served."

Quentin again expresses his sorrow about Pamela's death. He asks them to excuse him because he needs to check on April. Quentin feels relief because the initial questioning is over. With an evil grin on his face, he leaves his office and heads to April's home to offer her some comfort.

Chapter Seventeen

The Therapy Session

At 9:52 a.m. Amaya arrives at Ms. T.'s office. She is without makeup and dons swollen eyes, unable to muster up a smile. While sitting in the lobby, a pregnant woman and her husband walk past, holding hands and smiling as they leave the counseling office. She doubts her self-worth again. "I can't do anything right. I lost important tickets, I frustrate my husband, and I can't give my husband a baby. If I can't have children, what is the point of my existence?"

When Ms. T. enters the lobby, she greets Amaya and instructs her to follow her to the office. Amaya stands up, walks with a low stride, and keeps her head down as she follows Ms. T. Sitting in Ms. T.'s office, Amaya's eyelids droop and the corners of her lips turn down. She appears sad and overwhelmed. Ms. T., noticing this, asks Amaya how her week is going. Overwhelmed by emotions, Amaya breaks down in tears.

"I feel lost and I'm a disappointment to my husband," she says, her left leg shaking as she wipes tears from her eyes.

"You called yesterday with urgency, needing to get in today. Take a few deep elongated breaths and slowly tell me what's causing you this distress."

Amaya inhales deeply, stretches her neck, and exhales with an audible sigh before addressing her problems.

"I have so much going on that I don't even know where to start. I'm forgetting things, misplacing items, and feeling even more depressed than usual."

"Take your time and tell me more about your concerns," says Ms. T. as she places her hands on her lap and gives Amaya a warm smile.

"I think not being able to have a baby is causing me to experience a mental breakdown. I want to adopt a baby now, but Quentin is hopeful we will get pregnant and wants to wait."

"Does he still want to wait until you're thirty? It's less than a year away."

"Yes, but I can't help but feel impatient. I saw a pregnant couple leaving one of your offices today. They were holding hands, and she was gently rubbing her baby bump. The way they looked, so content and hopeful, it was truly heartbreaking for me to witness. It's hard for me to admit it, but I couldn't help but feel a pang of jealousy."

"Remember, jealousy is a natural emotion; take a moment to process why you're feeling that way and try not to hold on to it for over ten minutes. Now, I want you to close your eyes and recall the time when you received the news about your inability to conceive a child. Allow the memories to fill your senses as you process this sensitive time with me."

"Yes ma'am. When I was twenty-four, we decided I would stop taking my birth control pills as my husband and I were eager to build our little family. Despite our efforts for an entire year, we could not conceive. I have always had irregular cycles. I never considered it to be a hindrance to getting pregnant. My incredible husband reassured me that my irregular cycles were not an obstacle to having our sweet baby. He held me in his arms and promised to visit the doctor to see if there was any issue on his end.

"The doctor said there was nothing wrong with his sperm count, nor was there anything medically preventing him from getting me pregnant. The doctor gave my husband the name of obstetrician/gynecologist for me to see, Dr. Courtney Mitchell. About two months later, we had an appointment with Dr. Mitchell. She was so kind with her words when breaking the devastating news to us. I have primary ovarian insufficiency disease. I was like, what is that? She explained, and my husband and I cried. He wants to be a dad so badly.

"Discovering that I could never have a baby naturally was a devastating blow. The vivid images of my uterus, displayed by Dr. Mitchell, continue to haunt me to this very day. I can still hear my uncontrollable sobbing echoing through the office, and probably in the hallway, too. My tears cascading down my cheeks and Quentin holding my hand. In that moment, it felt like I was drifting in the air, looking down at myself and receiving the news. The weight of the sudden grief instantly settled upon me as I mourned the children I would never bear. In the depths of my despair, I couldn't help but feel inadequate for my husband, as if I was unworthy of his love. I still feel that way. This burden is unbearable, and it's controlling my every thought and emotion.

"I went as far to tell him I would let him go since I could not bear his children and I knew how much he wanted a little girl who looked just like me. We would lie in bed and talk about our little girl most nights. He laughed about how him spoiling her will make it hard for him. I truly believed I had to set him free so he could have the family he had always wanted. I told him I was a burden to him and he has so many burdens of my own. Then my husband said the most loving thing to me. 'There is no burden too big that I will not help you carry.' He asked me to never mention us separating again, and I haven't."

Amaya reaches out to the tissue box on the desk, her watery eyes blurring her vision. She delicately presses the soft tissue against her cheeks, absorbing any traces of her tears. With a sniffle, she brings the tissue to her nose and exhales. The sound muffled by the tissues. The air in the office feels heavy, as if the walls are slowly inching closer, suffocating her senses.

"How are you feeling, Amaya?"

"Not good. I used to play with dolls until I was twelve, pretending to be their mommy. In my little girl's imagination, I was determined to be a better parent than my own parents had been to me. It's such a tragedy that my unfit parents could have a child, while I can't."

"Did you get a second opinion about the diagnosis?"

"There was no need for a second diagnosis. Quentin and I saw the images of my uterus. He wasn't the problem. It was me all along. She is a thorough doctor. I totally trust her."

"Very well. I was just asking because people usually get a second opinion. Well, don't you have a special gala coming up in a couple of weeks?"

Amaya smiles and says, "Yes, I will receive the philanthropist of the year award."

"I'm certain stress is the reason behind your forgetfulness. Perhaps you should shift your attention towards the gala and the incredible contributions you are making to the community."

"I'll try my best. Maybe I can try to talk to my husband about adopting a baby again. Ugh, he is so against it. Thank you for fitting me in. I'll see you next Saturday."

Chapter Eighteen

BREE

It's early afternoon. The sunlight streams through Bree's living room. The house is quiet with Josh Jr. in school. She is finishing up housework. The dishwasher is humming faintly in the background. Dinner is in the oven, sending a savory aroma throughout the house. Making her way to her green room, she opens the closet door, revealing a box hidden in the very back, tucked away from casual view. Bree sits in her soft recliner with the back massager on, helping to relieve any tension. She opens the sacred box and pulls out a program. She weeps and says, "I'm sorry. I'm so sorry." She holds the program tightly to her chest and says, "I will make it right. I promise."

Bree receives a FaceTime call. She looks at the phone with a slight smile. She takes her hands and wipes the tears away before answering the call.

"Hey brother-in-law. What's up?"

"How are you doing, sis?" asks Jeff.

"It's all good this way. I meant to call you and Angela to thank you for Lil J's birthday gift. He loved the coat and the real wooden bongos. I have a special thanks to you two for that loud gift," she said with a chuckle.

"I'm calling to invite you to a small gathering we're having for Amaya before the gala. You know a pre-celebration before receiving her award? It was Kathy's idea. I was voluntold the party would be at my house."

"I don't know. I haven't felt like socializing lately. Let me get back to you about it."

"I know my brother won't come. I'm hoping you will. Angela would love to see you. This is going to be an unforgettable night for Amaya."

"Josh not coming won't stop me from coming. I'm attending the gala with him. I just don't want any conflict regarding me going to your house."

"Sis, the decision is yours. I extended the invitation, but I truly wish you would stop blaming yourself because my brother and I aren't speaking."

"I am to blame. I should have never told him Angela was a trans-female when you two started dating. It was not for me to tell. Plus, we have good friends in the LGBTQ+ community. I can't believe he has such a big issue with you and your remarkable wife."

"Stop blaming yourself," he says with warmth and reassurance in his voice. "Angela and I love both you and Josh. One day, he will come around. Josh didn't have a problem when we were dating. He is struggling to accept a trans-woman for a sister-in-law. It makes you wonder if your close friends in the LGBTQ community are really considered close friends to him. Friends don't judge one another. They accept them for who they are."

"I'll be there. I haven't really been enjoying going out lately, but you can count me in."

"I better get back to Kathy and the team. We have a project due tomorrow. I'll see you in a couple of weeks."

Bree tenderly presses her lips against the program, delicately placing it back inside the box, before tucking it away back in the closet. It's getting close to the time to pick up her son from elementary school. She takes the steaming dish out of the oven and places it on the stovetop. Unable to resist the tantalizing scent, she had to cut herself a corner of the broccoli and chicken casserole.

"Hmm, this tastes fantastic." She takes another bite, slips on her coat, gathers her purse, and proceeds to the front door to get her son. As Bree prepares to open the door, she catches sight of Pamela's picture on the afternoon news. The news anchor asks for help in finding the person responsible for Pamela's murder at the lake. Bree gasps, tilts her head and shrugs her eyes, questioning herself, "Where have I seen that poor lady before?" With Pamela's image lingering in her mind, she opens the door to leave.

Chapter Nineteen

Amber

Amber's partner, Larry, is being discharged from rehab. Amber is tidying up the new apartment before he comes home. Quentin will pick him from at the facility at 4:00 p.m. It's 3:20. Amber calls Quentin.

"Quentin, I need $300 to get some food."

"Let me pick him up and we'll stop by the store and get food for a couple of weeks."

"Listen, you don't know what we like. I want to give my man a good dinner when he comes home."

"You're out of your mind if you think I'm giving you that much money. Text me what you want."

"Never mind. You just stingy. I'll take care of my man."

Amber puts on her lime green coat. She walks for an hour to her old hangout. She arrives at her former corner. Her old friends, who are homeless and use substances, greet her. They ask her how it is living in her apartment. "You're all swanky now," says a woman with a cigarette in one hand and a beer can in the other. She tells them she loves the apartment and misses them at the same time. She asks one of her friends if they could spare something, just a little, to take the edge off because Larry is coming home from rehab in a couple of hours.

"You can have this, but you gotta pay me for this as soon as you get the money."

"Don't I always? My son-in-law is tight with my daughter's money. Give me a week, though."

She takes a quick snort of the black tar substance and heads home.

As Amber opens the heavy wooden door to her apartment, Larry, standing barefoot on the hardwood floor with his tall frame and silver hair glistening, greets her with a lingering kiss, sucking on her bottom lip. Quentin turns his head and looks out the apartment window. She says "Welcome home, baby! What do you think of our new place our son-in-law is renting for us?"

"Thank you, man! This is nice. You really stepped up for us."

"I'm glad to do it," says Quentin.

"I see you picked up some groceries. I'm going to put them up and give you a proper welcome home."

"On that note, I'm going to get out of here." Quentin drapes his arm around Larry's shoulder as they walk to the front door- "Remember, Amaya doesn't know about the apartment. I'm waiting for the right time to tell her. She is furious right now with Amber. She would not approve."

"Yeah, son-in-law, I know. I want to see her, though. I miss my baby girl."

Amber's yelling from the bedroom, "Baby, come check out this king size bed."

"Man, it's been a while. Let me go check that out," says Larry.

"You do that. I need to get home and start dinner. I hope you are serious about staying clean."

"I'm done with that mess. I plan to be the father my daughter needs."

Quentin taps him on the shoulder and leaves.

Chapter Twenty

Amaya

The voices

As the beautiful sunsets on the horizon, Amaya arrives home feeling drained after a long day at the office. Quentin calls her name. He tells her to come to the kitchen. She kicks off her heels and places them neatly in the corner. She also places her coat on the coat rack. "Coming babe," she says eagerly. She can't wait to see her husband.

"Taste this. I used a new recipe for mashed potatoes. What do you think?"

"Delicious."

"I thought you might like it. Dinner will be ready in about forty-five minutes. You look beautiful as always, but exhausted. Go upstairs, open the window, lie in bed and watch the sunset. If you fall asleep, I'll wake you up when dinner is ready."

She kisses him tenderly on his lips and heads upstairs.

Amaya pulls back the curtains and adjusts the blinds of the large bedroom window. Enjoying the vibrant hues of the sun's descent paints the sky, she stands at the window with amazement at the wonderful view. The tranquility of the view washes the stress of the day away. Amaya goes to the bathroom to shower before lying down.

Quentin enters the bedroom and notices that she is in the shower. He discreetly places his hands behind the headboard of the bed and presses a small black button. He then quietly exits the bedroom and heads back to the kitchen.

After stepping out of the shower, Amaya sits on the commode to dry herself off and apply lotion to her body. As she does, she hears wind whistling in her bedroom. Feeling a sense of unease, she stands up and walks slowly towards the closed bathroom door, gripping the wall for security. With a trembling hand, she opens the door, revealing the connection to her bedroom. Stepping through, a chilling breeze sends shivers down her spine as she steps into her bedroom.

She suddenly hears the faint sound of her grandfather's voice. It grows louder. "Princess. Princess. Can you hear me, my dear granddaughter?" Her heart is pounding in her chest. She stands still, unable to move. "Princess, we will be together soon." She screams. "AHH! AHH!"

Suddenly, the lights flicker, casting eerie shadows on the walls. Panic surges through Amaya's veins as she races out of the bedroom. Quentin hears her piercing screams and rushes upstairs. She leaps into his arms, unable to speak. Her shaking finger points towards the bedroom. He takes her back into the bedroom. The sound of her grandfather is still present in her ears. "Princess, no one understands you. Your grandmother and I are the only ones who ever understood you."

"Leave me alone! Please go away," she begs of the voices.

"Why are you screaming? Who are you talking to?" asks Quentin.

"It's my grandfather. Don't you hear him?" she asks with her eyes widening in terror.

"Your grandfather is dead. You don't hear him. Your grandparents have been dead for years."

In a state of panic, she desperately yells at her husband, pleading for it to go away. Fear grips her so fiercely that she buries her face into his chest, seeking comfort and protection.

"There is no one talking; it is only our voices that fills the silence of the room."

Leading her to the bathroom, he hands her a cold towel to place on her face. He instructs her to sit and relax for a few minutes. He promises to get a glass of wine from downstairs to help calm her nerves. She agrees and places the towel over her face. He leaves, shutting the door. He walks over to the headboard and discreetly presses the small black button once more before exiting the room.

He comes back with the wine and leads her to the bed. "Sit baby. There's no one in this room but us."

"He's gone," she says, rubbing her forehead.

"No one was here. Sip your wine."

"I know what I heard. I don't understand. What's happening to me?"

Quentin lies in the bed with her, cradling her body in his arms. He can feel the shivers coursing through her trembling frame. She pleads desperately, with a quivering voice, "I'm afraid. Please, don't leave me." He continues to spoon her as they fall asleep.

The next morning, Quentin gently places a steaming cup of freshly brewed coffee and an assortment of pastries on a tray. The rich aroma of the coffee fills her nostrils. As he approaches the bed, he hears a soft rustle of sheets. Amaya moves from under the warm covers, feeling a sense of comfort as Quentin sets the tray down beside her.

"Good morning, Babe. Are you feeling alright this morning? You had me worried last night."

There's a moment of silence as Amaya stares at him, her mind still reeling from the scare the previous night.

"No-no! I'm okay. My brain is playing tricks on me. There's no way I heard my grandfather's voice. Anthony Montgomery would never frighten me like that."

Quentin caresses her cheek with one hand and hands her a cup of coffee in the other hand. "Are you up to going into the office today?"

"Q, I need to talk to you this morning. I have been patient. I think I know why all these strange things are happening to me."

Quentin raises his eyebrows, places both hands on the back of his head, and leans back on the headboard. "What is it we need to talk about this early in the morning? Are you going to work today?"

"Yes, baby, I'm going into the office. Remember, I have a deadline tomorrow? I need to talk to you before we leave for work."

Quentin yawns loudly, his mouth stretching wide as he declares, "You have my undivided attention."

Amaya crawls closer to her husband and rests her head on his chest. "I'm ready for us to contact Bethany Christian Services to adopt a baby." He pushes her head off his chest. "Un uh, let me finish. I see your mouth opening to shut me down. Bethany is well-known and respected. They have been helping children find their forever homes for over seventy-five years. I've done extensive research on them. I need you to be on board. You wanted to wait until we were thirty-one to adopt. I will be thirty in a few months. It's time to get the process started."

Quentin touches her hand and explains, "I know you've been thinking a lot about adopting a child; honestly, I don't know if I'm mature enough to bond and love a baby we have adopted at this point in my life. You know how much I love you. My dreams were crushed when Dr. Mitchell gave us that life altering the news. I still want that little girl who looks just like you to have your big, beautiful eyes."

"He or she may not have my eyes, but they will have my heart," Amaya says, as she chokes with a quaver in her voice. The room is fuzzy as tears stream down her face, falling on the rumpled sheets. She jumps out of bed, spilling the coffee and the pastries on the sheets as she runs crying out of the room.

Chapter Twenty-One

The Gala

As Quentin and Amaya arrive at the grand gala in a black Lincoln limousine, the glistening moon shining brightly overhead. The limousine driver, dressed in a black suit and a black hat, steps out to open the door for the couple. Quentin, wearing a black tuxedo and a dark green tie, is the first to step out. He extends his right hand to Amaya, who gracefully emerges from the limo, revealing her black Vinca tassel stilettos and her alluring legs. Amaya is wearing a dark green mesh ruffle off-the-shoulder formal dress that's ruched with a split thigh. The garment is sheer and unlined, allowing the curves of her body to be clearly visible.

Amaya is still beaming from the surprise party for her at Jeff and Angela's home, celebrating her award. Amaya and Quentin, arm-in-arm, step into the stunning venue, a festival for the senses. The grand hall's sparkling chandeliers cast a warm, golden glow throughout the room. Soft music drifts through the air, elevating the mood of the well-dressed guests. The scent of fresh flowers travels from extravagant centerpieces, adding a touch of romance to the event. As they enter, the sight of the polished marble floor fills them with a sense of excitement for the evening's event.

Servers stroll gracefully through the gala, offering guests champaign in crystal glasses. One server, holding a tray of sparkling beverages, approaches

Amaya and asks, "Champagne, Mrs. Montgomery?" With a polite smile, she replies, "Yes, thank you." Quentin declines the offer, saying, "Maybe later." Amaya is admiring the surroundings. She turns to Quentin and says, "Wow! What a magnificent soiree. Oh, babe, look at the exquisite ice sculpture of my award. Let's get a closer look." Quentin agrees and says, "Now that's nice. Let's go look at the replica of our award."

The couple takes in the ambiance and listens to the joyful laughter of the guests. The sight of people dancing greets their eyes. Amaya is cherishing the comforting thought of having a great night and a glorious past two weeks. There have been no unsettling voices, no instances of forgetfulness, and no experiences of losing things. Her heart fills with pure happiness with her husband by her side, displaying emotional support, making her feel truly seen and understood.

Amaya's heart rate speeds up and her palms are clammy from anxiety as the attendees are now swarming towards her, eager to offer their greetings and accolades for her well-deserved recognition as the 2022 philanthropist of the year. Quentin is envious of the attention she's receiving. He skillfully masks his jealousy, concealing it beneath a facade of composure.

Ms. Guess, the director of Save the Children Charity, notices Amaya engaging in nervous and fearful talk with guests she doesn't know. Ms. Guess walks over to the couple, politely saying, "Excuse me. Excuse me," as she makes her way through the guests to reach Amaya. Understanding the situation, she rescues Amaya by informing the guests that she is ready to escort the couple to the table of honor. Amaya smiles gratefully and thanks Ms. Guess for rescuing her from the uncomfortable situation.

Amaya and Quentin take their seats at their table. Amaya touches the luxurious round glass charger plates trimmed with silver and gold braided metal. "The craftsmanship of this plate is beautiful," says Amaya.

"Not as beautiful as you, baby," says Quentin as he strokes the side of her face. Quentin signals a server with a tray filled with champagne glasses. "Could we please have two glasses of champagne?"

The server responds, "Certainly, sir." He hands Amaya a glass and then Quentin. He gives Quentin a nod before heading off.

"Sweetheart, go to the restroom and touch up your makeup. The lighting in this room seems to make your face shine a bit. We want to make sure we look our best for tonight."

"Thanks, babe. Please excuse me. I will be right back."

Amaya gets up from the table and asks a female server to point her toward the ladies' room. Once she is out of sight, Quentin discreetly scans the surroundings to ensure no one is watching. Seizing the opportunity, he sneaks a large amount of powder into her drink, skillfully stirring it to ensure there is no visible residue when she comes back to the table.

Amaya returns to the table. She reaches out and takes Quentin's hand, affectionately declaring, "I love doing life with you."

"Ditto," he says as he handed her the glass and picked up his own. "Let's raise a toast to us."

Mr. Johnny Devoe, the Master of Ceremony, gracefully walks onto the stage to welcome all the esteemed guests. With a charming smile, he begins by delighting the audience with a series of clever jokes, setting a lighthearted tone for the evening. In addition, he summarizes the exciting program that awaits them during this grand gala night. As the anticipation builds, Mr. Devoe invites everyone to find their designated seats at the beautifully arranged tables, as dinner is now prepared and ready to be served.

Amaya finishes her glass of champagne and then focuses on the tablecloth, rubbing its edge against her face and staring at it. "Feel this, baby. It's rapturous," she says, trying to put it on Quentin's face. "No-no. You enjoy it," Quentin says. Amaya suddenly notices the lights on the chandeliers, fixating on them. She bursts into loud laughter, capturing the attention of the guests. The couple receives their food, but Amaya remains preoccupied, contemplating which silverware to use.

Stepping forward once again onto the grand stage, the Master of Ceremony returns to announce the recipient of the prestigious 2022 philanthropist award. Addressing the crowd, the MC asks, "Are you all enjoying yourselves?" In response, the guests clap and enthusiastically respond, "Yes!"

"Mrs. Amaya Montgomery has dedicated over eight years volunteering with Save the Children. Her donations have been incredibly generous, showcasing her selflessness. Amaya is kind-hearted, compassionate, and passionate about helping others. It's our honor to present Amaya Montgomery with the 2022 Philanthropist of the Year award. This recognition is a token of our gratitude for her tireless efforts in assisting the children. We extend our deepest thanks for her unwavering commitment and exceptional contributions to Save the Children Charities.

"Ladies and gentlemen, let's give a round of applause to Amaya Montgomery, our 2022 Save the Children recipient." As the MC starts the applause, the other guests join in clapping.

Quentin nudges Amaya, encouraging her to make her way towards the stage. As she stands up and starts heading in that direction, she clumsily bumps into a food server who is busy collecting empty plates from the tables, causing her to drop the plates. The sound of the plates crashing against the floor fills the room, causing heads to turn towards Amaya and the food server. Broken shards of porcelain are everywhere. Amaya's face turns beet red while laughing. She quickly apologizes, her laughter now mixed with a tinge of embarrassment. The food server, a young woman with a kind smile, reassures Amaya that it's alright and that accidents happen.

The MC holds out his hand to help Amaya climb the stairs to the stage. Her balance falters while on stage. She catches sight of the overhead light. As she fixates on the light for a moment. Amaya tries to focus on her speech. She forgets the words. She just yells. "I feel great!" into the microphone and walks away from the podium. A few people in the audience laugh at Amaya's statement.

The MC is gazing at Amaya out of concern. He walks over to her and guides her back to the podium, and stands by her side, offering support. The audience senses that something is wrong, and whispers spread throughout the room as Amaya's speech becomes increasingly incoherent. Her once graceful but nervous demeanor is now a noticeable struggle to maintain composure. The haze of confusion makes her words get lost to the audience, leaving some with red faces and others shaking their heads. Silence is heavy in the ballroom.

The attendees exchange sympathetic looks, and the room falls into an uneasy silence. Despite her efforts, Amaya's incoherent speech of wandering thoughts and lack of focus makes it difficult for the audience to fully grasp her message. The drug in her glass of champagne has taken a toll on Amaya, turning what should have been a triumphant moment into a disheartening spectacle.

Bree and Josh exchange glances of astonishment as they observe Amaya's bewildering behavior. Josh leans in and whispers to Bree, "What on earth is happening? Is she drunk? This is mind-boggling. Just listen to how her words are slurring." They both shift their bodies to see Quentin at his table, their eyes mirroring his baffled expression, seeking answers for Amaya's behavior.

"Amaya usually has a composed and articulate demeanor. Now she's in the middle of the stage, swaying and struggling to maintain her balance. Her words are a jumbled mess," says Bree.

As they observe Amaya's erratic behavior, they can't help but wonder what's causing such a drastic change in her. "What in the hell are we looking at?" asks Josh.

Bree shakes her head, equally puzzled by the situation. "I don't know," she says, with her voice barely audible over the murmurs of confusion around them. "But I don't think she's drunk. It seems more serious than that."

Their attention shifts to others in the ballroom. They realize they are not alone in their confusion, as others in the room exchange worried glances and whisper amongst themselves. The atmosphere in the ballroom has become tense as the realization sunk in that everyone's equally perplexed. Some individuals discreetly point towards the source of the confusion, while others try to make sense of the situation by engaging in hushed conversations.

People furrow their brows, exchanging worried glances as they search for answers. Some individuals discreetly point towards the source of the confusion, while others try to make sense of the situation by engaging in hushed conversations. The once lively and joyous gathering has transformed into a room filled with uncertainty, as the confusion bonds the attendees together in a shared sense of bewilderment.

Amaya's slurred words continue to fall on confused ears, her gestures becoming increasingly erratic. Something is very wrong, and Bree and Josh know they need to find out what it is and help Amaya. "What she we do?" asks Bree.

"Hold on, Q is getting up from his seat to go up there and help her," says Josh.

Quentin relishes the joy of Amaya's confusion and the audience's noticeable reaction. As he takes confident steps towards the stage, Quentin can feel the excitement building within him. With a calm and collected demeanor, he addresses the audience, assuring them he will accept the award on behalf of his wife. His voice fills with a misleading hint of concern as he explains how Amaya has been acting strangely lately. The plan to gain control over her inheritance is unfolding flawlessly, he thinks. With the drug's influence on Amaya, it only strengthens Quentin's narrative of Amaya's supposedly mental instability.

Quentin continues his carefully crafted performance. He knows that every word, every gesture, must be with precision. The audience hangs on to his every word, drawn into his tale of Amaya's false decline. He describes her erratic behavior, mentioning sleepless nights, paranoia, and even hallucinations. Quentin's voice quivers with feigned concern, his acting skills on full display. He emphasizes how difficult it has been for him to witness his beloved wife's deteriorating mental state, all while maintaining a façade of unwavering support. The audience gasps and murmurs with sympathy, completely unaware of the sinister plot unfolding before their eyes. Quentin revels in their reactions, savoring the power and control he has over the situation. Deep down, he knows with each passing moment, his grip on Amaya's inheritance tightens, inching him closer to the wealth and influence he so desperately craves.

The couple arrives home early from the glorious gala, and Quentin opens the back door leading from the garage. Amaya gazes at him. Her eyebrows furrow in bewilderment. She feels dizzy and nauseous, and she realizes that something is wrong. "There's something happening to me. My mind feels off, and I'm feeling nauseous. I think I need to go to the emergency room."

"What were you doing tonight? I was sitting at our table, witnessing my wife act like a deranged person," Quentin asks while making himself a tequila on the rocks.

"I don't understand. Please help me, baby. I don't feel like myself," asks Amaya while waving her arms around, disconnected from reality.

"You changed into a different woman right before my eyes tonight. You think you don't understand? I don't understand what caused the change in your behavior tonight. It was distressing to see you act like that on our night in public. I tried my best to take control of the situation," Quentin says and takes a sip of his tequila.

"Why are you saying this to me?"

"Well, why do you always do this? You ruin everything. I just don't know what's wrong with you. Everything that happens to us is your fault. This is probably why you need Jeff and Kathy. You don't have the confidence in yourself to make the right decisions for your company. That's why you always fuck up! You're going to stop seeing that therapist. She is not helping you. I'm the only one who can help you. I'm your husband and that's my job."

Amaya walks away, stumbling with each step. "I'm still talking to you! Get back here!" Quentin yells, then hurls his glass of tequila and ice towards her. The glass shatters against the wall.

Overwhelmed with emotions, Amaya screams, "I should just end it all! I would find true happiness with my grandparents."

"You will not kill yourself because you're too scared to do anything, and you would even mess that up."

Quentin's harsh words cut through her, intensifying the already tense atmosphere. Amaya's hands clutch at her chest as tears stream down her face. The weight of her emotions crushes her, making it difficult to breathe. Quentin's hurtful remarks strike a nerve, fueling her insecurities even further. The pain she feels seems unbearable. Quentin's cruel response causes her to get her bottle of antidepressants from her purse and take them in with a glass of water from the kitchen. His words echo in her ears, reminding her she has no one on earth without her grandparents. The anxiety within her intensifies. He now has total control of her mind and actions.

Quentin walks towards the kitchen. "We were having such a good time at the gala and you had to spoil it in front of everyone." He notices the pills in her hand and knocks them out. "Are you really trying to kill yourself? How many have you taken?"

"None, yet. I don't want to be here anymore."

If she were to end her life before turning thirty, the entire plan would crumble. Quentin realizes he doesn't want to drive her to the breaking point so that she would actually kill herself. His intentions were never to push her to suicide, but to have control over her and the inheritance. *Shit, I'm going to have to rethink the holographic representations of her grandparents, which I had intended to unleash on her next month. Let me be a loving husband tonight. I can't have her killing herself in the middle of the night. That would ruin everything for me,* he thinks.

Amaya places the pills back in the container, still feeling confused by the effects of the molly drug. Quentin gently turns her around and embraces her tightly. "I love you, baby. Please believe how truly sorry I am for what I said earlier. I promise I'll never say those things to you again. You know you mean everything to me. Let me help you upstairs and get you into bed. Tomorrow will be a better day."

Looking at the clock, Amaya realizes its only 8:30. She hesitates. "I don't want to go to bed this early. I really think I should go to the emergency room. Something doesn't feel right."

"Let's wait until morning to see how you're feeling. But don't worry, I know just the thing to make you feel better." He reaches for the remote, switches on YouTube, and starts playing a mix of songs by New Edition, the Isley Brothers, Keith Sweat, and Charlie Wilson. Since she attends every new tour that New Edition does, most of the songs playing are from their repertoire. In fact, she's even attended some of their concerts twice.

"That will make me feel better. Thank you. I love you so much." She asks him to get the yellow cashmere blanket out of the closet and cuddle with her. He obliges. They're enjoying the music until they fall asleep on the sofa around 10:50 p.m.

Chapter Twenty-Two

Amber

At 10:55 p.m., Amber sits on the sofa, eagerly waiting for Larry to come home from work. It has been two weeks since his discharge from rehab, and he has remained clean throughout this time. Larry now works at the bowling alley just around the corner from their apartment, where he cleans up. Yesterday, he received his first paycheck and gave some of the money to Amber for groceries and to add minutes to his phone.

Larry comes through the door, takes off his coat and tosses it in a chair. "What you been doing all night? You said you would have the apartment clean before I came home from work."

"Our baby got that fancy award tonight. Quentin told us about it, remember?"

"Yeah-yeah, I remember. Why ain't the house clean? It's not like she invited you to go."

"Come over here and sit by me. I have a surprise for you." She places a spoon, a lighter, a shoelace, aluminum foil, heroin, and a hypodermic needle on the table.

"Get that stuff out of here. I'm not doing that shit anymore. It's time for us to be in our daughter's life. You know damn well that shit was killing us."

"Look Larry, we're just celebrating for Amaya. We can do this one last time."

"Hell, no!" says Larry, determined to get rid of it as he begins to pickup the paraphernalia and heroin from the table. However, Amber, fiending for the drug, starts hitting him and trying to wrestle it away. She even jumps on the back of his neck, striking him on top of the head with her fists, screaming, "Give me my shit! You ain't taking nothing from here!"

He forcefully flips her off his shoulders, causing her body to collide with the floor with a sickening thud. In a moment of shock, he drops everything in his hands. His eyes widen in disbelief at what she's doing. She frantically scampers around the hard, cold floor. Her heart pounding in her chest as she's collecting the tinfoil containing the heroin and the paraphernalia. She rises to her feet. Her voice fills the living room with anger as she fiercely confronts him about his actions.

Larry raises his hands in defeat, realizing he cannot prevent her from indulging in drugs. Feeling tired and hungry, he heads into the kitchen to cook himself dinner, only to find empty cabinets and a bare refrigerator. He knows she used the grocery money he had given her to buy drugs.

Returning to the living room to confront her, he sees her wrapping her arm with a shoestring, and using the spoon and lighter to melt the heroin. The black substance bubbling on the spoon causes a powerful urge for him to use again. He gives into the urge. He walks to the couch, grabs the other shoestring and wraps it tightly around his arm. "Make enough for me," he says.

"Let's celebrate," says Amber as she hands him the needle containing the drug. He injects it into his vein and removes the shoestring from around his arm. After Larry lies on the sofa, Amber prepares another spoonful for herself, melting it down before injecting it into her own vein. Her eyes roll to the back of her head as she smiles and reclines on the sofa, eventually closing her eyes and passing out.

As she wakes up, she notices the shoestring around her arm and removes it. Her eyes fall upon Larry, who is lying on the sofa with his eyes wide open and an eerie coldness coming from his skin. White foam is oozing from the corner of his mouth, sending a wave of panic coursing through Amber's body. She shakes him, desperately pleading for him to wake up. Amber's body is trembling uncontrollably. "Don't you die on me," she cries out, vigorously shaking his lifeless body. Amber rushes to dial 911. Her voice is tremulous as she begs for help.

"911, what's your emergency?"

"Help me! My man won't wake up. Please hurry!" she pleads, her voice filled with urgency. "When you come, bring that Narca stuff to save him."

"Ma'am, what is your name and address?" asks the 911 operator.

"Umm. Umm. My name is Amber Montgomery. I can't remember my address."

"We need your address to send the first responders. Go look at a utility bill or mail."

"I don't have no bills here. My son-in-law pays all the bills."

"Go to a neighbor's and get the address."

"Okay,"

Amber runs to a neighbor banging on the door. "What's the address here?" The neighbor refuses to open the door, but yells out the address, "27 Terrance Lake Drive."

Amber runs back to the phone that she threw on the couch. "It's 27 Terrance Lake Drive."

"Apartment number?" asks the 911 operator.

"I don't know."

"Mrs. Montgomery, open your door and look on the outside of your door for the number."

"Okay." She runs to the door with her phone in hand. "Thirteen, it's thirteen."

"We're sending someone now. I want you to stay on the phone with me until they arrive. Yes, the first responders will have Narcan."

"Hurry," says Amber.

In a mere five minutes, the first responders arrive at the scene, their sirens wailing through the air. They rush towards Larry, their footsteps echoing off the walls. As they gather around him, their eyes meet, acknowledging the grim reality. He has succumbed to a drug overdose. One of the EMTs with gloves on his hands delicately checks for a pulse, but his touch yields no sign of life. They observe his lips, now tinged with a haunting shade of blue. One EMT flashes a piercing light in his eyes, but there is no response in his pupils. A chilling sensation grips their hearts as they feel the lifelessness in his body, the stiffness of rigor mortis seizing his muscles.

A compassionate female EMT turns towards Amber, her voice filled with sympathy as she softly delivers the devastating news. "I'm sorry, but he is gone." In an instant, Amber's eyes widen in disbelief, her head shaking vehemently, desperate to deny the truth. She screams as she collapses to her knees. Tears stream down her face, mingling with the trails of mucus flowing from her nose, her every sob a testament to her overwhelming grief. As the coroner and the police arrive, the scene becomes an endless number of questions as they seek to unravel the events that transpired.

The coroner carefully places Larry's lifeless body onto a stretcher and prepares to transport it away from the scene. As the police approach Amber, who is visibly distraught and overwhelmed with grief, they gently guide her towards the waiting police car. However, Amber resists, her heartbroken cries echoing through the air.

Overwhelmed by emotions, she refuses to leave the spot where Larry died. Sensing her deep anguish, the compassionate female EMT, who had been attending to Larry's body, approaches Amber with understanding in her eyes. She softly speaks to Amber, offering her a comforting presence and support during this devastating time. With tears streaming down her face, Amber clings to the EMT, pleading for her to bring Larry back, as the police officers patiently wait, giving her the space she needs to process her immense loss.

Amber, feeling scared and sorrowful, finally steps into the backseat of the police car. The cold leather seats send a chill through her body, but she tries to focus on how she will answer the police questions. As the car pulls away from the scene of the overdose, she glances out the window, her mind replaying the events of the night. The flashing lights and the sound of sirens fade into the distance as they make their way towards the police station. Amber takes a deep breath, mentally preparing herself to give her official statement. She knows that this is happening and there's nothing she can do about it. As they approach the police station, Amber's heart races, unsure of what lies ahead. However, she is aware she must avoid going to jail.

Chapter Twenty-Three

QUENTIN

It's 6:30 the next morning. Quentin groggily rolls over and reaches for his phone. As he unlocks it, he notices a series of missed calls, all from the same unknown number. His curiosity piqued, he taps on the voicemail icon. As he presses play, a sense of unease washes over him. Quentin hears a voice on the other end filled with urgency and frustration. "Quentin, why haven't you been answering the damn phone? Come and get me! I'm at the Aurora Police Department." He can faintly hear the distant chatter of other people in the background, the sounds of a busy police station.

He feels the heebie-jeebies at the mention of Larry's name. "Larry died last night," Amber says, the weight of the words hanging in the air. Quentin's mind races, trying to comprehend what could have happened to Larry. And then, the mention of Amber being at the police station adds another layer of confusion and concern. As Quentin sits in the silence of his room, a flood of unanswered questions overwhelms him, and he feels the weight of the situation on his shoulders.

Quentin carefully slips out of his warm bed, trying not to disturb Amaya's sleep. He hastily slips into some clothes, feeling the fabric against his skin. A quick swipe of his hand across his face helps him shake off the remnants of sleep. Popping a piece of gum into his mouth, he savors the minty freshness.

Twenty minutes later, Quentin reaches the police department building. The sound of sirens wailing in the distance fills the air as he steps through the entrance. Approaching the desk sergeant, he inquires about the whereabouts of Amber Montgomery. The sergeant, with a nod, gestures towards the adjacent room.

Stepping into the room with a musty scent, Quentin finds Amber sleeping uncomfortably in a worn-out chair. He notices her tousled hair over her face partly concealing the lines of exhaustion on her forehead and her mouth, her body curled up to find a position to rest. "Amber, wake up. Let's go," he says, shaking her shoulder.

Confused, Amber mumbles, "Huh... What?"

He tells her, "I came to take you home." Slowly, she rises with a stiff body, stretching and yawning. Suddenly, her bad breath hits like a Mack truck.

On the car ride back to her apartment, she is crying profusely. Quinten is having a difficult time understanding her. "Amber, calm down. Tell me what happened to Larry. Amaya is going to be devastated," he says, looking in her direction while driving.

"We were celebrating Amaya's award last night. We just did a little bit of heroin."

Quentin steers the car to the left and speeds into a parking lot. "Heroin? Are you fucking kidding me? You did this?" he yells. "You forced him into it. Everything is being ruined because of you, you stupid dopehead."

"What do you mean 'ruined'? How is my man's death ruining something for you?"

"It's none of your business. I tried to help you both. Obviously, you don't want help. Your rent is paid for a year. I will continue to pay your bills and buy you groceries for a year. Don't ask me for cash. I will not give you any money."

"Let me out. I will walk the rest of the way."

"Woman, it's another four miles."

"I want to get out of this car. You're hurting my feelings."

"I bet your man wishes he were here for his feelings to be hurt. He's dead because of you! That man was doing good, and you took his sobriety and his life away from him. Yeah, get out of the car and walk home. I don't give a shit, anyway."

"You really hate me. You want me to walk home in this cold weather?"

"Isn't that what you said? Get out!"

Amber refuses to get out of the car. She defiantly clings to the car seat, her grip tightening as Quentin steps out and approaches her side. The screech of the door hinges rings through the air. With a sudden surge of strength, Quentin jerks her out of the car, her body stumbling backward. He slams the car door shut; the engine roars to life, drowning out any protests she might have mustered. A mix of anger and disbelief chisels across her face, leaving her standing there, motionless and bewildered, in a deserted parking lot.

Quentin calls Josh. "Hey, man. I need to come through right now. Be ready. I need to take you to my house. We have to tell Amaya that her father has died of an overdose."

"Oh no! I told Bree I would take Lil J to school today. But I know she will understand."

"I'll give you more details when I pick you up. I'll be there in ten."

"Okay, Q. I'll be ready." Josh hangs up after receiving the shocking news.

Quentin arrives at the house. He calls Josh and tells him he's outside. Quentin can hear Lil Josh crying, "Daddy, you promised. You promised." Lil J sniffs.

"Bree, I will pick him up from school and take him to get ice cream." Josh picks up his phone and tells Quentin he's on his way out to the car.

Quentin tells Josh what happened to Larry and how it's Amber's fault. "She may face jail time," says Josh. They arrive at the house. They see Sandra's car in front before pulling into the garage.

"I'm not in the mood for that nosey maid today," says Quentin. Josh and Quentin enter the house from the garage. "Let me go see if she's dressed and then I will bring you up," says Quentin.

"Okay," says Josh.

Quentin runs into Sandra. "Morning, Sandra," he says with a forced smile.

"Good morning, Mr. Quentin," says Sandra, her voice polite but distant.

Quentin, concealing his dislike for Sandra, walks upstairs to find Amaya. Amaya is already awake, the sound of rustling clothes in the walk-in closet showing she's up and alert. Quentin approaches her, handing her a soft silk housecoat.

"Baby, put your housecoat on. Josh and I need to talk to you," says Quentin, his voice tinged with urgency.

Amaya looks at him with curiosity, her eyes searching for answers. "Where have you been, baby?" she asks, her voice filled with concern.

"I will explain in a few minutes. Put your housecoat on," says Quentin, walking out of the bedroom. "I'm going downstairs to get Josh."

Quentin sees Josh talking to Sandra. Josh is telling Sandra about Larry. A frustrated Quentin tells Josh, "Man, come on upstairs." Josh follows Quentin upstairs.

Josh goes over and hugs Amaya. "We have some sad news, cousin. Sit down."

"I don't want to sit down. Just tell me, J,"

"Baby, come sit with me on the bed," says Quentin.

"Amaya, a devastating heroin overdose tragically took your father's life last night," says Josh, overwhelmed by an immense wave of grief. Amaya's anguished screams pierce the stillness of the room. She collapses onto her soft pillow, the tears streaming down her face with a forceful intensity. The sound of her cries fills the room. The pillow muffles her sobs, absorbing her anguish and offering a fleeting sense of comfort.

"Tell me what happened to my daddy."

Quentin finds himself with no other option than to reveal the truth to her. "I rented an apartment for Amber and Larry," he says. "She was living on the streets. I love you so much, which is why I helped your parents. I wanted Larry to have a safe and clean environment to return to after completing his rehab program. He had stayed clean for two weeks and even found a job. However, devastatingly, he injected heroin and tragically passed away last night."

Amaya's eyes well up with tears as she glares at Quentin. Her face flushes with bereavement. Devastation washes over her like a tidal wave, leaving her feeling helpless and broken. Amid her turmoil, her thoughts spiral, presenting self-doubt and self-blame. She can't escape the negative words that spill from her trembling lips, tainting her already wounded soul.

Quentin, with a false look of concern on his face, reaches out his hand towards her, hoping to offer some false comfort. However, as his hand inches closer, she instinctively flinches away, her body language clearly expressing her reluctance. Quentin immediately withdraws his hand, understanding that she doesn't want any physical contact at the moment from him. Instead, he shifts his approach and focuses on using his words to console her, offering words of support and understanding. In front of Amaya, Quentin tells Josh he respects her boundaries and strives to find alternative ways to be there for her during this difficult time.

Quentin tells her he loves her, then says. "I'll call Kathy and tell her you will not be in for a few days." Amaya remains silent, staring into the distance. Quentin exchanges a discerning expression with Josh before they exit.

On the drive back to Josh's, they discuss Amaya's father's death and how she is handling it.

"You're going to have to be there for her during the loss of Larry. I will be there for her too," says Josh.

Quentin pulls into Josh's driveway so he can retrieve his car and make his way to the office. Afterwards, Quentin gives Debra a call to inquire about an update on his project. He informs her of the recent passing of Amaya's father and mentions that he won't be able to come into the office today.

"I'm sorry for your loss. Please give Mrs. Montgomery my condolences," says Debra.

"I will. I need to stop by the gas station. The gas light just popped on. I'm going to fuel up and get back home to be with my wife. She hasn't been herself lately. Her father's death may push her over the edge. I must be there for her," says Quentin.

"You're such a good husband. I hope I'm as lucky as your wife one day. You go take care of her. Everything is running smoothly with the account," says Debra.

Quentin, wearing his black Ray-Ban hexagonal flat lens sunglasses with gold trim, to keep the sun out of his eyes, pulls into the Fuel Mart. He parks at pump ten and inserts his black card to pay, all while noticing a girl he knows from high school. Meanwhile, his car is fueling, and the lady approaches him, recognizing him as well.

"Hey there!" Lea asks with raised corners of her mouth. "Q, how the hell are you doing?" He reaches out to hug her in a friendly manner. "Good to see you. I'm doing okay," says Quentin.

The two engage in small talk. Lea sees her husband coming out of the gas station eating ruffles potato chips and carrying an unopen sprite. "AJ, baby, come over here. Guess who I'm talking to?" says Lea.

The man walks over, and Quentin, with one side of his mouth raised, says. "AJ, it's Quentin, our friend from high school. How long has it been since we all have been together? Quentin, you didn't make it to our ten-year class reunion," says Lea.

"My wife and I were out of the country and couldn't make it." Quentin extends his hand for a handshake at AJ. "It's good to see you, man." AJ quickly alters his stand with his right hand squeezed into a fist. His left foot moves forward and swings his fists, connecting to Quentin's nose with a powerful blow. Everything goes black.

"That's what you get for breaking my little sister's heart freshman year of high school, all for the rich girl," says AJ and he walks away.

Quentin feels a sharp pain in his nose. He brings his palm up to wipe it. When he looks down, he notices the crimson stain of blood on the palm of his hand. Simultaneously, he catches sight of Lea, frantically trailing behind AJ. "AJ! AJ!" Lea's voice rings in the air as she hastily calls out to her husband. "What was that?"

Quentin is stunned after a former friend punches him in the nose in a semi-crowded gas station, causing his pride to be hurt and his face to flush with anger and embarrassment. The sharp sting of the blow continues to repeat in his mind. He ignores the curious gazes of onlookers. Determined to escape from their judgmental eyes and regain his composure, he makes his way to his car and drives straight home.

Chapter Twenty-Four

THE FUNERAL

A week has passed since the tragic event. It is now 9:30 a.m. on a Thursday, and Amaya is preparing for her father's funeral in four hours. Dressed in a black pants suit, she sits on the soft sofa, clutching the only two pictures she has of her and her father. Meanwhile, Sandra is in the kitchen, busy preparing for the repast. Kathy, Bree, and Angela are heading to Amaya's house, where they will join Amaya in the family car. Quentin and Josh are on their way to Amber's apartment. She will ride with them to the funeral.

Sandra steps out of the kitchen to check on Amaya. "Can I do anything for you?"

"No, I'm fine at the moment. However, I can't guarantee that I'll feel the same way later."

Amaya pulls her hair to the left side and lays back on the sofa. Angela is the first person to arrive at the home. She rings the doorbell. Sandra answers the door. "Good morning, Mrs. Angela," says Sandra.

"Good morning, Ms. Sandra. How is Amaya doing this morning? I don't know what to say to her to make her feel better."

"She's doing as well as to be expected. Don't worry so much about what to say. Just follow her lead," Sandra says with a soft smile.

"Amaya, please let me know if there's anything I can do for you," says Angela as she sits next to Amaya and gives her a kiss on the forehead.

"I'm okay, sis. Thank you. I'm just ready to get this day over with," says Amaya with a trembling voice.

Bree, Tanya, and Kathy arrive at the home and ring the doorbell. Angela gets up and goes to answer the door. After she opens it, all three of the ladies embrace each other in the doorway. "How is she? I called and texted her last night, but no response," says Kathy.

"I think she's trying to keep it together. Come on in. Let's show her some love," says Angela.

The ladies settle comfortably into the plush sofa in the living room. Angela takes her place on the left side of Amaya, while Kathy sits on the right. Meanwhile, Bree sinks into the embrace of the upholstered armchair, finding it incredibly cozy. The aroma of the tea fills the room even before Sandra enters carrying a tray with steaming chamomile tea for everyone.

With careful precision, Sandra arranges the hot water, teacups with tea bags, and a variety of sweeteners: sugar, honey, Sweet'n Low, and milk. Finally joining the ladies, Sandra wearily sits on the love seat. The living room is softly lit, as per Amaya's request, to have the blinds closed over the French windows. Lost in her own world, Amaya continues to stare at the pictures, completely oblivious to the other ladies' presence.

Amaya looks up at the ladies and gathers their attention. "I have something important to tell you all, but my husband has expressly forbidden me from sharing it with anyone."

Intrigued, the ladies collectively ask, "What is it? What's going on?"

"Sandra, you could not make it to the gala because you were sick. I know you heard about what happened."

"Yes, I did. I was waiting for you to tell me. I'm worried about you."

Amaya lets out an audible sigh. "I have been losing things, forgetting things and hearing things. I heard my deceased grandparents' voice a few weeks ago.

Scared the hell out of me. I think I'm losing my mind. Quentin wants me to stop seeing my therapist. He does not believe she's helping me. I think she has helped me a lot. Maybe he's right, it's time to find someone new. He wants me to let him help me because...."

Kathy abruptly interrupts. "Quentin does not have the training to help you. If you want to find another therapist, that's fine. Do not let your husband mess with your mental health."

"How has your therapist been helping you with the voices and the other things?" asks Angela.

" I haven't told her."

"You didn't tell her?" Sandra exclaims, sitting up in her chair.

"No, Quentin told me she would admit me to the mental hospital and the stocks for our agency would plummet."

"That's not true. That's a misconception some people have. You won't be admitted to a behavioral hospital unless you are a danger to yourself or others. Quentin is wrong," says Angela.

Amaya looks down, and with a soft-spoken voice she explains, "I know it sounds crazy, but Quentin is convinced if I tell my therapist about the voices and other things, she will deem me unstable and have me admitted to a mental hospital. And he's worried about the impact it will have on our agency's stocks. He's always been concerned about appearances and maintaining a certain image."

Kathy shakes her head in disbelief. "Amaya, your mental health should be your top priority. Your husband's fears about the stock market should not dictate your well-being. It's important to have a therapist who can help you navigate through these experiences and provide the support you need, especially now after losing your father."

Angela leans forward, her expression filled with concern. "Amaya, keeping this from your therapist will only hinder your progress. They're trained professionals who can help you understand and cope with what you're going through.

You deserve to have someone in your corner who can provide the guidance and support you need."

Sandra's voice is firm as she adds, "You need to prioritize your own mental health, Amaya. Don't let Quentin's worries hold you back from getting the help you deserve. You have every right to have a therapist who can address these issues and provide the necessary support."

Amaya nods, tears welling up in her eyes. "You're right. I can't let fear and appearances dictate my well-being. I need to stay with Ms. T, who will understand and help me through these experiences, regardless of what my husband thinks."

At 12:30 p.m., the family car, its engine humming softly, has arrived to take them to the funeral. Amaya's quivering body feels weak, as if she might collapse at any moment. "I don't know if I can do this," she says, with a shaky voice.

Sandra wraps her arms tightly around Amaya, guiding her towards the door. Amaya touches the doorknob; its coolness offers a brief distraction. "You can," Sandra reassures her, her voice gentle yet firm. Amaya's tear-streaked face reflects the anguish in her heart. Her sobs drown out the distant chirping of birds.

The weight of Amaya's grief feels heavy on her chest, causing her heart to speed up. Amaya's mind replays good and bad memories of her father, who they are about to bid farewell to. The car ride to the funeral feels like an eternity, each passing moment a reminder of the finality of her loss. The sound of the engine provides a comforting backdrop, a constant hum that seems to help calm Amaya's emotions.

Sandra's presence is a lifeline, her arms offering both physical and emotional support. The family car arrives at the funeral. Amaya looks toward the church and sees Amber, Quentin, and Josh walking in. She exits the car. With each step towards the church, Amaya's body grows weaker, her legs threatening to give way under the immense weight of sorrow. Yet Sandra's unwavering strength and love guide her forward, a beacon of hope in the darkness.

As the mourners gather, Amaya and her family don't join the mourners. Instead, they quietly make their way inside, finding their seats in their respective areas. The air is full with the gentle melody of soft, somber music resonating through the hushed atmosphere of the church. Amaya notices Amber sitting in the front row. Quentin and Josh escort their wives to the front row.

However, Amaya refuses to sit on the same church bench as her mother. She tells Quentin she will sit in the row behind the first row. Amaya makes her way to her seat, Tonya, Vonne, and Anne, Amaya's colleagues from work, approach her and lean in to give her a hug. Amaya hugs Tonya particularly tightly because they share similar stories.

The funeral begins as an unfamiliar pastor, representing the funeral home handles Larry's arrangements, steps forward to deliver the eulogy. With a voice traveling through the somber church, the pastor recounts Larry's tumultuous journey, emphasizing that he has finally found peace. The scent of freshly cut flower arrangements provides solace for Amaya. She looks around at all the people at the funeral, hearing their muffled cries that envelop the atmosphere in profound sadness.

Amaya cannot handle going to the graveyard to witness her father's burial. Instead, she plans to return home and await everyone for the repast following the graveside service. Amaya expresses her reluctance to see Amber. She tells Quentin, "Don't bring Amber back to the house for the repast. I appreciate you and Josh offering to pick her up for the funeral."

Amaya and her friends walk slowly towards the family car parked nearby. The weight of Amaya's grief still hangs heavy in her body. The ladies make their way back to the car, their steps filled with a mixture of exhaustion and sadness. Their eyes are red from tears shed, and their faces still show the remains of sorrow. The ladies have all decided not to attend the graveside service. Instead, they choose to be there for Amaya, providing her with the support and comfort she needs during this difficult time. They know that being present for her, offering their love and understanding, is more important than any formalities at the gravesite. As they finally reach the car, they exchange glances filled with unspoken understanding, silently reaffirming their commitment to Amaya and their shared journey of helping Amaya to heal that lies ahead.

Chapter Twenty-Five

SANDRA

Sandra watches as Josh and Quentin leave the house. She hears their footsteps fading away. She gives Amaya some space, understanding the need for solitude in times like these. Slowly, she walks into the kitchen to make chamomile tea to help calm Amaya. She turns on the stove, the soft hiss of the gas burner breaking the silence. Sandra carefully pours hot water into a delicate China teacup, the steam rising and swirling in the air.

She gently places a tea bag into the cup, the scent of chamomile intensifying. Adding just a touch of lemon and a hint of sweetness with a bit of Sweet'n Low, she gradually stirs the mixture, the clinking of the spoon against the cup providing a soothing rhythm, while the comforting aroma lingers in the kitchen. The warm cup in her hands brings a sense of comfort, and Sandra knows this small gesture may help ease Amaya's troubled mind.

Amaya is still in shock about Larry's death. She knew he would have been clean years ago if it wasn't for Amber's influence on him. Sandra sheds tears for her sweet Amaya and Larry. *I must be here for Amaya.*

I need to comfort Amber during this time of loss. I can't tell her to be strong or everything is okay. It's important to avoid telling her to be strong, or that everything is okay, as that won't truly console someone who has lost a loved one. Instead, I should allow her to process the pain of her loss. I can let her know that I also feel hurt by Larry's death, but I must be careful not to make her forget about her own grief. It's crucial to support Amaya without causing her further distress.

Sandra walks upstairs with the chamomile tea in hand. She opens the door and notices Amaya sobbing on her pillow.

"Amaya, I'm truly sorry to hear about the passing of your father. Please know that I'm here for you during this difficult time. If you feel the need to vent your anger and sadness about your father's death, I'm here to listen and support you in any way I can. Can I give you a hug, sweetie?"

Amaya wipes her face and blows her nose, then looks at Sandra and whispers, "I really need a hug."

Sandra leans over with tears in her eyes and gives Amaya a hug. Sandra sees her hug is comforting Amaya.

"How is the tea?" asks Sandra.

"It's soothing," says Amaya as she takes another small sip.

"Do you feel like processing Larry's death and what you're feeling? If not, I can just sit with you."

"I have so many feelings right now. My grief has me feeling shocked, sad, and angry, you know? We were not close, but when my husband told me Larry had a job and was clean for two-weeks, only to overdose, it completely shattered me."

"I can't imagine," says Sandra as she wipes tears away.

"I'm so glad you're here. I don't really want to talk anymore. Can you stay with me?"

"Of course, I'm always here for you." She gets into bed with Amaya, pulls her close, and allows Amaya to lie on her chest. Sandra put on soothing meditation music to help Amaya's sadness and anxiety. As the music fills the room, Sandra gently stroked Amaya's hair, offering her a comforting presence. She whispered words of reassurance and love, reminding Amaya that she's not alone in her grief.

With every soothing melody, Sandra can feel Amaya's tension gradually easing, her breathing becoming steady. Sandra's embrace provides a sense of security, allowing Amaya to let go of her present worries and find solace in their shared moment. Amaya's eyelids grow heavy. Sandra continues to hold her, knowing that sometimes all we need is someone to be there, to listen, and to offer unconditional support. Eventually, Amaya's breathing slowed, and her body relaxes into a peaceful rest. Sandra remains by her side, watching over her, silently promising to always be there, no matter the circumstances.

Amaya opens her eyes for a moment, offering a brief glimpse, and softly utters, "Thank you for the chamomile tea and the empathetic ear."

Chapter Twenty-Six

Amber

Drug Court

It's springtime, and the fragrance of the sweet scent of blooming flowers drifts in the air. Vibrant colors paint the landscape, as petals unfurl under the warm sun. The gentle breeze carries the sound of chirping birds, harmonizing with the rustling leaves. Spring has arrived, announcing its presence through all the senses.

Amber enrolled in drug court for eight months instead of serving jail time. The court found her guilty in connection to Larry's death and heroin in the apartment when the first responders arrived. As part of her drug court program, Amber attends day treatment five days a week and has weekly check-ins with her probation officer. She undergoes drug testing twice a week.

Amber has arrived for her third time at the drug court. Judge Braswell is the presiding judge. Amber is sitting in the gallery area at the back of the court, waiting to go in front of the judge. "Amber Montgomery," says the tall bald male bailiff.

Amber heads to the table in front of the judge, pulls the chair out and sits at the table. "Morning Judge," says Amber with a grin on her face.

Dressed in a black robe and with his gray hair adding to his distinguished appearance, Judge Braswell directs his attention towards his papers. "Ms. Montgomery, can you please explain why you have failed to attend your last two urine screenings?"

"Judge, I ain't missed my testing. I have been going to treatment every day except that one day I was sick. I have been doing everything I supposed to do to keep myself clean," says Amber.

"Ms. Montgomery, Amber, I was just joking with you. You gave this court quite a hard time when you initially began the program. So, do you have any news to share with the court?" the judge asks, sporting a grin.

"I have been sober for three months."

A resounding wave of applause sweeps through the spacious courtroom. Amber's bright, glowing face looks around the room, her expression a combination of surprise and delight as the sound of hands clapping washes over her. A sense of pride swells within her.

"Thank you. I haven't felt this good about myself in years. After losing my man, I'm through with the streets."

Judge Braswell, with a warm and encouraging smile, leans forward and delivers some good news to Amber. After carefully reviewing the progress notes from her day treatment, the judge announces Amber will attend Day Treatment three days a week now rather than five days. Amber's face lights up with relief and gratitude as she realizes the judge understands the effort she's been putting in.

"Amber, it is now time for you to work a part-time job on the two days when you do not have your day treatment program. Ms. Cynthia has provided a list of suitable jobs for you, and she will assist you in arranging interviews and providing any necessary support as you begin your new job. I would also like to congratulate you on your three months of sobriety. Please continue to embrace your days of recovery."

As Amber rises from the court table, a burst of excitement fills her. She can't help but feel a rush of energy coursing through her body, fueling her determination to make the most of this opportunity.

With a beaming smile and a genuine appreciation for the chance she's given, she follows Cynthia, her new mentor, to receive the list of jobs. Amber's lively attitude pushes her forward, ready to embrace whatever challenges are ahead.

Chapter Twenty-Seven

Amaya

Amaya reclines on her soft, cozy bed, the orange glow of the sunset seeping through her bedroom window. As she crunches on cheesy Cheetos, the sound of one of her favorite drama series, "Will Trent," brings her enjoyment, the funny dialogue mingling with the sound of the air conditioner calming her nerves. Determination is building as she places the half-eaten Cheetos bag on the nightstand and makes her way to the bathroom. The cool water cascades over her hands, washing away the residue of the cheesy snack, leaving behind a refreshing scent of lavender soap. Returning to her bed, she fixes her eyes on the door. The weight of the impending conversation lingers, creating a mix of nervousness and hope, knowing that this moment will change their lives forever.

Amaya hears Quentin coming down the hallway, and as he enters the room, he takes off his tie and jacket before sitting on the bed beside her.

"How was your day, babe?" Amaya asks, looking at him with concern, raising her eyebrows.

Quentin sighs, "It's been a long day. I'm going to meet the guys for drinks in an hour. I came home to change clothes and shower."

"Can you give me a few minutes? I really need to talk to you," Amaya says with a serious look on her face.

Sensing the urgency in Amaya's expression, Quentin says. "Okay, let's talk."

"I understand you don't want me to continue seeing Ms. T, but I want you to know that I've been seeing her consistently, especially after losing my father. It has been crucial for me to have a therapist during this time to help me process my grief and navigate the other challenges I've been facing. I have been open with her about the voices I've been hearing and the issues I've been having with memory loss. I've also discussed the out-of-character behavior I exhibited at the gala."

Quentin's nostrils flare. "We discussed she's not a good therapist for you. You have been talking to me. I don't understand why you lied to me."

"Baby, I needed you and her. Thank you for your love and support. I feel safe with you. I needed Ms. T., too. She helped me to find new ways to face my challenges."

"What did Ms. T. say about what's been happening to you?"

"She's referring me to a psychiatrist for hallucinations. She finds it strange that the voices only happen at home."

"Maybe you're under more stress at home. Has she sent the referral?"

"I don't know. Why?"

"No reason."

"I have a conference I'm going to in Miami in a couple of weeks. Kathy is going with me. She doesn't want me to be alone. I wanted to tell you now. I've made a decision that I have been pondering over for months. When I turn thirty, I'm giving the inheritance to St Jude's and the Trevor Project. I've thought about it long and hard. We do not need the money. I have more money than I can spend in a lifetime."

Quentin has a lump in his throat. He leans towards Amaya and interrogates her. "Who put that idea in your head? What about the children we're going to have? I believe a miracle can happen and we can have that beautiful little girl who looks like her gorgeous mother. You can't make a unilateral decision like that without talking to me," Quentin says, teeth clenched.

"Baby, Ms. T. said I should talk to you, but ultimately, it's my decision. I know you didn't marry me for the money. We have more than we need. It's time to face the fact that I will never get pregnant. I'm going to schedule us a meeting with Bethany to adopt a baby."

"You're the one making all the decisions that affect both of us, and I've had enough of discussing this. Right now, I just need to take a shower and meet the guys for drinks. I know I really need it right now."

Amaya is upset because he walks out before she finishes talking to him. As a result, she cries and cannot stop her tears. Meanwhile, Quentin comes out of the bathroom and gets dressed without saying a word to Amaya.

"What time will you be home? I would like to finish this conversation with you. It's important."

"Don't wait up," he says, slamming the bedroom door as he leaves.

Chapter Twenty-Eight

JOSH

Elevations Nightclub

At 7:10 p.m., the dimly lit Elevations night club buzzes with excitement. Josh settles in the VIP section and sinks into a luxury black camel back couch while drinking a vodka soda. He eagerly awaits Quentin's arrival. Meanwhile, their friend Idris leans against the bar, cold beer in hand, as his eyes trace the movements of passing women. Josh looks dapper in a sleek grey suit that makes him look confident, complemented by a gold wheat chain necklace around his neck.

Quentin steps into the club. A cloud of smoke from his cigar follows his every step. The DJ takes command of the mic, and the infectious beats of high energy music pulsate through the club. The music fills the room. Bodies sway and feet tap in synchrony. Bartenders pour lines of colorful drinks for eager customers at the bar, the sounds of blenders crushing ice for frozen drinks mingling with the lively chatter.

Strobe lights flash, casting a mesmerizing display across the room. The lights create an electric ambiance, heightening all the senses and immersing everyone in a visually stimulating environment.

Josh discreetly slips a handful of cash into the server's hand, the sound of paper rustling softly. He whispers in her ear and points to Quentin. She makes her way towards Quentin and Idris. Her eyes meeting theirs. The server's fingers gently brush against the smooth surface of the bills as she carefully tucks the money away into her worn money bag. The server gives Quentin and Idris the message and points them to the VIP section.

Quentin and Idris walk over to Josh's table. Josh gets up and gives them a mix of handshake and hug, with a pat on the back after letting go.

"Good to see you, Idris. It's been a minute," says Josh.

"I had to get out of the house. My mother-in-law is visiting, and she seems to have forgotten that it's my house. She and my wife are changing our bedroom around. That's something my wife and I were planning on doing together this summer." Idris takes a big sip of his vodka soda.

"That's crazy," says Quentin.

"Only good vibes tonight, guys," says Josh.

"The club is hopping tonight, wall to wall people. How did you get us VIP seats?" asks Quentin.

Josh smirks and says, "You know, I know people. I'm VIP!"

The guys sit and talk for a while. Josh looks up and spots Elena in the crowd. He weaves through the people and makes a beeline for the short-hair brown-skinned young lady looking around the club sitting with two females.

"Hey Elena! You look nice tonight," says Josh, looking into her eyes and smiling.

"It's so loud in here. I can't hear you."

Josh moves close to Elena, leans into her ear and tells her again she looks nice.

"Aww thank you. You look pretty good yourself."

"Can I get you a drink? You're almost dry."

"Sure."

"What are you drinking?"

Elena raises her nearly empty glass and replies, "In between the sheets."

Elena laughs at his expression. "It's a drink." She lightly pushes him towards the direction of the bar, a luxurious setting with comfortable seating.

"Aaah, okay. I'll be right back. I'll get one for myself too, and then we can both enjoy being 'between the sheets'," says Josh. He heads to the bar.

When Josh returns with the drinks, he casually suggests, "Hey, would you and your friends like to join me and the boys in VIP?"

Elena asks her friends if they would like to sit in VIP. They quickly agree, their bodies swaying to the music while raising their glasses in the air as they follow Josh through the crowd, showing a mix of excitement and disbelief. As they enter the VIP, the luxurious setting amazes them with comfortable seating, a private bathroom, exclusive servers, and drinks on ice amazes them.

The atmosphere is vibrant, with music pumping and people dancing to the beat. Elena and her friends settle into their seats, sip on their drinks, and enjoy the elevated view of the dance floor. They can't help but feel a sense of special treatment, reveling because they are part of an elite group within the club. The night takes on a whole new level of excitement, and they can't wait to see what other surprises await them in the VIP area.

Josh introduces Quentin and Idris to the girls. As the night goes on, Josh puts his arms around Elena's shoulders. However, Josh notices that Quentin, who is usually very sociable and flirtatious, isn't interacting much with the women. Quentin seems to be lost in his own thoughts, occupying himself with drinking and making small talk. Idris is in high spirits, cracking jokes and reveling in seeing the ladies laugh.

Josh asks Elena to step outside. They both get up and head outside. Standing outside of the nightclub, Josh asks, "Can I take you out this weekend?"

"Does your wife really know you have extramarital affairs?"

"To be honest with you, my wife is aware I've been unfaithful. Believe it or not, she doesn't seem to care. Deep down, I really wish she cared. Elena, I married her because she got pregnant while we were still in our first year of college. She was my high school sweetheart, and I had feelings for her. I couldn't bear the thought of another man being called 'daddy' by my child. So, I asked her to marry me. Over time, my feelings for her grew, and I genuinely love her. But she keeps me at bay. She's been struggling for a while. I've tried my best to support and assist her, but she's become angry with me for my efforts."

"Wow, I never expected you to be that kind of guy," she says. "I was actually considering sleeping with you, but I can't do that. There's love in your marriage, and I can't be a part of interfering with that. Well, I'll see you in the elevator, friend!" They hug each other with their arms around each other's waist. She walks back into the club. Josh stands outside, taking a moment to process their conversation. It was the first time he has been so honest with a woman about his marriage. He wasn't upset when Elena turned him down.

He confidently strides back into the dimly lit club. The thumping bass of the music pulsating through his chest. Ignoring the thoughts of his conversation with Elena, he heads straight towards the exclusive VIP area, where his friends and the girls await his return. Settling back into the luxury couch, he dances in his seat to the rhythm of his favorite BBD song, feeling the beats of the music distract him from the uncomfortable conversation.

Chapter Twenty-Nine

QUENTIN

Removing an Obstacle

Quentin is sitting in VIP making small talk, thinking about what Amaya said about her therapist sending her to a psychiatrist. He tries to mask his anger while around everyone.

Quentin thinks to himself, *I can't let her go to a psychiatrist. And she has told her therapist about the issues she's having with hearing voices and losing things. I need her to trust me so I can eventually drive her insane and then they'll have to make me her power of attorney. Now she's talking about giving the money away. I can't let that happen.* Quentin is staring in space, lost in his thoughts. Idris calls Quentin's name several times. "Q. Q. Q, where you at, man?"

Quentin snaps back to reality. His brows furrowing in annoyance. "Man, what is it?" he grumbles, his irritation clear in his tone.

A woman with a curvy body, naturally curly hair, and a mole on her nose catches Quentin's attention. He quickly sits up and recognizes her as Ms. T, the therapist. He remembers Amaya showing him an article on Ms. T. Anger wells up within him as he realizes she is interfering with his plans to drive her to the brink of madness before she donates it all to charity. Driven by twisted determination, he vows to get rid of that therapist once and for all.

Quentin tells everyone he's ready to call it a night. One by one, his friends bid their farewells, their voices fading into the background. The cool night air greets him as he steps into the parking lot. A desire to rid himself of the intrusive therapist consumes his thoughts. He slides into his car; the leather seat is cool to the touch. Contemplating his options, a breeze brushes against his face, causing him to roll up his windows. Perhaps removing the license plate and running her over as she crosses the street? He dismisses the idea as too risky.

He accesses his phone and conducts a background check on the therapist. Discovering her address, an unsettling satisfaction washes over him. Igniting the engine, the faint smell of gasoline lingers in the air as he speeds away. "It's time to pay this therapist a home visit," he says, with a firm grip on the steering wheel looking straight ahead with his eyebrows lowered and drown together, "She will not interfere with my plans."

Arriving at Ms. T.'s house, he contemplates his plan. He drives around the corner and parks a couple of houses away. Before exiting the car, he grabs his Chicago Bulls cap from the backseat and reaches for some leftover Covid masks from the glove compartment. Feeling lucky there are only a few streetlights, he believes he won't be easily spotted as he approaches her house.

As he opens the gate to the backyard, his eyebrows raise in surprise because there's a ladder there. Seizing the opportunity, he takes the ladder and climbs through the second-floor window of Ms. T's house, feeling confident that there's no alarm on a second-floor window. Using his ball cap to protect his elbow, he breaks the window and enters the dark room. Checking his surroundings with his phone's light, he notices no clothes or personal items. It has to be a guestroom.

He searches for Ms. T's bedroom. Once he finds it, he goes downstairs to the kitchen and returns to the guest room, waiting for her to return home. His plan is to physically assault her with her meat mallet from her kitchen, ensuring she can no longer provide therapy to his wife. While in the guest room, he thinks about his plans, particularly his control over his wife's finances, when she turns thirty. Methodically, he plots each step of his mission, his mind consumed by deep-rooted rage and resentment towards Ms. T. The thought of his wife's dependence on this woman and the trust she has placed in her fuels his rage even further.

Hours seem to crawl by, but he remains steadfast in his resolve. The sound of a key turning in the front door finally breaks the silence, sending a surge of adrenaline through his body. He readies himself. Quentin grips the meat mallet he took from her kitchen drawer. The moment of reckoning is now for Ms. T.

Downstairs, Ms. T. flicks the light switch on in her living room, takes off her high heels, almost losing her balance, and walks into the kitchen, the cool linoleum floor soothing her aching bare feet. She reaches for a Styrofoam cup from its package and fills it with water from the faucet. With a gentle twist, she turns off the kitchen lights and heads upstairs.

Entering the bathroom, she removes her clothes, washes the makeup off her face and brushes her teeth. She slips into her favorite nightgown with white polka dots, that read, "Let me sleep," and takes the extra pillows off the bed.

Ms. T. nestles in her bed with an enormous yawn and settles beneath the covers, the soft sheets embracing her tired body. As she closes her eyes, the room falls into a gentle hush, the only sound being her steady breaths.

Fifteen minutes pass and Quentin exits the guest room, his every movement hushed. He enters her bedroom. The floor squeaks, but she doesn't wake up. He approaches her bed, where her body is curled on her side. Quentin abruptly yanks her cover, causing her to awaken in terror. A blood-curdling scream pierces the air as he brandishes the meat mallet high above her head. With a swift and forceful swing, he strikes her jaw with unrelenting power. Grabbing her by her hair, he violently drags her out of bed, her feeble attempts to crawl away proving futile. A brutal kick sends her sprawling onto her back, the impact stealing her breath away.

Seizing the mallet once more, Quentin mercilessly strikes her knees repeatedly, her arms instinctively raised in defense. He makes his escape from the room, glancing back, only to witness her desperate crawl towards her cell phone. With determination, he keeps retreating and quickly reaches the guest room. He exits through the window and descends the ladder. He walks back to his car, takes off his disguise, and feels a wave of satisfaction knowing that Ms. T. is no longer an obstacle for him.

Chapter Thirty

SANDRA

7:00 a.m., Sandra plays amateur chauffeur for her friend and boss. Driving Amaya and Kathy to the Aurora Municipal Airport to catch their flight to attend the 2023 Global Resource Management Conference in Miami. Sandra listens to the ladies in an animated conversation about the latest trends and challenges in their field. Sandra arrives at the airport. She smoothly parks the car in the drop off area of the airport, ready to assist Amaya and Kathy with their luggage. Sandra wraps her arms around both ladies, squeezing tightly, and whispers in Amaya's ear, "I love you. Have a good time."

Sandra returns to Amaya's house for her cleaning duties, but she can't seem to shake the nagging feeling that Quentin is behind all the recent troubles Amaya has been facing. Driven by determination, she searches for any evidence that might expose Quentin's deceit.

Quentin arrives home a few hours early. Sandra has to pause from her search through Quentin's office. Quentin enters the home from the garage, walks into the living room, and speaks to Sandra.

"Sandra, did you get the girls off to the airport?"

"I did. They're headed to sunny Miami."

"I'm going upstairs to lie down. I have a headache. You can skip our room today."

"Will do. I'll clean the master bedroom tomorrow."

At 5:00 p.m., Sandra finishes work and leaves her phone behind on the kitchen counter so she can have a reason to return later in the evening. Quentin has a weekly tradition of going out with the boys every Thursday. Sandra finishes gathering her purse and then she leaves.

As Sandra is driving back to Amaya's later, a storm hits and rages over Aurora. The sky hangs ominously as the thunder roars with a deafening force. Bolts of lightning tear through the sky with a tempestuous blackness that engulfs the city. The rain pours relentlessly, drenching everything in its path. The ferociousness and fright are reaching everyone, and out of the darkness emerges an inexplainable horror.

Sandra returns to Amaya's home drenched from the rain. Quentin's car is gone. She dries herself off and begins her careful footsteps in the silence. She feels desperate as she searches for any evidence against Quentin, hoping to unveil the truth behind the bizarre occurrences that have plagued Amaya.

Sandra climbs the staircase, her heart pounding in her chest. The upstairs is heavy with the odor of secrets long kept hidden. She places her purse on the console table in the hallway. Her pulse quickens, a mix of hope and fear. She approaches the bedroom door and pushes it open. The sound of her own breathing drowns out the sound of rain pounding against the windows.

Sandra searches the bedroom, looking for any clue, any shred of evidence that could shed light on Quentin's involvement in the unexplained happenings that have haunted Amaya's every waking moment. The thunder booms outside, shaking the house to its very foundation, as if nature itself is urging Sandra to uncover the truth. She continues her search, her mind racing with anticipation and the fear of what she may discover.

Sandra continues her relentless search with caution, navigating through the darkness. The absence of any light ensures she won't attract attention. She peers behind the dresser and scrutinizes both closets. Sandra flips the mattress on the bed, feeling the musty fabric from the mattress beneath her fingertips. She stretches her arms behind the headboard, exploring every inch. Suddenly, her hand brushes against a hidden button. As she presses it, a deafening boom of thunder startles her, sending shivers down her spine.

She hears wind in the room and Mr. Montgomery's voice talking to Amaya. He's calling her Princess, the name he called her when she was a little girl. "What the fruit is happening here?" says Sandra as she presses the button to turn the wind and voice off. She shakes her head. "I always knew my girl wasn't losing her mind." Realizing the gravity of the situation, Sandra knows she must contact the police immediately.

As lightning illuminates the bedroom, a brilliant flash fills the room. In that fleeting moment, she catches sight of a mysterious silhouette, a man standing in the doorway. But as quickly as the image appeared, it vanishes into the darkness. A wave of relief washes over her, for she had mistaken the figure for Mr. Quentin coming home early.

She swiftly exits the bedroom and grabs her purse from the console. Heading downstairs, her heart rate increases. She's paralyzed, and her chest is tight as she sees lights on downstairs. "Quentin is home! Did he notice my car?" she wonders, feeling scared.

Fear gripping her, she hurriedly heads towards the front door. To her surprise, she finds the deadbolt locked, realizing that she doesn't have a key for it, as it's only used when the couple goes to sleep. A sense of horror overwhelms her as she realizes she can't leave. Just then, Quentin's voice calls out to her, "Oh, Sandra, why don't you come to the kitchen and join me for dinner?"

"No, thank you. I should get home, and I only returned to finish up your room and to get my phone," says Sandra, hoping to find a way out of this situation.

"You're cleaning in the dark now? Sit, have dinner with me. I insist. We need to talk. I reheated some leftovers," says Quentin, with a hint of malice in his voice.

"I need to head home."

"It's not safe out there. The storm is treacherous, that's why I came home early. There are no signs of it easing up right away," Quentin says.

Sandra understands it might be safer to be in the storm than in the kitchen with Quentin, but she reluctantly agrees to have dinner with him.

He presents her with a plate of quesadillas and Spanish rice before taking his seat across from her with his own plate. Carefully, he pours them each a glass of water.

"Excuse me for just a minute. I need to make a call. You eat," says Quentin.

She takes a bite of the quesadillas and nods her head. She looks at him walk to the sink as she takes a second bite and listens to his conversation.

"Hey, get up. I need you to come through for a minute. Listen, I don't care what you're in the middle of. Come through now!"

Sandra's eyes blink quickly as she opens her mouth, stuttering her words. "Mr. Quentin, who was that on the phone?"

"You shall see," he says with a malicious grin.

Sandra is itching. She's scratching her arms, now her hands, and neck. Hives have spread across her entire body. She begins to cough. "What's in the quesadillas?" she asks with a tingling in her throat.

"You know, the usual: chicken, cheese, Pico de gallo, and some minced shrimp." He looks her straight in the eyes.

"Shrimp? You know I'm allergic to shellfish." Frantically, she runs to retrieve the EpiPen from her purse. She can't find it. She empties all the contents in her purse, but it's not there.

Quentin stands in the hallway with the EpiPen in his hand. "Is this what you're looking for?" he asks, taunting her.

Sandra pleads, "Give it to me," but Quentin refuses. She coughs and vomits, collapsing to the floor, barely able to move. The doorbell rings.

"Don't get up. I'll answer the door."

He returns with Josh. Sandra feels relief. Struggling to speak through her coughing and vomiting, she begs for his help, "Thank God it's you, Joshua. Please help me."

"What is going on here?" asks Josh. He runs over to Sandra, who croaks out, "Please get my EpiPen from Quentin."

Josh grabs the EpiPen out of Quentin's hand and kneels next to her. Anxious, she urges him to use the EpiPen on her leg. But Josh hesitates, "I'm sorry. I've always liked you, but you're interfering with our plans."

"Not you, Joshua? You've always been Amaya's rock," she says, shocked at Josh defending himself. He explains Amaya doesn't need or want the money, and he feels neglected by being left out of the will. A disappointed, Sandra compares him to Quentin, unable to bear looking at him.

Quentin slowly approaches her. Sandra's breath grows shallow, causing a faint rasp in the air. She musters her strength to accuse him of being evil, but he reveals an even darker side, his words dripping with malevolence, "Sandra, you thought I was bad. I'm a lot worse."

In the final moments before her consciousness slips away, a montage of memories floods her mind, each accompanied by a vivid sight, the laughter of Amaya and Annie as children echoing through her ears; the gentle touch of the grocery store manager, who she's been secretly sleeping with for over ten years. And the comforting talks with Amaya. Sandra's fading consciousness meets with the passage of time, thirteen agonizing minutes, until she succumbs to death's embrace, her final breath escaping silently.

Chapter Thirty-One

JOSH

"What the hell, man?" asks Josh, as he paces back and forth in front of the body.

"I went upstairs to my bedroom and discovered her snooping around. She had stumbled upon the button that activated the voice over of Amaya's grandparents. It was clear she had found some incriminating evidence, which she would've shared with Amaya and the police. This situation would have had dire consequences for us."

Damn, Q! This has gone too far. I cared for Sandra; she was the sweetest person I knew. Honestly, she was right about you, anyway. We had been planning this for years, ever since Uncle Anthony and Aunt Genevia died in that car accident. I know she could be nosy as hell, but she didn't deserve this. If she had to go, couldn't you have made it more humane? I admit, I've done some terrible things myself, but all this could have been avoided. You could have just threatened Annie and her grandchildren or something. Now, how are you going to explain this? And what about disposing of the body?

"If you can let me get a word in, I can explain," he says with frustration etched on his face. He leans over towards Josh. "But first, let's address how we are going to dispose of the body. We are deep in this together. It was your twisted plan in the first place, for me to marry Amaya, drive her insane, gain power of attorney over her, and split the money. So, it's 'we,' not just me. First, how stupid are you? She loved Amaya as if she were her second daughter. I wouldn't have been able to threaten Annie and her brats. She would have called the police," says Quentin.

"Let's address the body in the room. How are we going to handle this?" asks Josh with his eyes intensely staring at Quentin.

"She's allergic to shellfish. I'll put on gloves and pack the rest of this food in a to-go box with chicken quesadillas written on the box. We'll leave it in the passenger seat. Her EpiPen isn't in her purse. The storm has calmed, but it's foggy outside. I'll follow you to her house and park a few houses away. You will drive her body home in the back seat of the car. Drive into the garage and put her in the front seat. Go into the house, change into some of her clothes, put a wig on, put your shoes and clothes in one of her purses, then come to my car. When they find her, the cause of death will be determined to be anaphylaxis."

"There's one problem with your plan. You have me doing all the work!" says Josh in a boisterous tone. "Let me be really clear. So clear that you can see it through a silk screen. I'm not doing it!" Josh purses his lips.

"Yeah, you are," says Quentin. He slams his hand on the mantel of the fireplace.

"You killed her," says Josh, his voice trembling with anger, as he slams his hand forcefully against the cold stone fireplace. "I would have found another way to keep her quiet," he says, his eyes filled with outrage. "You can drive her lifeless body, with the stench of death lingering in the car, and dress yourself in her clothing and wig to deceive anyone who may see. I'll follow behind you with the weight of our actions heavy on my conscience."

"How about we do...," says Quentin as Josh rudely interrupts him.

"No. We're doing it this way. You always believe you're the cleverest person in the room, but let me tell you, you're not!"

Josh retrieves her keys from her purse and drives the car into the garage. Their muscles strain as they lift her lifeless body and place her in the back seat.

They both position themselves as they embark on the macabre plan they hashed to get her body home.

As the two men drive away from Sandra's home, they notice streaks of red, resembling blood, painting the sky that stretches across the western horizon above Sandra's home.

Chapter Thirty-Two

Amaya

Miami

The weather in Miami is all sunshine. The forecast predicts a high of 86 degrees Fahrenheit, with 92% humidity. At 8:00 in the morning, Amaya and Kathy enter the first day of the conference. As they settle into their seats, they exchange friendly greetings with the others at their table, who are also professionals in their field.

The speaker, an expert in legal compliance, starts the presentation, and his voice reverberates clearly through the room, capturing everyone's attention. The slides on the projector provide visual aids, enhancing the speaker's explanations. A whiff of freshly brewed coffee fills the air, invigorating Amaya and Kathy, who had woken up early to attend the conference. They lean forward, fully engaged, as the speaker delves into various strategies for ensuring legal compliance, sharing real-life examples and practical tips.

The speaker has just concluded his captivating presentation, leaving the audience impressed and inspired. As the surveys for his performance are being handed out, the people at the table engage in a lively discussion about which workshop they should attend next. Each person shares their preferences, highlighting the topics they are most interested in.

The table buzzes with excitement as they weigh the options and consider the potential for gaining valuable insights and knowledge from the upcoming sessions. Someone suggests the idea of getting together later in the evening to unwind and enjoy some downtime. They make plans for a gathering in the hotel's downstairs lounge.

It's 6:30 p.m., Kathy and Amaya make their way back to their cozy hotel rooms. Their laughter fills the corridor as they recount the delightful dinner they shared with their newfound friends at the conference. They enter their hotel rooms and enjoy the fresh scent of flowers and the stylish room. The ladies step into a soothing shower in their rooms and then make their way downstairs to meet up with their new friends at the vibrant lounge enjoying music they can vibe with and sip on drinks.

With cocktails in their hands, they excitedly approach their friends and exchange greetings. As they smile at each other, their arms instinctively reach out for friendly hugs. The music blares as people are dancing and laughing, ready to party. With each taste of their cocktails, the ladies feel a surge of energy, ready to engage themselves in the night's festivities.

"I'm dry. I'm going to get another drink," says Amaya as she shakes her empty glass and moves her hips to the music. On the way to the bar, she trips over someone's foot and lands in a man's lap.

"Well, hello," says the gentleman, his mouth raised at both corners.

A startled Amaya says, "Oh my goodness! I can't believe I literally fell into your lap!" She nervously bites her bottom lip. Feeling embarrassed, she quickly gets up and begins apologizing profusely. He reaches out. His fingers curling around her delicate left hand while applying a gentle pull to draw her closer. As he does, his eyes catch a glimmer of a magnificent diamond wedding ring on her left finger.

"Just my luck. You're married."

"Yes, I am. Happily married," she says, waving her ring in his face.

He looks at one guy sitting at the table. "Hey, hey take your phone out and take a picture." The guy takes a big gulp of his beer. "Take a picture of what?" he asks.

"Hey, take a picture of this beauty so I can show Santa what I want for Christmas."

"Dude, that has to be the corniest pickup line I've ever heard," the man says as he struggled not to choke on his beer.

"No, no. I better go," she says and pulls her hand away. She walks to the bar in need of a strong drink after that awkward interaction.

Amaya rejoins the group of girls. She immediately shares her experience with Kathy. "I was so nervous falling in that man's lap," Amaya admits, "I thought I was going to throw up."

"Girl, where is he? Is he cute?" Kathy asks playfully.

"Shut up! I didn't pay attention to that man," says Amaya, tossing her lustrous hair to the side, her auburn highlights reflecting in the neon lights. Laughter bubbles from her lips as she joins the girls on the dance floor. After a few minutes, Amaya excuses herself from the group to call her husband. She weaves through the crowd, looking for a somewhat quiet corner. The persistent calls and unanswered texts from him throughout the day have left her unsettled. A knot of nerves forms in her stomach.

As she calls her husband's number, the pulsating beats of the music fade into the background. Doubts creep into her mind, a bitter taste of suspicion clouding her thoughts. She can't shake the feeling he is purposefully pulling away from her, leaving her alone in a sea of unanswered calls. With there being no answer, she returns to Kathy and the group.

An hour has passed, and Amaya and the girls are tipsy from the drinks. Amaya feels a gentle nudge on her shoulder and turns to find the man she had accidentally fallen into earlier, a mischievous glint in his eyes. "Dance with me," he says.

Amaya's inhibitions drown temporarily in a wheelbarrow of alcohol, and she replies without a hint of anxiety, "What's your name?"

"I'm Tyler. What's your name, sexy?" he asks with a sly grin.

In that moment, Amaya momentarily forgets the vows she made, and playfully flirts back with Tyler. He takes her hand and leads her onto the crowded dance floor. Tyler continuously replenishes her glass with more drinks throughout the night. Kathy notices a change in her friend and pulls Amaya aside, with a look of concern on her face. "Are you okay?" she asks, her voice barely audible above the music. "This isn't like you. Where is my shy friend?"

Amaya takes the last sip of her drink and says, "I haven't felt this good in a long time."

"Why don't we head back to our rooms?" Kathy asks.

"No way," says Amaya, and she dances back to Tyler. Together, they slip out of the lounge and take the elevator to the sixth floor, where Tyler's hotel room is located. Amaya, struggling to walk in her high heels, takes them off. She's clearly intoxicated. Amaya stumbles as Tyler pulls her closer and passionately kisses her. Lost in the moment, she wraps her arms around him and kisses him back. With a quick motion, Tyler hangs the "do not disturb" sign on the door and closes it behind them as they enter his hotel room.

It's morning. Amaya has missed several calls and texts from Kathy and Quentin. She has a severe headache and feels nauseous. The room is spinning. She turns over and there is a strange man lying next to her. She takes a big gulp. What has she done? She jumps out the bed and calls Kathy.

"Where are you? The conference began over an hour ago," asks Kathy.

"I need to get out of here. Last night, I made a mistake—I slept with that man. I think I had too much to drink or something. Right now, I'm feeling nervous and nauseous. I don't know what to do. It's hard to catch my breath, and I feel another panic attack is coming on."

"Get out of there, now! I'm headed upstairs. I'll meet you in your hotel room."

"Umm, okay."

"Wait! Before you go, look around for a used condom. You don't want Tyler to have given you a STI."

"Oh, that's his name?"

"Girl, look for that condom and get the hell out of there."

"I don't see one."

"Look in the bed and on him."

"I did. I don't see one."

"Alright. Alright. Leave now, leave nothing behind. I will take you to my doctor in three days for a thorough examination for any diseases. I know you; you will not feel comfortable going to your doctor about this."

"You know me, but is this necessary?"

"Hell, yeah! And don't sleep with Quentin until all the tests come back. You only have to hold off having sex with Quentin for about six days."

"I'm going to my room. I can't go to the conference hung over."

"You've never drunk like that before. I'm sure you feel awful. I'm coming to take care of you, and I'll head back to the conference after I get you settled."

Amaya swiftly gathers her belongings and rushes out of the hotel room. As she steps outside the room, tears stream down her make-up smudged face. Her heart feels heavy. Walking towards the elevator, she can't help but lower her head, burdened by guilt. Every step she takes feels like the walk of shame.

Chapter Thirty-Three

QUENTIN

Quentin arrives at his office, while sitting in the parking garage, he tries to call Amaya, but there is no answer. Frustrated, he sits in his car for a minute to gather his thoughts. Eventually, he calls Kathy.

"Hello."

"Hey, Kathy. Is Amaya with you?"

"No, she's not with me. She's still asleep. She's not feeling well."

"Oh, really? Was she sick last night?"

"I'm not sure. She went to bed before me. I checked on her in her hotel room about twenty minutes ago."

"Got it. Thanks, Kathy. I'll try to call her later. Take care of my girl."

"I'll let her know you have been trying to reach her."

"Bye," says Quentin.

On his way to his office, he quickly grabs a bagel with cream cheese from the cafeteria in his office building. He heads straight to Josh's office and closes the door behind him. "Josh, we need to talk."

"I don't have time for this right now. My meeting with Mrs. Wright is in an hour."

"Make time!" Quentin says as he pushes Josh's laptop to the side of his desk.

Josh exhales an audible sigh. "What is it, Q?" He furrows his eyebrows and locks eyes with Quentin.

"I can't get Amaya on the phone. It's important I tell her that Sandra didn't show up for work and is ignoring my calls. I left a couple of messages on Sandra's phone to cover our tracks," says Quentin.

"You and this 'we' and 'our' are killing me. Killing Sandra before talking to me makes this a 'you' problem."

Quentin feels a faint twitch in his left eye as he watches Josh reach for his laptop and begin typing.

"Are you going to just stand and watch me?"

"Yeah, I'm man enough to ask for help."

"I forgot the world revolves around you. My bad," says Josh.

"Man, does this drama have an intermission?" asks Quentin.

"Dude, you're my best friend. I'm pissed with you right now, but I gotcha. Don't call Sandra's phone again. You don't want to make it too obvious that we're trying to cover our tracks, especially since you dragged me into this mess. Here's the plan: when Amaya gets home, she'll go to Sandra's house and find her dead in the car. Remember, Amaya has a key to her place. That moment will really push her over the edge, and then our plan will be complete."

"That's a damn good plan," says Quentin.

Chapter Thirty-Four

Amaya

Homecoming

Amaya and Kathy sit side by side on the airplane. Their journey back home is underway. Amaya looks out the window, where the billowy clouds calm her nerves. She loses herself in the thoughts of the convention and wonders how she could get so drunk and have a tryst with a stranger. A wave of self-disgust washes over her.

Sensing Amaya's turmoil, Kathy reaches out and gently clasps her hand. "I know what you're thinking about. We will keep this between us."

"I have to tell Sandra. I tell her everything."

"Understood, but no one else, okay?"

"Well, I have to tell Ms. T. when I see her on Saturday."

"Okay. That's it."

"I know. Yes, I know. I'm not sure how I'll face my husband after what happened. This struggle with infertility is taking a toll on me. And I'm still experiencing forgetfulness, hearing things, and now I give my body to a complete stranger. Memories from that night are coming back to me. I remember enjoying the attention he was giving me. But something just crossed my mind. I couldn't find a condom. Perhaps we didn't have sex. It's possible that we simply went to sleep naked and intoxicated." Kathy looks at her, rolls her eyes, and puts her headphones on.

After returning to Aurora, they take an Uber home. Quentin greets her and then tells her Sandra hasn't shown up for work since Thursday. When Amaya tries to call Sandra, it goes straight to voicemail. Realizing something isn't right, Kathy offers to ride with Amaya to check on Sandra. She suggests Amaya drop her off at her own home afterwards.

Amaya appreciates Kathy's offer and agrees. The two friends drive through the familiar streets of Aurora, their conversation filled with worry and speculation about Sandra's sudden disappearance. As they approach Sandra's house, an eerie feeling consumes Amaya, intensifying her concerns. They park the car and make their way to Sandra's front door. Amaya reaches out to ring the doorbell, but there's no answer. Amaya takes out her key and opens Sandra's door.

"Sandra. Sandra. Are you home?" yell both girls as they walk through the house.

Amaya looks around. "It doesn't appear that anything is out of order. It's as if she hasn't been here at all." Determined to investigate further, Amaya says, "I'm going to check the garage to see if her car is there." She steps into the garage. The sight that greets her is horrific.

Amaya's piercing screams echo through the garage, desperate for Kathy's attention. With trembling hands, Amaya yanks open the car door, her voice filled with anguish as she calls out Sandra's name. Amaya's fingers brush against Sandra's lifeless body. A wave of coldness washes over her, the clamminess of the skin sending shivers down her spine.

The stiffness of Sandra's form, a telltale sign of rigor mortis, confirms the horrifying reality. Overwhelmed by the sight before her, Amaya cannot bear witness to Sandra's corpse. Sensing the need to shield Amaya from the heart-wrenching scene, Kathy rushes to her side, urging her to look away. Collapsing into Kathy's arms, Amaya's legs grow weak, her sobs of despair falling on Kathy's supportive shoulders.

Kathy walks Amaya to the living room to sit down. Kathy gets her a drink of water and then calls 911, reporting the finding of Sandra's lifeless body.

Amaya is now home, still trembling from the loss of her friend and mother-figure. Kathy is there to support her. Amaya picks up her phone, scrolling through her contacts to find Annie's number. She knows she needs to call her before the police do, as she doesn't want Annie to hear the devastating news from a stranger. Amaya takes a deep breath as she hears the other end click.

"Hello," says Annie.

"Annie, it's Amaya. I have to tell..."

Annie interrupts. "Why are you calling me?"

"Annie, please listen. I have some news to share with you, sad news. If you're not sitting down, please do so," Amaya says with tears in her eyes and a shaky voice. "I'm sorry to inform you that your mother has died. A couple of hours ago, I discovered her in her car in her garage. We are currently unaware of the circumstances of her death."

"No...no! she's not gone," screams Annie.

"Quentin and I are here for you and the kids for whatever you need. I will purchase your plane tickets to come back home."

Amaya hears the trembles in Annie's voice as she breaks down on the phone. "Mommy, I'm so sorry for how I treated you. Can you hear me from Heaven, mommy? I should have never treated you the way I did. Mommy, I love you."

Amaya and Annie are spending a few minutes on the phone, both in tears. Amaya says, "Call me with the information so I can pay for your flight home."

"I'm truly sorry, Mya. Can you find it in your heart to forgive me for my jealousy? We used to be so close, like sisters, before I let my actions ruin our bond. This is a tough way for me to learn that life is too short to hold on to grudges. I want you to know that I love you, my dear sister."

"I miss you so much, and I love you even more," says Amaya with a slight smile on her face.

Amaya looks up as Quentin and Josh rush in through the back door. "We tried to get here sooner, but we had meetings we couldn't miss," says Josh as he runs over to Amaya, setting himself beside her and giving her a big hug. "Sandra was so wonderful. Many people will miss her." Quentin thanks Kathy for staying with Amaya and pushes Josh out of the way so he can be with his wife.

Later, Amaya takes some sleeping pills to go to sleep. Exhausted and emotionally drained, she collapses onto her bed without even bothering to change out of her clothes. The weight of losing her father still lingers heavily in her heart. And now Sandra, her closest friend. The pain and grief have become overwhelming, leaving Amaya feeling utterly defeated and unable to cope with the world around her.

Beads of perspiration form on Amaya's forehead as she awakens, and her clothes become drenched with sweat. Confusion clouds her mind as she grapples to decipher the dream. Sandra issued her a warning, yet there was no clarity when revealing whom to be cautious of. Instantly, Tyler, the man with whom she slept with in Miami, flashes into Amaya's mind. A nagging suspicion takes hold of her, intertwining with the lingering remnants of the dream.

Amaya, feeling lost, sad, and unable to find peace, reaches for the bottle of sleeping pills on her nightstand. With a sigh, she takes a couple more than the recommended dosage, hoping that this time the extra pills will help her remain asleep. She lies back down on her bed, the heaviness of drowsiness slowly creeping over her. Closing her eyes, she tries to will her racing thoughts to subside, hoping that sleep will grant her a temporary escape from what she witnessed today.

Chapter Thirty-Five

QUENTIN

At 7:30 a.m., Quentin is standing at the stove, cooking breakfast for Amaya and Kathy. He asked Kathy to spend the night to assist him in caring for Amaya. The air fills with the sizzling sounds of eggs and turkey sausage, as well as the aroma of whole grain toast and freshly squeezed orange juice. As he cooks, Quentin picks up his phone and calls Josh to discuss the next step in their plan.

Josh groggily answers his phone. "Yeah, what's up?"

"I think it's time to start the hologram of her grandmother and grandfather," says Quentin.

"If Kathy goes home tonight, it's the perfect time for you to do it."

"I tested it out when Mike first installed it. It will scare the hell out of her."

"How will you hide the projector?"

"It's small. I'm going to hide it behind the air purifier in our dresser bureau. There will be a book by the mirror where she can't see the machine."

"That's a good plan. Bree and I will be over this afternoon so that Kathy can go home and get some rest, and be out of our way for tonight's festivities."

"Cool, we will be here."

Quentin prepares a stunning breakfast, beautifully garnished with a twisted orange slice, a strawberry, and a blueberry. Making his way up the stairs, he carries the food to the rooms where the girls are sleeping. He gently knocks on the door to the guest room. "Good morning. I have breakfast cooked for you. Are you decent? I can bring it in."

"Good morning. Please come in. I'm famished," says Kathy.

Quentin enters the room and places the bed tray table on the bed for Kathy.

"This looks exquisite. You have always been a divine cook."

"Thank you again for staying last night, Kathy. This is an awful shock. I know Sandra didn't like me. We went head-to-head, but I respected that woman. I promise you I'll be here to support Amaya during this sad time."

"I'll take you home this afternoon when Bree and Josh come over."

Kathy says, "That's fine. As long is she's not alone for a few days."

Quentin enters their room with a bedside tray table. Amaya awakes with dried tears on her face and red puffy eyes.

"Good morning, baby. I need you to eat some breakfast."

She pushes it out of the way. "I'm not able to eat anything right now. Thank you, anyway. I will drink the orange juice." She takes a drink. "Umm baby, this is refreshing."

"Let me take some of the load off of you. Give me Annie's number and I will get the flight information and pay for the tickets. We can ask Jeff and Angela to pick them up."

"That's so thoughtful, babe. Can you hand me my phone?"

He reaches for the phone on her nightstand. She unlocks the phone and gives it to Quentin to find Annie in her contacts. He calls Annie and listens as she tells him she has a flight departing tomorrow at 1:40 p.m. and arrives at 7:25 p.m. He gives her Jeff and Angela's number and informs her they will pick her up from the airport. "Amaya and I insist you and the children stay here while you're in town."

"Your gesture is very much appreciated. We will kindly take you up on the offer. I'll see you all tomorrow. Quentin, I have to say, it's going to be difficult for me to come back knowing I pushed my mother away because of greed and jealousy."

"Sandra always loved you. You're her daughter. I know she forgives you for your actions."

He gives Amaya the flight information and tells her that Josh and Bree will be over this afternoon to sit with her.

"I need Josh right now. Do you know what time he will get here?"

"Not sure. He is coming into the office today. He said early afternoon."

"Okay. Can you wrap up my plate? I'll eat it later."

Quentin leaves their bedroom carrying the tray. Walking down the staircase, he reaches the final three steps, and his foot catches on a loose edge, causing him to lose his balance and crash down onto the cool floor. The plate of food hits the floor. Pain shoots through his right ankle as he struggles to rise, his palms pressing against the smooth surface. As he lifts his head, his eyes meet the stares of Amaya and Sandra, frozen in time within the confines of a portrait, their gazes following his every move.

"That damn Sandra is playing havoc with me from the other side," he mutters as he limps to the couch and turns on the morning news. "I'll clean that mess up later."

Chapter Thirty-Six

Amaya

The therapist

It's 8:30 a.m. Amaya is still lying in her bed. Kathy gently knocks on the door. Amaya says, "Come in."

"How are you feeling this morning?"

"Honestly, not good. I would feel worse if I didn't have you and my husband last night."

"I think you better call Ms. T. this morning. You're struggling with so many challenges and now the death of Sandra. You cannot wait until Saturday."

"I will call later."

Kathy hands her the phone. "Call now."

Amaya dials Ms. T.'s number and it goes directly to voicemail. She and Kathy lie in bed and talk for a few minutes. Amaya tries reaching out to Ms. T once more. This time, Amaya sends a text but notices that the recipient doesn't receive it. Amaya calls the office.

"Good morning. Thank you for calling the Wellness Therapy Center. How can I direct your call?" says the receptionist.

"Hello. This is Amaya Montgomery. Can you please connect me to Ms. T.?"

"Mrs. Montgomery. Ms. T. will not be in the office for a while."

"Why is that? I really need to schedule an appointment with her."

"There was a home invasion at her house a few nights ago. She's in an induced coma now. It's devastating to our clinic family. The intruder broke her jaw, dislocated shoulder, and both of her knees are broken. It's unimaginable. Ms. T. has a long recovery journey ahead of her."

In total disbelief, Amaya struggles to understand the gravity of this situation and the recent losses in her life. Amaya's voice fills with concern. "How can all this be happening?"

"Mrs. Montgomery," the receptionist responds gently. "We understand how difficult this is for you. But please know that we have several great therapists here who can see you while Tiffani is recovering. I highly recommend Ms. Candacon, Mrs. Nita, and Mrs. CJ. They're experienced and compassionate therapists."

Amaya's face contorts with a mix of emotions, her mouth drawn down in deep thought. "I need to think about it," she says. She finally says, "I will call you back in a week."

Kathy asks what happened. Amaya explains what happened to Ms. T.

"We will get through this together. I want you to know that I am praying for you and Sandra's family. It's wonderful to see you and Annie working on your friendship. You need to recognize your strength and resilience as a woman. I've noticed a difference in your anxiety levels this past week. You appear more in control of things happening in your life. Remember to continue using the coping skills you've learned in therapy. I know you don't want to hear this, but I'm your friend and I'm going to tell you, anyway. Please consider trying one of the therapists the receptionist recommended. You need a safe place to process everything that's happening."

Amaya lies on her soft pillow. Kathy gently wipes her tears. Her nose is red and runny. The weight of these losses becomes an unbearable burden for Amaya. Exhausted from the grief, Amaya becomes drowsy and falls back to sleep.

Chapter Thirty-Seven

JOSH

Josh sits in the living room, deep in thought about his life and his desire to mend his marriage with Bree. Just then, Bree comes downstairs, carrying Lil J's overnight bag for grandma's house. As Josh looks at her, he couldn't help but admire her attractiveness, her gentle manner with their ten-year-old son, and her straightforward nature.

He invites her to sit down so they can have an open conversation about how to revive their marriage. "Let me know what's in your heart," he says. He acknowledges he needs to change his life. Feeling lost and unsure, he admits seeking sex from other women is wrong, but emphasizes his plea for a fresh start with his wife. "Is there a ray of hope for our future?" he asks, staring at Bree intensely.

Josh mentions how Bree only reaches out to him when it suits her needs, leaving him feeling neglected. He longs for her forgiveness and wonders if this forgiveness is too much to ask. "Please say something, sweetheart. I want to save our marriage."

"You are saying a lot and asking questions without giving me a chance to respond. That is not healthy communication. That is just one of our problems," she says.

"Is there a chance for us? I love you and Lil J with all my heart."

"I can't stand to look at you most times. You're holding me hostage in this marriage. If I leave you, you threaten to turn me in and I go to jail. You know I'm not leaving my son. He means everything to me. He's the only thing that gives me joy in this life of mine. I don't know if I can ever forgive you."

"Yes, I'm to blame for letting you have everything your way. Allowing you to do shop therapy, as you call it. I have made so many mistakes, but loving you is the one thing I've done right. I have something in motion now that will set us up for life. You can buy your own clothing store if you like. You know you're a shopaholic," he says while pulling her close to him in a loving embrace.

"So, you're saying your son and I can leave right now, and you would not turn me into the police?"

"You're not leaving me!"

"You didn't love me when you married me. I know you cared for me because we were high school sweethearts. Chante and Symone told me you were planning to break up with me during our freshman year of college, but I got pregnant. I made the mistake of telling you the truth about..."

"I will not lie. Yes, I was going to break up with you. I wanted to experience the college lifestyle. Something changed within me and I developed a deep love for you while you grew to detest me after we had the baby. If you give me a chance, I can make our world spin on its axis. Please, baby, give me another chance. I'm through with the other women. It's only you I want," he pleads.

"Let's drop Lil J off at grandma's house so we can go check on Amaya. She's the one you love. Every time she calls, you run. I've noticed you have always been more attentive and supportive to her than to me, your wife. I'm not mad, though. She is easy to care for."

"Are you willing to give me a chance?"

"No. You are controlling me. I don't like that. I especially don't like you holding our secret over my head, and that you're willing to send me to jail if I don't stay in line."

Lil J comes running down the stairs to put his Spider-man action figure in his overnight bag, and then stomps back up the stairs. "Son, stop stomping up the stairs," says Josh.

Lil J crawls up the stairs the rest of the way. "Is this quiet enough for you, Daddy?" he asks, laughing as he ascends each step.

Bree shakes her head. "He's definitely your son. A jokester, just like his dad."

He hugs her and runs his finger through her long natural brown curls. Lil J quietly comes down the stairs and says, " Mom, Dad, come on, I'm ready to go to grandma's."

"Okay, son. We're ready," says Josh as he releases the embrace from Bree.

"Let's get in the car," says Bree.

Josh whispers in her ear, "I can show you better than I can tell you. I will fix this: I promise you this."

Josh gently takes Lil J's hand as the little boy excitedly heads out to grandma's house.

Chapter Thirty-Eight

Amaya
The Hologram

As the clock strikes 10:00, the night envelop the couple in a serene tranquility. Amaya expresses her joy at spending time with Josh and Bree, and her eagerness to see Annie and the kids tomorrow. Quentin's footsteps, barely making a sound, turn off the lights downstairs. With a gentle strength, he scoops up Amaya, their bodies entwined, and gracefully ascends the spiral staircase. Amaya's laughter fills the air. She plants a passionate kiss on Quentin because she feels safe in his arms and loved.

As they enter the bedroom, Amaya pulls out her phone while Quentin heads to the bathroom to brush his teeth and change into his pajamas. Wanting to reassure Kathy that she's doing fine and not to worry, Amaya dials her assistant's number. After several rings, the call goes to voicemail and Amaya hangs up and searches for her night clothes. Just then, her phone rings, and it's Kathy calling back.

"Hey Kathy. I was just calling you to tell you I'm doing fine. Were you busy?"

"No, not at all. I was just drying my hair and getting ready to look at a couple of episodes of 'Friends' before I call it a night. I'm glad you're feeling better."

"I am. I can't wait for you to meet Annie tomorrow."

"I'm glad to hear that you and Annie are working on rebuilding your relationship. I need to remind you about tomorrow's appointment with my doctor. We need to ensure that you didn't contract a disease from Tyler, so I'll be picking you up for the tests at 9:30 a.m."

"I didn't forget. I'll be ready. Love you and I will see you tomorrow."

After Quentin comes out of the bathroom, Amaya heads in to shower and brush her teeth. A few minutes later, she emerges from the bathroom and joins her husband in bed. He attempts to start foreplay, but she gently explains that she's not in the mood for it tonight. "Damn it! I want to make love to my husband tonight. I have to hold off until I take these tests," she thinks to herself, feeling hot and horny. As they both fall asleep, they turn their backs away from each other, creating a sense of distance.

The clock reads 4:25 a.m. Amaya awakes feeling Quentin shifting restlessly beside her. His unrecognizable words fill the room as he talks in his sleep, and his jolts to awaken her.

Amaya tries to go back to sleep when she hears her grandfather's voice. "Princess. Princess," says her grandfather. Then she hears her grandmother's voice. "Mya boo, we miss you, honey."

Lying in bed, Amaya refuses to sit up, her body weighed down from apprehension. "No... No! Not again," she whispers to herself, her hands instinctively covering her ears, blocking out any external sounds. "This isn't real. It's merely a manifestation of the mounting stress in my life," she whispers to herself.

Amidst her uneasiness, a sudden burst of brightness travels through the bedroom. Slowly, she musters the courage to sit up, her heart pounding in her chest. As her eyes adjust to the unexpected light, she finds herself confronted by the apparitions of her deceased grandparents. Standing before her bed, their ethereal forms sway gently, their arms outstretched, beckoning her towards an unknown realm beyond mortal existence.

Breathing heavily and feeling nauseous, she stutters the words, "What the hell?" she screams as she stares at her dead grandparents standing in her bedroom. Her muscles tensing up as she screams, "No...no! I'm not coming with you. I don't want to die." She wets the bed. Quivering, she pushes Quentin's back to wake him up. "Q, look, my granddaddy and grandma are in here with us," she says. Her hair is erect on her arms.

"I see nothing. I'm worried about you. Here, lie in my arms and let's go back to sleep."

She pulls the covers over her head. "I can't look. They want me to come with them. They want me to kill myself," she says, pleading for his help from under the covers. "Princess. Princess," calls her grandfather.

Amaya is under the covers, shaking and sitting in her urine. "Hear that? He keeps calling me by the nickname he gave me as a little girl."

"There's nothing there. Get out from under the covers. There are no ghosts in this room," says Quentin. She cautiously peeks out, scanning the darkness, but there's nothing to be seen. Confusion washes over her as she recalls the vivid image of their figures and the echo of their voices, now lost in the silence.

Quentin's hand brushes against a warm, damp spot, and a disgusted look forms on his face. "Gross! Let's find one of the guest rooms to sleep in and you can clean yourself up," says Quentin, with his upper lip curling towards his nose. Amaya, still disoriented, relies on Quentin's muscular arms to navigate her through the dark room. She remains on high alert, scanning for any potential threats. Quentin guides her carefully towards the guestroom.

As they reach the guest room, she is still feeling nauseous. She throws up on Quentin's feet and on the carpeted floor. "I'm so sorry," she says, feeling a mix of fear and embarrassment.

Quentin glances down at the mess she made and gags. "Let's just go to another room quickly so I can wash off my feet. You can clean this vomit up in the morning," he says, as he aggressively turns her around to leave the room.

"Ugh! Babe, I didn't mean to do that," she says with remorse.

"Hush! Just be quiet." He frowns. He takes her to another guest room, gives her double the dosage of sleeping pills again, and goes to wash his feet.

Amaya lies in bed, tears streaming down her face, unable to escape the weight of her negative emotions. Fear grips her heart as the beats speed up. The overwhelming feelings of loneliness and fear consume her. The darkness of the room seems to mirror the darkness within her, amplifying her despair. Thoughts of Sandra, Larry, and possibly losing her mind are tormenting her with a sense of hopelessness. The silence of the night only deepens her sense of loneliness, as she yearns to talk to her therapist, the person who truly understands the battles she fights within herself. In this vulnerable moment, Amaya finds relief in her tears as they offer a temporary release for the pent-up emotions that consume her.

Chapter Thirty-Nine

Amaya

Sandra's Repast

"What a beautiful service for Sandra," says Amaya. As they enter Sandra's church for the repast, the delicate fragrance of flowers fills the rooms of the fellowship hall. Amaya and Annie can't help but feel a surge of joy upon discovering Sandra had had a secret love interest all these years. When he rose to speak, a collective gasp of astonishment echoed through the room. He confessed to having proposed to Sandra multiple times, but she always replied, "When I have my two girls together to walk me down the aisle." Amaya couldn't help but feel a twinge of sadness deep within her heart at this revelation.

Amaya asks Annie to stay a few days longer. She's enjoying Annie's company and her children are delightful. Annie says she has to return home but will be back in a couple of weeks to settle her mother's estate and says she would love for Amaya to help her. Amaya happily agrees and gives her a hug.

"Having you back in my life, Annie, has brought a sense of peace that I haven't felt in a while. Not to mention the carefree spirits and laughter of your children bring me great comfort."

"I will be back, and I'll never allow jealousy to come between us again. Love you, Love you, sister. You know Mama is looking down and smiling. Her girls are back together again."

Amaya smiles and gently grabs her hand. "I know she is."

"I still don't understand how shrimp got into her chicken quesadillas. The food was not in a bag so we can't trace where she bought it. A careless mistake on someone's part."

"Quentin and I were discussing it the other night, and we couldn't figure out why she didn't have her EpiPen with her. She always keeps it in her purse, no matter what," says Amaya.

"I guess we will just have to ask her about it in when we are all together again in," says Annie with a soft loving smile on her face.

"My birthday is in three months. Quentin is throwing an elaborate party at the Hilton Chicago/Oak Brook Hills Resort for my Dirty Thirty. You must be there, sis. You remember how uncomfortable I get around crowds?"

"I will be there, never been the one to miss a party. I'm going to head back to your house with the kids. The celebration of my mama's life was glorious, but I'm overstimulated."

"I'll see you at home later. I actually have an appointment with my new therapist in a couple of hours. It's the earliest slot she could get me in."

The ladies embrace once again a warm hug, in a warm hug, which fills their hearts with mixed emotions, gratitude for the time spent together and a sense of somberness for the impending departure of Annie. They hold each other tightly, cherishing the precious moments they have shared. With a heavy sigh, they release their embrace and turn to face their loved ones and friends, who have gathered to say a last goodbye to a woman of courage and faith. Tears well up in Amaya's and Annie's eyes as they express their gratitude and heartfelt goodbyes to each person, thanking them for sharing their memories of Sandra and the love they have given.

Amaya sits down in the office of her new therapist, Ms. Candacon, who she hopes can her help until Ms. T.'s return.

"Good afternoon, Amaya."

"Hello, Ms. Candacon."

"How are you doing? I hope you're coping well. I understand you attended a funeral today for a loved one."

"I'm making it, I guess."

Amaya is short with her answers, and her leg shakes with anxiety. The distress she feels when talking to a new therapist is clear.

"How about we do some deep breathing exercises?"

"Okay. I think that will help me."

The therapist provides guided meditation to help Amaya feel calm and to overcome her emotional distress while in the session. Amaya feels relaxed but is hesitant to talk.

"Amaya, it's okay if you do not feel like talking. May I say that coping with the loss of a loved one is difficult? Loss is an emotional event in our lives. Grief is private and personal. We all cope with grief in our own unique way. I will not lie to you. The hardest part of the grieving process is allowing yourself to feel your emotions and not avoid them. Feeling your emotions is an integral part of your healing journey. I notice you're holding back your tears. That's not helpful.

"Allowing yourself to cry activates your parasympathetic nervous system, allowing your breathing and heart rate to slow down, bringing a feeling of relief. Reading your progress notes from Ms. T. I know Ms. Sandra meant a lot to you. She will always live in your heart and your memories and recognizing the mark she left in this world. Amaya, how can you honor her life?"

Amaya wipes away her tears. "Thank you for your help. I appreciate your guidance and I will try to follow your advice. Is it alright if we end the session a bit early?"

"That's totally fine. Please reach out if you need me before next week."

Amaya reaches for her black leather purse, the gold clasp glistening in the soft light of the room. She stands up from the cushioned chair. With a warm smile, she looks at her new therapist, Ms. Candacon, who sits across from her, her attentive eyes filled with empathy for Amaya. Adjusting the strap of her purse on her shoulder, Amaya says, "I will probably see you next week. I will let you know for sure on Monday. Goodbye." And walks out of the office.

Chapter Forty

JOSH

Amaya's Thirtieth Birthday Celebration

On this delightful summer late afternoon, the gentle summer breeze rustles the lush green leaves of the trees surrounding the venue, creating a soothing atmosphere. The air carries the sweet scent of blooming flowers, enhancing the mood for Amaya's birthday party. The warm touch of the evening sun on Josh's skin as he stands outside the venue adds to the overall feeling of high ambition for the celebration.

Josh enters the ballroom and meets Quentin. The two men stand in the hotel's ballroom, overseeing the final preparations for Amaya's extravagant birthday celebration. Streamers and balloons fill the room in various spaces, creating a festive and cheerful vibe. Soft fairy lights twinkle overhead in the ballroom, and centerpieces of her favorite flower, pink orchids, grace the tables. Josh and Quentin listen to the hushed whispers of three of the staff diligently arranging the tables and chairs.

"It's the big night. Amaya's thirtieth birthday. The last chance to drive her out of her mind," says Josh as he kicks one of the decorative party balloons on the floor.

"She went to the lawyer's office this morning, where she signed the papers and received the rest of her inheritance," says Quentin as he looks around at the staff.

"I still can't understand the barrage of scare tactics, manipulations, and mind-altering situations we subjected her to. All of this perfectly crafted in to gain control over the money. Years we planned this. Besides that, I'm still pissed that my great aunt and great uncle failed to leave me even a single penny in their will. I was always by Amaya's side, fighting off bullies, listening to problems about that damn Amber, and offering my support in every way possible. No, they had to give money to the maid and her kid," says Josh as he stomps on a balloon. He adds, "I have the hallucinogenic for tonight."

"No more parlor tricks, man. We're going to have to kill her," says Quentin with a stoic facial expression.

"You said 'kill' her? Are you out of your damn mind? I'm not killing my cousin."

"J, that's all we have left to do. She's going to give the money away to St Jude's hospital and to the Trevor Project."

Josh thinks for a minute. "Let's just accidentally throw her down the stairs or something. Give her brain damage. I can't kill my cousin. That's off the table."

"She has to die. When we all go on the cruise next week. We'll put poison in her food. She can die on the ship because they will not get her to the hospital in time," says Quentin.

Quentin's chilling words ring loud in Josh's head as he listens to Quentin's sinister plan to kill his cousin. Surprise overtakes him as he witnesses his friend's cold and calculated tone, sending shivers down his spine. He struggles to find his words. Josh recognizes the severity of Quentin's intentions and the potential consequences that could follow.

Taking a deep breath, he finds his voice. "You are out of your damn mind. No more killing! You've fucked everything up. Why did I think you could carry out my perfectly laid out plan to drive her bonkers so that you could control the money?"

Amid the rant Josh is on, Quentin implores him to reconsider his dangerous plan. "There's no other way. I didn't stay in this marriage for eleven years for nothing. You're with me or not. If not, you will not see a penny of this money." Quentin storms off, his frustrations palpable.

Josh, dressed in a baby blue button-down shirt, paired with a cream-colored jacket with a blue handkerchief in the front pocket, blue jeans and dark blue shoes, sits at a table. Lost in thought, he tries to process what the hell has just happened. He calls Bree and reminds her to have Amaya there in an hour, allowing enough time for most of the guests to arrive. He tells her not to facilitate a conversation between him and his brother Jeff.

Josh rises from the table and approaches Quentin. "I'll take care of disposing of the hallucinogenic in the restroom, and I'll devise another plan to convince her to grant you power of attorney over her estate. We will not kill my cousin. I honestly didn't think you were that savage. Besides, so many people have witnessed her erratic behavior. We can definitely get away with this."

"Okay, my guy. We will try it your way for now. We may only have a few days before she signs the money away. Hey, people are arriving. It's time to put on our party face and party."

Quentin and Josh are walking to the front to welcome the guests to Amaya's birthday party. Josh sees his brother, Jeff and his wife Angela are in line. Josh leans over to Quentin. "My brother is in line. I'm going to step away for a few minutes and let you greet the two men."

"Come on, man, you're going to have to get over this crap about the woman he married," says Quentin.

Josh is feeling disgusted. "I'm going to get a drink. I will be back."

Josh, holding a vodka tonic, mingles with the guests as he engages in small talk. Suddenly, he hears applause and turns around to see Amaya entering the room. She looks stunning in a royal blue dressy/casual romper, featuring a

V-neck, sleeveless ruffle, and backless design. Josh walks over to her and hugs her. "Happy thirtieth cuz!"

Josh has made sure Amaya's favorite songs are on the playlist. It's going to be a "New Edition" night, he says to her with a giggle.

"You know it, NE 4 Life," says Amaya

There's laughter and chatter as friends and family gather, their smiles reflecting the happiness of the occasion, from finger foods to delectable desserts. Josh assures Amaya the menu for tonight is a culinary delight. Amaya, dressed to impress, beams with excitement as she takes Josh's hand to mingle with her guest, thanking them for their presence on her special day.

"I see a difference in you. You're not as anxious as you usually are. You're working this room like a boss," says Josh.

Amaya leans in close to Josh. She places her index finger to her lips. "Shhh," she whispers, her eyes darting around the room. "Don't tell Quentin, I recently saw a psychiatrist. She prescribed me an antidepressant to help me with stress and anxiety. I don't feel as afraid or on edge as I usually feel since being on the meds for six weeks. I've never felt this good. Please don't tell my husband. He vehemently opposed to me taking meds, insisting medication doesn't work."

Josh is in complete shock. He knows there isn't a plan that he can think of to drive her crazy or trick her into signing the power of attorney over to Quentin now that she is taking meds. He looks at her and says, "I'm happy for you. What made you try medication?"

"Well, I gave Ms. Candacon a chance to be my temporary therapist. I plan on returning to Ms. T. once she is well enough to resume counseling after being attacked by that animal who invaded her home. I have to say that Ms. Candacon has been a great therapist. She has helped me understand how medication can be beneficial for my anxiety, past trauma, and all the losses I have experienced. And you know what? She was absolutely right."

"It's great to hear that. I'll let you enjoy your guests. We've been inseparable all night. Now, I want to give Quentin a chance to show off his wife. I need to go find Bree. Did you know she thinks she's second to you?" They giggle and part ways, heading off to different corners of the party.

Josh walks over to Quentin, who is talking to Jeff and Angela. His voice filled with urgency. "We need to talk. Now!"

"Hello, brother," says Jeff. Josh acts like he didn't hear Jeff and he feels tension rising within him. He demands again that Quentin leave the conversation and come talk to him.

Angela casts a quick glance between the three men, but Josh's mean look catches her eye. She discreetly excuses herself, giving them the space they clearly need. Meanwhile, Quentin tells Jeff that he will catch up with him later before leaving with Josh.

"Don't overreact, but we have a problem. Amaya is taking medication for her anxiety and what the hell ever she has going on in that head of hers."

"What?" says Quentin.

"I haven't talked to her in a while. I'm trying to work on my marriage, as you already know. How could you not see a drastic change in your wife?"

"I guess I noticed she wasn't afraid of her shadow anymore. I just don't pay that much attention to her."

Josh scoffs. "That's your problem. All the attention has to be on you. We're going to have to kill her on the cruise, but in the most humane way possible." Josh walks away with adrenaline surging through his body.

A week later and the two couples have packed their bags and are heading to the airport to catch their flight to Orlando, where they will board the cruise ship. Josh is having second thoughts about their plans for Amaya's demise on the cruise ship. He thinks it's too risky. He remains quiet on the plane. Bree asks him, "Are you excited about the cruise, considering this is the first time you're not cracking jokes or monopolizing the conversation?"

"No, baby, I'm good. I have some business stuff on my mind." He takes her hand and tells her he loves her and he will do anything for her. She smiles at him and says, "You have changed. I'm willing to fight for us." He smiles big and says, "Thank you, my love. Everything I'm doing is for our family."

Arriving at the embarkation of the cruise ship, the staff warmly directs the two couples, who hold platinum status, to the VIP line. The staff examine their documents and check their identification cards for accuracy. Josh notices Bree and Amaya radiating a spirited vibe, ready to celebrate. As the couples step onto the promenade deck, holding hands, fingers intertwined, they relish the gentle breeze coming from the water.

Josh and Quentin, their minds filled with treacherous thoughts, abandon their wives just as everyone gathers on the side of the ship, ready for it to set sail. Walking on the deck, the two men discuss their sinister plan to poison Amaya on the third day of the seven-day cruise. Josh wants Amaya to have some enjoyment before her untimely demise.

The plan is to slip the poison into her food during dinner, while the wait staff entertains everyone with singing and dancing. Their strategy involves Quentin and Amaya arriving late, ensuring that they would receive their meals later than the rest. While Amaya and Bree enjoy the show, Josh will discreetly add the odorless and tasteless poison to Amaya's dish.

On the third day of their trip, the couples enjoy an exhilarating excursion, zip lining and snorkeling. Now, on deck, Josh finds himself seated next to a focused Amaya, engrossed in her romance novel. Meanwhile, Bree and Quentin are engaged in a game of sports trivia in the atrium. As Josh glances around, he notices a woman a few deck chairs away, staring in their direction. Puzzled, he wonders why she's staring at them. However, before he can establish eye contact with her, she turns her head.

"Cuz, put the book down for a second. How does it feel to be a multimillionaire?"

"I mean, it's no different from how I felt last year."

"You have it all. You should let me invest the money for you."

"I have other plans. I'd rather not discuss work or money during our vacation. Let's relish our time together as a family."

"I'm here if you need help," says Josh, hoping he can spare her life.

"I need you right now."

"I gotcha. What do you need from me?"

Amaya jumps up from the deck chair filled with energy. She pulls Josh out of his chair. "Go on the twister water slide with me."

Josh pulls his hand away from hers. "Hell no. You own your own for that. I can see myself flipping off the side of the slide and just dangling in the air. Uh-uh, not me," he sits back in his chair with purse lips.

Amaya throws her head back, laughing so hard she can feel it in her belly. "You're useless, cuz."

"I'm not totally useless. I can be used as a bad example," he says, sitting straight up in the chair and laughing.

"Facts, J." says Amaya with a slight grin.

Josh and Amaya lounge by the pool for another thirty minutes until their spouses return, then they all decide to go to the casino before getting ready for dinner. Tonight is dinner with the captain, so it will be an elegant affair on the ship. Amaya stands up. She suddenly feels a wave of dizziness wash over her. Josh reaches out to steady her. She assures everyone that she is fine. She explains she has felt dizzy the past couple of days.

"Are you sure you alright?" asks Josh as he glances at Quentin.

"I'm fine."

"It could be the bumpy waters," says Josh.

"I'll be fine. Please don't make a fuss," says Amaya.

Josh and Bree, along with Quentin and Amaya, eagerly make their way to the cruise ship's casino. They try their luck at various games like roulette, blackjack, and slot machines. The sound of spinning wheels, clinking chips, and the few cheers of winners fill the air as they play for a couple of hours. As the evening approaches, they decide to return to their luxurious cabins to shower and prepare for the elegant captain's dinner awaiting them. With their hearts still filled with excitement from the wonderful day, albeit with pockets filled with lint instead of tokens from unfortunate losses, they can't wait to dress up and continue the memorable day.

Josh notices the plan taking shape as he observes the animated crowd gathering for the evening's dinner and entertainment. After dinner is when the staff begins their lively singing and dancing in costumes, which will be the perfect cover for their nefarious act. Timing is crucial; Quentin and Amaya must arrive late to ensuring a delay in serving of their meal.

When the server arrives, he greets the couple. However, instead of providing menus, he provides bread and water. The guests are now required to use the cruise ship's phone app to view the menu.

"J, I miss the hard covered menus. My app keeps acting up. Can I look at the menu from your phone?"

"Here, sweetie, I know what I'm going to order."

"I wonder what's taking Amaya and Q so long for dinner? I'm famished," says Bree.

"Let's order," says Josh, feeling conflicted as his inner voice whispers, *You don't want to do this to your cousin. Can you live with this? She trusts you.* The knots in his stomach tightened, signifying his growing unease. Realizing there was no turning back, he moves closer to his wife, and puts his arms around her for a sense of comfort.

Quentin and Amaya arrive Twenty minutes late. "We're so sorry to keep you waiting. My husband got a little frisky," says Amaya and they all laugh.

Josh tells Amaya how good the mashed potatoes are. "Here, taste mine," he says as he takes her fork and gives her a taste of his mashed potatoes.

"Mmm...you're right," Amaya says, her eyes scanning her menu app filled with tantalizing options. The aroma of sizzling prime rib from the table next to her, tease her senses. "I'm going to order the succulent prime rib with creamy mashed potatoes and asparagus."

"Great choice," says Josh as he gently kicks Quentin under the table.

Josh observes Amaya's pale skin, knowing that it will soon no longer be a concern. In a few hours, she will peacefully drift into sleep, never to awaken. He plans to put in just the right amount to ensure she will not suffer from any cramps or nausea caused by the poison when the show starts. His sole intention is to ensure her passing is painless.

Quentin and Amaya's food arrives, just as the show is about to start. Josh leans over to Amaya and tells her she's going to enjoy her meal. Meanwhile, the serving staff, dressed in their colorful costumes, are ready to entertain the guests with songs and table dancing. Amaya and Bree leave the table to better see the show. The captivating show immerses the ladies, making them unaware of the impending danger.

Josh retrieves the tasteless and odorless poison, a small vial filled with a lethal dose. He has spent days researching and planning, ensuring that his plan would go off without a hitch. With calculated precision, he carefully sprinkles the poison over Amaya's mashed potatoes.

"Are you sure this will work?" asks Quentin, his voice filled with doubt.

Josh smirks confidently, his eyes gleaming with determination. "Look," he replies, holding up the vial, "this is the right amount. It's gonna work. You just make sure you act distraught in the morning when you can't wake her up. We need to make it convincing."

Quentin nods in agreement. Little do they know their actions will set in motion a series of events that would forever change their lives.

The ladies return to the table, bragging about the show. Amaya looks at her food and feels a wave of queasiness, then pushes it aside.

"What's wrong?" asks Josh.

"I'm feeling queasy now that I'm looking at the food," says Amaya

"Baby, just eat your mashed potatoes. You know that's your favorite side."

"No, I think I'm going to lie down."

Curious, Josh looks behind her ear and notices she's still wearing her sea sickness patch. "We will just get it to go for you," says Josh.

Quentin calls the server over to the table. Josh asks Bree to escort Amaya to her cabin after they get her food to go. He and Quentin are planning to see the adult comedy show after dinner. Bree agrees.

The server comes to the table. "Are you all ready for dessert?"

"Does anyone feel like having dessert?" Josh asks. They said they're full from dinner.

"I will take a cognac. My cousin needs a to-go container for her food. She's not feeling well," says Josh.

The server apologizes and informs the table that the restaurant doesn't permit taking food out. "The restaurant doesn't have to-go containers," says the server.

Quentin angrily asks, "What is my wife going to eat later? All that will be open is the pizzeria. She will not eat pizza in the middle of the night. Just give me a napkin to put over her plate."

The server appears nervous, unsure of how to handle the request. In response, Josh stands up and politely addresses the server, asking, "Could we possibly make an exception? I'd like to apologize on behalf of my friend. He's quite worried about his wife, who recently lost her father and a close friend. Would it be possible to allow us to place a napkin over it for my sick cousin?"

"Let me ask my manager. Maybe we can make an exception." He picks up the plate.

"You can leave the plate here. She may nibble a bit," says Josh.

The server says, "Please give me just a minute." He then takes the plate and heads towards the kitchen.

The server comes back without the plate. "We can't allow food to leave the restaurant."

"Where's her plate?" asks Josh.

"We trashed it. We can't bring a contaminant back out to the dining room," says the server.

Josh and Quentin, though fuming, are attempting to maintain their composure.

"Thank you, babe and J. I really appreciate both of you looking out for me. Honestly, I don't think I'll be able to keep anything down tonight. I'm not sure why this patch isn't working. Once I'm back at the cabin, I'll change it out for another one. You both take such good care of me." She hugs both men before she and Bree head back to her cabin.

"This is bullshit. I'm just going to throw her overboard. I'm going back to the states a widower, by any means necessary," says Quentin.

"She must have gotten a placebo patch or something, Q. She's never been sick on a cruise before. Did you see how pale she's looking?"

"No, but what I'm seeing now is my wife giving away all of our money," says Quentin with frustration seeping into his words. Standing up from the table, he throws his napkin down. "Enjoy your cognac." He storms out of the restaurant.

Sitting alone at the table, Josh sips his cognac, deep in thought about how the night went to hell in a handbasket.

Chapter Forty-One

Amaya

As Quentin and Amaya step through the back doorway, home from their cruise, Amaya feels a frigid chill from Quentin's icy demeanor. Her heart aches, feeling wounded and fragile. She can't fathom why her husband has become so distant, refusing to engage in even the simplest conversation since their cruise. His lack of interest in her causes unsettling thoughts to swirl in her mind. She questions how enjoying the breathtaking excursions and captivating shows hadn't brought them closer as a couple. His coldness ignites painful memories of Amber. Determined, Amaya knows she must confront the five-hundred-pound elephant that looms in their relationship.

"Quentin, I need to ask you something important. Are you upset that I'm donating the remainder of my inheritance to charity?" she asks, her voice filled with concern.

"I don't know what you're talking about," Quentin says dismissively. "I'm going to grab a beer."

Frustrated by his lack of engagement, she persists. "We're still in the middle of a conversation, Q. Your beer can wait. Our marriage can't. We barely connected on our vacation, and things changed when I told you I wasn't keeping the money."

Quentin sighs and sits down on the sofa, slapping one pillow to the side. "We should have made that decision together," he says.

Amaya stares at her husband, her stomach twisting in revulsion. The present sight of him sends waves of nausea crashing over her, forcing her to race to the bathroom. Where she clings to the toilet while uncontrollably vomiting. Moments later, he enters the bathroom. His insensitive words cut through her. "Make yourself a doctor's appointment. I don't want to catch what you have." Dismissing her with a callous indifference, he turns and leaves the bathroom, leaving her confused and hurt, wondering why he has suddenly turned so cold towards her.

The night feels never-ending for Amaya, as she cannot fall asleep. Her emotions are calm now and she gazes at her husband sleeping, lost in his dreams. She questions whether giving away the money is a mistake. The thought of losing her husband over the inheritance troubles her deeply, leaving her tormented and unsure of what steps to take next; with heavy eyes, she finally falls asleep.

As the soft morning light filters through the curtains, a brand-new day unfolds, brimming with endless possibilities. Quentin quietly leaves before Amaya wakes up. Amaya gets dressed and resolves two things: to save her marriage and to visit a doctor to address her persistent vomiting and dizziness. There's a two-day wait at her primary care physician. She opts to go to an urgent care clinic instead.

Amaya reaches urgent care, completes the forms, and promptly receives medical attention.

"Good morning. My name is Liz. I'm one of the nurse practitioners here. I see you're having stomach issues and dizziness?" says Liz.

"Yes, it appears to be worsening. I started feeling nauseous and dizzy maybe a couple of months ago. I tried taking antacids, and they gave me some relief. But they don't seem to help anymore."

"It says here your last period was two months ago. We'll take a urine sample for a pregnancy test and some blood work."

"I'm infertile. I can't get pregnant. My husband and I are discussing adoption within the next couple of years."

"There are so many children whose only wish is to find parents and a home. Good for you and your husband."

The nurse practitioner draws blood and takes away the tube. She returns and has Amaya lie back on the table. She feels Amaya's abdomen, her belly is firm. "Have you noticed your breast feeling tender?"

"I do. I know that means my period is coming. It's just running late."

"Hmmm," Liz says aloud, reaching for a urine cup on her table. She turns to Mrs. Montgomery. "Could you please provide me with a urine sample in this cup? The bathroom is right outside this door. Once you're done, simply leave the cup in the designated window."

A hesitant Amaya grants her request without asking questions. Amaya returns to the room. She can't help but wonder if she should have waited to see her doctor. Just then, Liz return, breaking the silence, "You're pregnant! Congratulations.

Amaya's eyes widen in disbelief, her mind racing to comprehend the news. "I can't be pregnant. It's impossible," she says.

Undeterred by Amaya's doubts, Liz retrieves a fetal Doppler, its smooth surface glinting under the fluorescent lights. With a gentle smile, she says, "Let's start by listening to your baby's heartbeat. After that, we can perform an ultrasound to determine how far along you are." Amaya, still convinced that there must be a mistake, reluctantly agrees to undergo the tests. Her heart pounds in her chest.

Liz carefully places the fetal Doppler on Amaya's belly. It's cool touch causes her to flinch. At that moment, a hushed anticipation fills the room. Seconds pass, but it feels like an eternity. And then, Amaya hears the rhythmic sound of her baby's heartbeat, a tiny thumping that resonates through her entire being. Overwhelmed with emotion, tears of joy stream down her face. "It's true!

It's true!" she yells, her voice fills with joy and gratitude fills her heart. "Thank you, Jesus, for this incredible blessing."

She feels the warmth of the gel on her belly and the gentle pressure of the ultrasound wand as the Liz moves it around to get the best view. Amaya witnesses the tiny, perfectly formed features, the fluttering of its little limbs, all captured on a screen.

"Look at your baby. You are sixteen weeks along and into your second trimester! It's important to start your prenatal care, so here's a list of obstetricians in the area. Stress or the food you're eating could cause the severe nausea you're experiencing. Also, you're a little dehydrated. Try drinking milk, sixty oz of water, and healthy smoothies. Congratulations to you and your husband. The nurse will come in with your discharge papers."

"Thank you so much. I can't express how much this miracle means to me," says Amaya as she takes Liz's hand for a gentle shake. Amaya carefully gets off the exam table and reaches for her purse to call Sandra and share the good news, then remembers Sandra has passed away. With a heavy heart, she stares up at the ceiling, cradling her belly. "Sandra, I wish you were here to share this miraculous occasion with me. I miss you so much. Continue to fly high, my angel."

Amaya walks out of urgent care and glances at the list of obstetricians. After considering her options, she will remain with Dr. Mitchell. She has seen Dr. Mitchell for annual exams and she's the doctor who diagnosed Amaya with deeply infiltrating endometriosis. Amaya's excitement grows as she realizes she is ready to tell her husband about the miracle pregnancy. However, she wants this moment to be a special occasion, where she can surprise him with the amazing news.

Driving to work, Amaya can't help but smile as she recalls the moment she first saw her baby on the ultrasound monitor. She's driving and daydreaming of holding her precious bundle of joy in her arms. With every red light, she looks over at the ultrasound picture in the passenger seat. When she arrives at the office, she walks directly to Kathy's office and closes the door.

"Good morning, sunshine," Kathy says as she pauses her work and glances up at Amaya, who is grinning uncontrollably.

"I have to show you something. You're the first to know."

"Show me what? Girl, stop moving around. You're giving me motion sickness." Kathy furrows her eyebrows.

Amaya holds up the sonogram with both hands shaking with excitement.

"Is that what I think it is?" Kathy asks with curiosity and excitement.

"I'm sixteen weeks pregnant." They both scream, hug each other, and jump up and down.

Amaya touches her stomach with the corners of her mouth raised. "This precious being growing inside is the reason I've been pale, dizzy and nauseous."

"Sit down," Kathy says softly, her voice carrying a gentle yet firm tone. Kathy's eyes meet Amaya's. "You said I'm the first to know. We need to keep it that way for now. I don't mean to spoil the blessed occasion, but if you're sixteen weeks pregnant, it's possible Tyler is the father and not your husband."

Amaya rises from the chair, pacing the floor and huffing. She panics, bending over towards the floor, shaking her head. "Oh shit. Oh shit. I pushed that night out of my mind. This baby has to be my husband's."

Kathy notices Amaya's distress and reaches out to comfort her, grabbing both of her hands. "Come here," she says soothingly. "Look at me. Pace your breathing. We're going to get through this together."

Struggling to catch her breath, Amaya can barely speak. "My husband can never know about the affair. But if the baby isn't his, I have to be honest with him. A paternity test is what I need before I tell him. I can't go to Dr. Mitchell for my prenatal care. I'll find another doctor. Once I have the results, I'll tell Q. Maybe I'll have to get a DNA test from his toothbrush or something."

"You've been watching too much TV," says Kathy with a chuckle. "Let's look at this list and see which doctor can get you in ASAP."

Chapter Forty-Two

QUENTIN

It is a clear summer evening, with beautiful stars sparkling in the sky. Quentin arrives home from work and relaxes on the deck, trying to enjoy the outdoor string lights and colorful potted plants while partaking in a refreshing margarita on the rocks. Yet he can't stop thinking about the change in Amaya's demeanor. How she appears less anxious and exudes a newfound confidence in herself. Her transformation leaves Quentin feeling frustrated and defeated. He questions how he can control the inheritance after their failure of the planning all these years. It baffles him how this once insecure woman has suddenly become so strong. Quentin suspects that her transformation may be because of her new therapist and the medication she's taking.

Josh arrives and makes his way to the deck, where Quentin is on his third margarita.

"Where's Amaya?" he asks.

"I talked to her earlier today. She and Kathy are going to dinner," said Quentin as he casually places one knee over the other, licking the salt from the rim of his glass.

"I'm going to grab a drink. Thanks for offering," says Josh, his voice dripping with sarcasm as he reaches for a glass and heads toward the 3.5-gallon margarita dispenser.

Quentin frowns. "Man. you know you're welcome to drink. What have you come up with? I didn't sign up for this."

Josh's body language becomes more purposeful. He sits down and leans slightly forward towards Quentin, his posture conveying an air of authority and persuasion. "I'm going to convince her not to give the money to charity." He speaks with a steady and confident tone. The muscles in his jaw tighten, emphasizing his determination to resolve their problem.

"She's going to want to adopt a baby now that's she's thirty," says Quentin. "I don't want no damn kids. I can't stand them. They're messy and way too loud. That's why I got a vasectomy before we got married. You know, just another secret from Amaya."

"You're too selfish for kids and that's precisely why I drove you to the appointment," says Josh, as he casually adds ice cubes to his margarita glass and laughs.

"You always have jokes, but right now, I have to deal with Pamela's investigation and all the other shit we're facing. Let me enjoy my drink with no wisecracks."

"Any updates on Pamela? It's probably going to be a cold case," says Josh.

"The men in blue will never trace that murder back to me," he says with a smug smirk forming on his face.

Josh warns him. "Don't get too cocky. You could have paid her off. I think you enjoy having the power in your hands to control someone's life. Remember, you got caught putting firecrackers in your neighbor's cat's butt in high school, and lit the stem? Don't say you won't get caught."

"I don't enjoy killing. It's a means to an end. Pam had to go. She was about to reveal our affair to Amaya. And for that cat, it hissed at me and jumped off the counter and scratched me. It had to go," he says in an unsympathetic manner, brushing his hand against the scar on his arm, a reminder of the cat's attack.

"Changing the subject. I'm going to ask Bree to marry me again."

"Why? Isn't once enough?"

"I want us to renew our vows and move away from here when this money comes through. Get your best man tux ready."

Quentin lounges back in the chair. "Let's just get this money first."

Chapter Forty-Three

Amaya

Two weeks have flown by, and Amaya still feels like she's floating on cloud nine ever since discovering her pregnancy. She and Kathy are driving to Amaya's very first obstetrician appointment. A sense of excitement takes over the two women as they listen to Ciara's song "I Got You." The sound of their singing echoes through the car. Amaya's bliss remains unwavering, refusing to allow Quentin's apathetic attitude to diminish her joy.

She has in hand her medical records and images from Dr. Mitchell's clinic that she downloaded this morning before the appointment with Dr. Newton. Excitedly, she looks forward to sharing the news of their baby with her husband, hoping that this will reignite his attention and love for her. She wishes it was her husband with her for this doctor's appointment.

"Amaya. Amaya. Where you at, girl? We're here."

"I was just thinking about how happy Q will be when I surprise with news. This is surreal," says Amaya as she exits Kathy's car.

Amaya sits in the waiting room, nervously tapping her foot. She can't help but feel a mix of emotions as there is a small possibility Tyler is the father.

Amaya leans her head on Kathy's shoulder. "My pregnancy is a secret I have to hold for a few more weeks until I can get a paternity test. You remember how

Q used to dote on me, showering me with affection and attention? I want us to get back to that."

"May I tell you what I think?" asks Kathy.

"Of course."

"I think Quentin believes there's a power imbalance in your marriage. Your money maybe causing some resentment within him. He agreed to sign a prenup before you two were married. Therefore, the $750 million dollars is yours, not his. He may not feel as though you two are financial partners."

Amaya listens attentively to Kathy. Her words make sense. "I never thought about that. Maybe the baby news will shift his focus to our future family and bring us closer together as we once were."

"Mrs. Montgomery," calls the nurse.

"Coming," Amaya grabs her purse and the medical records. "Kathy, come with me."

In the exam room, Amaya undresses, puts the exam gown on, and sits on the table. Dr. Newton enters the room.

"Good morning, Mrs. Montgomery. How are you feeling?" asks Dr. Newton.

"Please, call me Amaya. You will see more of me than others. I'm feeling better. I don't know if it's the excitement of being pregnant or is it just the all-day morning sickness is subsiding."

The doctor looks at her labs. "You're eighteen weeks along now. There may be only a few instances where you feel nausea and regurgitation. More than likely from certain smells or foods."

"Dr. Newton, I'm barely showing. I can still wear my clothes. You can only see my baby bump when I hold up my shirt. Is that normal?"

"There's nothing to worry about. All your labs are in range. For some women, their baby bump will not be noticeable until the end of the second trimester or the beginning of the third. This is not uncommon with first pregnancies. Now let's get a good look at this little one."

The doctor, Kathy, and Amaya look at the 3-D ultrasound. "Your baby is on target. No need for concern," he says as he pats her arm and smiles.

"Oh, my God! Look at the baby moving around. I can't feel anything."

"Close your eyes and be in tune with your body for one minute; mainly focusing on your abdomen," says the doctor.

"I...I feel fluttering. I feel my little baby moving. Oh little one, I love you so much," says Amaya as she gazes at her stomach.

"Your baby has been moving for a few weeks. You just hadn't felt the somersaults in your belly. But it's coming," says the doctor with a chuckle.

The doctor is finishing up the examination while Amaya thanks Kathy for being a part of this experience with her. Kathy assures Amaya that she wouldn't want to be anywhere else. During their conversation, Kathy reminds Amaya about the question she needs to ask the doctor.

The doctor can't help but overhear the conservation. "What question do you need to ask?"

Amaya hesitates, feeling embarrassed, but eventually speaks up. "Dr. Newton, about eighteen weeks ago, I was under the influence of alcohol at a conference and may have slept with a man other than my husband. I can't remember, and I left the hotel room before he woke up. Is it possible for a paternity test when it's safe for the baby? I guess it's a good thing I'm not showing."

"There is a non-invasive DNA test. We will take a small sample of the amniotic fluid, draw blood from you and your husband. Or a cheek swab from him."

"No...no...no! He can't know. I can bring in his toothbrush," says Amaya as the room grows small. She feels suffocated and jittery.

"We can certainly try with the toothbrush. However, it will not be as accurate while you're pregnant."

"I'll take that chance," she says.

The doctor tells Amaya he wants to discuss her images. "I see no evidence of you ever having deeply infiltrating endometriosis." He places the images she brought and put them side by side to the current images.

Amaya, look at the image you brought in to me. "See, right here, there is severe scar tissue between the cul-de-sac and the outer uterus. The scar tissue serves as an adhesive between the two organs." Dr. Newton says as he points his finger at the screen.

"Miracles happen all the time. Maybe it went away after all these years," says Kathy.

Dr. Newton gestures for both ladies to lean in and examine the image of Amaya's uterus displayed on the screen. "There's no scarring. This is a healthy uterus." As they peer closely, the image revealing an unblemished uterus from the images taken a few minutes ago. With a gentle yet firm tone, Dr. Newton points out the stark contrast. "Now observe closely, ladies. The uterus you presented to me is an inverted uterus. It leans towards the spine instead of the usual sitting upright position. Amaya, this is not your uterus despite your name being on the image. This uterus belongs to a woman in her mid-thirties, whereas your image was captured when you were twenty-six. These are unequivocally two different uteruses."

Amaya is speechless. Kathy says, "Something weird is going on. How can a mistake this big happen? Amaya, who referred you to Dr. Mitchell?"

Amaya takes a moment to collect her thoughts before responding to Kathy's question. "It was actually Quentin's doctor who highly referred Dr. Mitchell," says Amaya, her voice filled with confusion. "We researched her online. She had excellent reviews and success rates with couples struggling to conceive. We were desperate for answers, so we scheduled an appointment and I have been with her ever since."

Kathy's eyebrows furrow in concern as she processes this information. "But if Dr. Mitchell misdiagnosed your uterus, then what does that mean for all the other treatments and procedures she recommended?"

Amaya's mind races with the possibilities. "I'm not sure, but it makes me question everything now. From the invasive tests we underwent, were they all based on incorrect information? And what about the emotional toll this has taken on Q and I? The hope, disappointment, and heartache we've experienced..."

Dr. Newton remains quiet. He tells Amaya he will see her in four weeks, and she can get dressed and make her next appointment with the receptionist.

Kathy places a comforting hand on Amaya's shoulder. "We'll figure this out, Amaya. I, personally won't let this mistake go unnoticed or unaccounted for. We'll file a complaint on your behalf, gather all your medical records, and consult with another specialist. This is too important to just let go. Dr. Mitchell has done something shady. I can feel it in my bones," says Kathy.

Amaya nods, grateful for Kathy's support. Yet, she feels it's a mistake and doesn't want to cause trouble for Dr. Mitchell because she has always been kind to her and a great gynecologist.

Kathy tells Amaya as they leave Dr. Newton's office, she's ready to embark on a journey to uncover the truth behind the misdiagnosis and seek justice for the emotional and physical toll Amaya has endured.

Chapter Forty-Four

JOSH

As the clock strikes 6:00 p.m., Josh, feeling a warm sense of hope about his marriage. He handpicks his attire for an evening of dinner and ax throwing. The clatter of axes hitting their targets and the cheers of other patrons isn't exciting to him, but it's an outing Bree wants to try, and hopefully will heighten the excitement of the night. The sweet sound of his wife's laughter and surprise comes to his mind as he imagines their evening ahead.

Lil J's grandma is on her way to pick him up for the night and give him a ride to school in the morning. The couple will have the evening to themselves. Josh plans to ask Bree to renew their vows after they come home from date night. He has a bouquet of three dozen pink and red roses in a crystal vase. Josh's eyes gleam with affection as he gazes upon the Leo princess-cut, a breathtaking four-carat diamond ring with all its brilliance captivating even in the dimmest light. With a gentle touch, he traces the inscription inside the fourteen-karat white gold band, "It was always you."

Josh calls out from the bedroom, "Bree, it's time for you to get ready for our date night."

Bree responds, "I'm coming. Just give me a sec. Lil J is packing for his sleepover with grandma, and I'm making sure he has everything for school."

As Josh slips on his socks and shoes, he turns on the evening news. Bree finally enters the bedroom, her voice filled with affection. "You have proven to me you can change and love me. It's been years since I've said this. I love you, J." She wraps her arms around him and kisses him passionately, igniting a spark within him.

He removes his clothes. "Lock the door. We can get a quickie in," says Josh.

"Later. I'm hungry and ready to go throw some axes."

"I'm glad you love me, otherwise, I wouldn't let you near me with an ax," says Josh with a chuckle.

Josh reluctantly puts his clothes back on, feeling disappointed that a quickie is out of the question. However, he understands and will wait to make love to his wife later that night. Meanwhile, Bree sits at her vanity mirror, applying her makeup. She glances over at Josh, who is patiently waiting for her to get ready for their date night.

"I've been thinking about something lately," said Bree, catching Josh's attention. He gets up from the bed and gently strokes her shoulders as she continues to apply her makeup. Curious, he asks, "What's on your mind, sweetheart?"

Bree gazes at him intently for a second. "You should start a company of your own. You're much smarter than Q, you bring in the most accounts, and he doesn't respect you. He doesn't respect anyone, and he doesn't try to see your perspective. He has to always be right, even when he's wrong. And he can't stand constructive criticism. It seems like he's unable to feel guilt or empathy," she says while meticulously putting on her eyeshadow.

Josh listens closely, conflicted by Bree's words. "But Q is not just my business partner, he's also my friend. Yes, he has his flaws, but he's been like this since the day we met. We have a plan in place that will secure our little family's future. I can't achieve it without him."

"Shhhh," whispers Bree, her attention drawn to the breaking news on the television. Setting her makeup brush down, she listens intently as the local news reported, "There has been a breakthrough in the six-month-old case of Pamela

Hester. An eyewitness, who wishes to remain anonymous, was walking towards the lake when they noticed a dark luxury car speeding away. According to the witness, it appeared to be a BMW. The police department will review the traffic cameras in that area during the specified time frame. If anyone else has any information regarding the murder of Ms. Hester, please contact our anonymous hotline."

Josh switches off the TV and says, "It's really unfortunate about that lady, but right now, I just want to focus on enjoying a fantastic night with my amazing wife."

Bree springs up from her vanity chair, a sudden realization crossing her face. "I remember now! I knew she looked familiar. It was that same afternoon when Lil J and I tried to surprise you at the office after you texted me about the big account. I noticed her in a heated conversation with Quentin, but I paid little attention to them. He killed that woman," she says, and accidentally throwing her eyeshadow brush across the room, hitting the bathroom door.

"You don't know that. Don't be saying things like that without evidence."

"I know because he was driving his black BMW that day. I'm calling the police." She reaches for her cellphone and Josh demands she put the phone down.

"What's wrong with you? If he's innocent, he can prove it," she says.

"Sweetheart, let it go. This will screw up our big plans. We could lose everything. You wouldn't know what to do if you couldn't buy clothes every day."

A furious Bree shouts, "Clothes over a woman's life?" She storms towards her closets, hurling clothes and shoes at him. One heel hit him above the right eye, causing a knot to form. The room is in disarray as Josh tries to gather the scattered clothes while being called a coward. Lil J rushes into his parents' room upon hearing their argument, witnessing the chaos. He looks at the mess and his distraught parents and asks, "What wrong? Why are you two always shouting at each other?" he asks, with tears forming in his eyes.

Josh gently puts his hand on his son's shoulder, offering a reassuring smile. "I'm sorry mommy and I upset you. Let's go downstairs and wait for grandma. She will be here soon. You go ahead. I will be right behind you, son." Lil J wipes his tears and leaves the room, headed downstairs. Bree is standing in the corner of the room with her nostrils flared as she looks at Josh before leaving the room. Josh reminds Bree that she can be in a jail cell next to Quentin. "So, think about it before doing something you will regret!"

Chapter Forty-Five

Amaya

At 6:39 p.m., Amaya tiptoes quietly into the house, careful not to disturb her husband, who's working in his home office, busy working on a project. He looks up and sees his wife walking towards him. Amaya meets Quentin's icy stare. She takes a deep breath and refuses to let his frigid behavior ruin her joy about her surprise pregnancy.

Still grappling with the shock of her misdiagnosis, Amaya seeks solace in the attic as she climbs the squeaky stairs to the place of forgotten treasures. The musty smell of the attic hits her like a ton of bricks, making her feel queasy, but the wonderful memories fill her heart. Boxes filled with her faded baby pictures, and the delicate clothes stored by her grandparents put a smile on her face.

Time seems to slip away. Thirty minutes have passed, and Amaya's lost in a sea of nostalgia. Amaya embraces the warm memories of her time spent with her beloved grandparents and Sandra. The weight of these cherished moments wraps around her like her grandfather's hugs, providing a mental break from the emotional detachment of her husband and the pain of her infertility misdiagnosis.

Amaya goes through some of Quentin's dusty boxes, eager to find baby pictures of him and explore his memories. As she's rummaging, she comes across his high school yearbook. Intrigued, she flips through the pages and notices a familiar face in one of the basketball team photos: Quentin, standing tall and proud with his teammates.

She can't help but smile at the sight of her husband, imagining him running up and down the court, showing off as usual. She reads the heartfelt messages left by his friends. Amaya realizes how important basketball was to Quentin during his high school years. The words of encouragement and praise from his friends only fuel her hope that their baby will inherit the same athletic skills as her husband. Amaya's fingers trace over the faded signatures, and she sees a name that she knows. Courtney Mitchell, her gynecologist.

Amaya reflects on her past visits with Dr. Mitchell, brooding over the shocking connection between the doctor and Quentin. Dr. Mitchell's signature in Quentin's high school yearbook, suggesting a friendship that neither of them mentioned during their first visit. They behaved as if they were strangers, which now seems calculated to Amaya.

It strikes her that Dr. Mitchell misdiagnosed her intentionally. How convenient that Quentin was the one who found Dr. Mitchell. The revelation hits her hard, especially considering that Dr. Mitchell lied to her about being infertile. Amaya can't fathom why someone she trusted would purposely hurt her like this, especially when all she ever wanted was to have a baby. The anger and betrayal boil within her, as she feels someone she trusted has held her life hostage. Amaya immediately heads downstairs to confront Quentin.

Chapter Forty-Six

BREE

Bree sits on the bed, livid, surrounded by clothes on the bed and floor. She wonders how Josh has the audacity to say she will be in a jail cell next to Quentin if she reports what she suspects about Pamela Hester's murder. Josh returns to the bedroom, informing Bree that Lil J has left for Grandma's house.

With an enraged glare, Bree looks into Josh's eyes, radiating pure wrath. If looks had the power to kill, Josh would be on a one-way trip to the morgue. Her voice, slow and unwavering, carries a stern edge as she confronts him. "How can you dare threaten me with exposing my secret, the very thing you begged me to keep hidden? For years, I've carried the weight of guilt and self-loathing, all because you wanted to maintain our twisted pact. You've held me captive, a hostage to this dark secret. But no more. I'm ready to face the consequences, even if it means leaving my son to make this right. I'm contacting a defense attorney first thing in the morning."

"Sweetheart, I didn't mean what I said," says Josh, his voice filled with remorse. "I would never turn you in. It was just a stupid scare tactic. Our son needs both his parents, and that's all I've ever wanted." As he walks slowly towards Bree, being careful not to add fuel to the fire. "I just want Lil J to feel safe and loved by both of us," says Josh.

Bree rises from the bed and tries to walk out of the bedroom. Josh reaches out and gently grabs her arms to get her to stay and finish the conversation. She forcefully snatches her arm away from his grip so hard she hears a pop in her shoulder accompanied by a shooting pain. "Get your hands off of me! I'm going downstairs to my green room," she said in an unwavering tone.

Josh trails behind her, his footsteps silent but persistent. She spins around, her long hair whipping across her face, the strands brushing against her skin. "And don't you think about following me," she says, her eyes wide and intense.

Josh takes a step back, using both hands to gesture for her to leave. Bree huffs and says, "That's what I thought!" before storming out of the bedroom. The slamming of the bedroom door reverberates through the house, leaving behind an eerie silence.

Bree sits in her green room, in silent and deep in thought, contemplating if she can really confess and leave her son for a prison cell. "I can't turn myself in. It was an accident. J wouldn't turn me in. He wouldn't betray me like that. Family is important to him. Josh will not stop me from making an anonymous report on Quentin. Josh acts like he owes Q something. If anything, Quentin owes Josh everything. He is nothing without Josh. Josh is the brains behind their company."

Bree nestles against her soft pillow, sinking into the comfort of her reclining chair, as she tries to soothe her racing thoughts. The room is dimly lit with a lavender scent coming from her plug-in, creating a calming state of mind. She whispers to herself, "Josh and Q are up to something, and this shit doesn't feel right."

Chapter Forty-Seven

Amaya
The Reckoning

Amaya's heart is pounding as she runs from the musty attic down the spiral stairs. Determination fuels her as she storms into Quentin's office and demands he stop what he's doing because they need to have a serious conversation. Quentin, engrossed in his work, remains hunched over his desk. The sound of his fingers tapping on the keyboard infuriates Amaya. Without lifting his head, he dismisses her, his words dripping with contempt. "I don't have time for your neurotic behavior."

Furious by the deceit she uncovered, Amaya's anger ignites. With a swift, powerful motion, she swipes her hand across his cluttered desk, sending papers flying and knocking his laptop to the floor. His cup of coffee splashes everywhere.

A surprised Quentin springs to his feet, his eyes wide with the shock of Amaya's behavior. His voice rises, laced with outrage, "What the hell do you think you're doing?"

Undeterred by Quentin's words, Amaya stands her ground, her voice filled with rage. "Sit your ass down. You ain't running shit right now."

Quentin walks out of his office. "You're having another one of your episodes. Now you're getting violent. Your symptoms are worse. I think we should discuss me having power of attorney until we can get you stable."

Amaya stands firm, looks him in the eyes and says, "I'm pregnant."

"Baby, have you forgotten you can't get pregnant?" says Quentin, pretending to be sad.

"No. Have your forgotten you said miracles happen every day, and I could get pregnant and have a little girl who looks just like me? That's what you always said when I brought up adoption."

Amaya paces angrily around the living room, her thoughts racing like a marathon. She's finally able to articulate what she needs to say. "I was in the attic, looking through boxes, and I stumbled across your high school yearbook. I looked inside and I saw a picture of someone we both know."

Quentin, visibly aggravated, leans against the wall, his exasperation clear in his slouched posture. He sighs heavily. "I don't have the time or energy to play guessing games with you."

She refuses to back down. "Oh, come on. Just take one guess."

"I don't have time for this. You need to get busy cleaning up my office since you came in acting like a lunatic."

She points her finger at him. "You're not listening to me," she says, slowly in a sarcastic tone.

Quentin snaps, his tone sharp and impatient. "You need to go clean up my office."

Amaya, unable to contain her emotions any longer, steps closer to Quentin, their faces just a few inches apart. Her voice rises with anger, causing tiny droplets of spit to escape her mouth as she yells, "I said take a guess!"

Quentin walks away from Amaya and the conversation. In a fit of rage, she picks up his cell phone and chucks it with all her might against the wall, causing the phone screen to shatter into a web of fractured glass.

Quentin turns around, his eyes widening in disbelief. "Have you gone mad?" he asks as he grabs her. His grip tightens around her arms, firm and forceful. "Have you been doing drugs with your mama? You have lost your damn mind." He pushes her backwards, and she lands on the chair when he lets go of her arms.

Amaya, silent and disturbed, reaches for her phone to call Josh. He answers, and she wastes no time in pleading, "Josh, please come to my house. Use your key to unlock the front door. Quentin just forcefully put his hands on me." As she speaks, Amaya adjusts her disheveled clothes.

Amaya stands up and shares her realization. "Courtney Mitchell and you were friends in high school, and you both acted as if you were strangers. I trusted you," Amaya continues, her voice filled with a mixture of anger and hurt. "You both deceived me about not having the ability to get pregnant. Why manipulate me into seeing her as my fertility specialist and gynecologist?"

Quentin's face becomes pale, his eyes darting nervously. The weight of his deception being discovered proves too heavy for him to handle.

"Dear husband, I'm eighteen weeks pregnant. You will be a father." Amaya's eyes harden as she confronts her husband. "What I don't understand is why go through such a farce? And don't lie about it. I have the ultrasound images from the so-called Dr. Mitchell. The image is not my uterus, and it's that of a woman many years older than I."

The room buzzes with tension. The weight of his betrayal is suffocating Quentin. Amaya stands there, her emotions raw and exposed, awaiting Quentin's response. As she locks eyes with him, a chilling realization is apparent. "The depth of his soul is pure evil." Amaya's hands and feet are trembling, and her forehead is drenching in sweat. Amaya's chest is tight as she looks around, her eyes moving from one shadowy corner to another with a growing unease.

Suddenly Quentin yanks her by the hair, forcing her to the sofa. With a menacing glare in his eyes, he forcefully pushes her down onto the cushions. "Ouch! You're hurting me. What did I ever do to you, but love you?" She tries to stand up from the couch. Halfway to a standing position, he delivers a brutal punch to her face. The impact knocks out a tooth accompanied by the taste of copper in her mouth.

Fear grips her, her heart pounding in her chest. Blood is dripping on her clothes from the punch in the mouth. His rage fills the room from the venom of his words. "You stupid bitch! I've had enough of you. Look at me when I'm talking to you." A frightened Amaya, desperately looking for a chance to escape. Amaya's once perfect marriage has turned into a terrifying battle for survival.

"Did you ever love me?" Amaya asks, sobbing, as she avoids looking at him. Quentin's true identity as the devil is now revealed, and the suffocating heat of hell engulfs Amaya.

"I loved having sex with you, but I didn't fall in love with you. We had some great times together."

She looks up with tears streaming down her face. "Why in the hell did you marry me?"

"Now...now. You're a smart girl. How many guys did you have running after you? You kept your wealth a secret in school, no friends, and you jumped at the sound of your own voice. Come on now. You know I only married you for your money."

Amaya pulls up her shirt and shows her baby bump. "This is your baby growing inside of me."

"I have to say, I would have never thought you would cheat on me, but you did. Wife of mine, I got a vasectomy two months before our wedding. Truthfully, I can't stand kids. Even Lil J gets on my nerves. I'm not mad, though, because I've been cheating on you for years. I'll give you that one. Yeah, before you say it, Sandra was right about me. You should have listened."

"Our relationship and marriage were all a lie! You will pay for this!"

Quentin squats on the floor, positioning himself directly in front of Amaya. With a mischievous glint in his eye, Quentin leans forward. "I have a question for you. What happened to the cowardly lion? Did you go see the wizard and get you some courage? Because, you know, if you were more confident and assertive, I might have fallen for you." Quentin laughs after asking the question.

"Throughout all these years, I have loved you so deeply, only to discover tonight it was all a ploy for my wealth," says Amaya as she's shaking her head.

Quentin stands up grinning. "You're dying tonight. I'm going to allow you to make the choice. Suicide, or I kill you and dump your body somewhere."

"You're going to kill me? What is wrong with you? I'm carrying a child. You will be responsible for taking two lives."

"Don't blame me. Blame Ms. Candy Corn, your new therapist. It's her fault. All that EMDR, DBT, and LMNOP therapy stuff. Those interventions helped your crazy ass." Quentin bows in front of her, behaving petty. "I concede. Therapy actually helps black folks. Too bad you can't be an advocate for mental health."

Amaya is in total shock. She's wondering what is taking Josh so long. "Q, you can have everything. Just spare me and my unborn child. You're not a killer."

"Allow me to share a bedtime story with you, just before you enter eternal rest. Once upon a time, there was a nosy ass maid who stumbled upon one of the tricks I used to drive you crazy. Oh, and by the way, you were right about the lights being on in the guest house. Speaking of which, did you enjoy the reunion I arranged for you and your grandparents? No need to thank me. It was my pleasure. The most amusing part for me was when I made you believe you were forgetting everything. That was hilarious."

"So, you call me crazy? You're certifiable, all for the sake of money?"

"You're being rude. Let me finish the story. It's to die for. Back to the maid. She found evidence and was going to tell you and the police. I caught her and then fed her shrimp quesadillas. It was a painful death for her. Silver lining, before she departed from this earth, she saw that she was right about me all alone."

"You bastard. She did nothing to you, nothing. I hate you."

"Boo hoo. I'm heartbroken. Okay, let's talk about Ms. T., note that I didn't kill her. I needed her out of the way. But then came that new therapist. I'm going to have to visit her and..."

"You stay away from Ms. Candacon. You won't get away with this."

"Don't worry, my dear, Candy Girl is safe, at least for now." He sneered. "It all depends on you. Will you join me upstairs, where I'll tempt you to consume your entire bottle of anxiety medication with a glass of wine?" asks Quentin with a twisted charm. "I'll make sure it's your favorite bottle."

A shiver runs down her spine as his words pierce her ears. The thought of dying from his sick game is grisly. Amaya thinks to herself. "I'll get out of this. He will not win. J should be here any minute now."

"Or," he continues, his tone growing darker, "I will be forced to resort to more physical measures, killing you. Disposing of lifeless bodies has become a tiresome task for me."

Josh hasn't come. Time is running out. *Think, girl. Think. Yes, I got it!* "Q, all condemned people deserve a last meal. Can we go in the kitchen and reheat the mashed potatoes and salmon? Then I'll go upstairs. Please don't hurt anyone else."

"You always loved my cooking," says Quentin in a conceited tone.

With a firm grip on the back of her neck, they enter the kitchen. He pushes her into the wooden kitchen chair. He keeps his eyes on her until he sets the timer on the microwave. In a split second, she seizes the opportunity, rising swiftly from the chair, her adrenaline surging throughout her body. With a swift, impactful swing, she brings the wooden chair crashing down upon his head. He falls to the floor.

She runs into the living room. He gets up from the kitchen floor, runs after her and grabs her by the blouse and punches her over and over in the head. Her eyes fall upon the fireplace. Reacting on instinct, she seizes the iron poker, it's cool weight in her trembling hands. Summoning every ounce of strength she has left; she plunges it deep into his right leg.

"You bitch!" Quentin screams, letting her go.

He lunges towards her once more, his fingers barely holding onto her. With a swift motion, she swings the poker, the cold metal handle pressing against her sweaty palms. The force of her blow resonates through the room as she hits him across the face, a sickening thud echoing in his ear. His body crumples, collapsing onto the floor, facing downwards. Anger fuels her as she relentlessly strikes him on his back, the poker connecting with bone and muscle. A fierce cry escapes her lips, punctuating each punishing strike. "This is for Sandra," she yells.

Quentin can't move. He pleads, "Stop! Stop!"

"And this is for Ms. T." Another brutal swing follows. A momentary pause for Quentin as she catches her breath, her eyes fixed on the broken, disgusting man beneath her. "And this, my dear sociopath of a husband, is for all the torment you inflicted upon me." Quentin's body lies motionless, his feeble pleas for mercy falling on deaf ears. "Stop! Stop!" he continues to implore, his voice trembling with fear. Yet, Amaya's rage remains unquenched.

Amaya's adrenaline surges through her veins as she relentlessly unleashes her rage upon Quentin. Each swing of the iron poker carries with it a mix of fear, anger, and liberation. As she continues to beat him, Amaya's mind flashes back to the countless nights of emotional torment she endured at his hands. The years of manipulation, gaslighting, and psychological abuse fuel her determination to make him suffer as he made her suffer.

With each strike, she releases the pain that has consumed her for far too long. Her voice trembles with a combination of hatred and triumph as she screams, "I will never let you hurt me again! Your reign of terror is over!" Each strike of the poker serves as a cathartic release, a symbol of her reclaiming her power, mental health, and asserting her strength.

Amaya, feeling tired, stops and thinks about her baby. She looks at her tummy, rubbing her baby bump, and asks herself if her baby is okay. Concerned, she picks up the phone to call the police. Exhausted, she almost faints but catches herself. Just then, Josh bursts through the front door and quickly assesses the situation. He looks at Amaya and the trashed living room. "Are you okay?" Then, he rushes over to Quentin and checks for a pulse. Relieved to find Quentin still alive, Josh inquires, "What happened here?"

A distraught Amaya rushes into Josh's arms, tears streaming down her face as she desperately recounts the events of the night. She gestures towards her round belly, displaying her baby bump. "I'm pregnant, but tonight has cost me so much."

Josh guides her to the sofa. "Sit down. I'm calling 911 for you and Quentin. Stay here, I'll be right back. I'm going to the kitchen to get you some water." A relieved Amaya sits down on the sofa, looking away from Quentin's body sprawled on the floor. Josh comes back into the room. "I called 911," he says.

"What took you so long? And where's my water?"

Josh pulls a knife concealed behind his back. Amaya's words catch in her throat, speechless and terrified. "I can't believe this," she says, her words are barely audible. "You're involved in all of this? It was your plan, wasn't it?"

A bitter confession spills from Josh's lips. "Yes, it was. You never cared about the money. We did. Your grandparents didn't leave me anything. I was always by your side. I had to figure out a way to get what I deserve."

Desperation takes over Amaya as she reaches for a lifeline, snatching a picture of her and Josh from the wall. The frame is gold and solid in her grip, a tangible reminder of the love they'd shared as family. "Look at us," she pleads. "This isn't fake. We love each other, cousin. You do not have to do this. I will sign all of it over to you." But Josh remains resolute, unaffected by her words as he advances closer.

"We have cameras," she says, hope flickering within her. "You will not get away with this."

A sinister smirk appears on Josh's lips. "I was in the control room erasing the footage," he confesses, his voice chillingly calm. "And I disconnected the cameras, too. It will all look like a robbery gone wrong."

"Your mother would be so disappointed in you, J," Amaya cries, her voice trembling. But Josh's response leaves her stunned.

"Probably not as disappointed as she is that I shot her in 2019 and watched her bleed out on the kitchen floor. There, the mystery of my mother's murder is finally solved."

Shocked by his words, Amaya pinches herself repeatedly with one hand while clutching the picture of her and Josh in the other. "This has to be a bad dream," she says as she desperately tells herself, "Wake up, Amaya. Wake up."

"Mom knew too much by eavesdropping on Q's and my conversation. She overheard the plan and was going to tell you."

Amaya knows she must protect her baby and herself. Amaya slams the picture against the wall, shards of glass scattering across the floor like fragments of her shattered world. One jagged piece catches her eye. Without hesitation, she snatches it up, her grip tightening around the sharp edge.

She swings the glass towards him, but he swiftly kicks her, blocking her attack. The glass slips from her hand, clattering to the ground. Josh lunges at her with the knife held high towards her stomach. The world seems to slow down as she instinctively raises her hands, desperately shielding her unborn child from harm. The searing pain runs through her left hand as the knife mercilessly pierces her flesh. A scream tears from her throat, a desperate plea for help that echoes into the void.

Josh pulls the knife out of her hand. She's screaming for help. "No one can hear you," says Josh. He looks at her straight in the eyes and says, "I'm sorry." As the blade descends towards her heart, a deafening bang reverberates throughout the room. The knife slips from Josh's hand, falling to the floor. He collapses onto Amaya, his weight pressing down on her fragile form. With every ounce of strength she has left, she pushes him off, gasping for air.

Bree stands there, a guardian angel amidst the chaos, holding a smoking gun in her hand. Relief washes over Amaya as she looks into her friend's eyes, knowing that she is no longer alone and is safe. Darkness envelops her vision, and she succumbs to unconsciousness, the pain from her hand and mouth fading away.

With Amaya passed out on the floor, Bree runs over to her and dials 911, her voice steady as she calls for help. The nightmare is finally over. "I got you, friend," says Bree with unwavering loyalty.

Chapter Forty-Eight

Hospital Room 334

The night of fright has ended. Darkness giving way to the flickering fluorescent lights of Hardy General Hospital. The shrill sirens pierce the air as first responders urgently whisk Quentin, Josh, and Amaya inside. Bree accompanies Amaya, offering her comfort during this difficult time.

As they arrive, the hospital staff swiftly admits all three patients. Quentin's injuries are severe, demanding immediate surgical intervention. Two hours have passed. Bree remains steadfast by Amaya's side, patiently waiting for her to regain consciousness. Amaya, still groggy, stirs from her sleep, her hand tender and sore from the recent surgery.

In a surprising turn of events, two doctors enter Amaya's room, which is numbered 334. One doctor is Quentin's physician, while the other attends to Josh. Two police detectives accompany them. The doctors are asking the wives for verbal consent to discuss their husbands' injuries in front of both women to aid in the police interrogation.

Dr. Finn Drake, Quentin's doctor, carefully explains the extent of his injuries. "The loss of movement, lack of control over his bodily functions, and other symptoms indicate severe damage to his spinal cord. Our prognosis is that Quentin may spend the rest of his life in a wheelchair."

Dr. Tracy Britt, Josh's doctor, delivers a more hopeful update. "The bullet passed through his shoulder. After stitching him up and administering antibiotics, he will be ready for discharge by morning." The women express no emotions from the doctors' updates, and the doctors leave the room.

Filled with tension, the courageous Bree provides an account of the events that unfolded that night. Bree's voice trembles slightly as she bravely tells the detectives about Quentin's cold-blooded murder of Pamela Hester. Josh's mother's murder, Sandra's murder, and Ms. T.'s brutal attack are all pieces of a twisted puzzle, finally solved. The realization of the heinous crimes committed by Josh and Quentin, all for the sake of money, hangs heavy in the air, smelling like the foul odor of rotten eggs.

Bree's fear of her husband and Quentin is obvious. She takes a few deep breaths. Being mindful of her chest rising and falling in sync with her breathing, she requests protection for her family and Amaya. The police officer responds with a reassuring voice, explaining the protocol to keep them safe.

The police officer assures Bree they will lock away the two men responsible for the crimes for a long time, bringing a sense of ease to her troubled mind and providing a glimmer of hope for both women. Bree feels a wave of relief washing over her, as if someone has lifted the weight of the world from her shoulders. She exhales audibly in relief.

Amidst her relief, Bree's mind shifts to her young son, Lil J. She can't help but be concerned about how she will explain everything to him. With his innocent admiration for his father, the news will be shattering for him, further complicating an already challenging night. Deep down, Bree realizes it is time to come clean and confess her secret.

Agony twists Amaya's face as she squeezes her eyes and furrows her brows. A low, raspy moan escapes her lips as she tries to get comfortable.

"Can I get you something?" asks Bree.

"The throbbing in my hand is pretty uncomfortable. I don't want to use the nurse call button and have to wait. Do you mind asking the nurse if they can increase my pain medication?"

"I will do that now. Just lay back."

The nurse enters the room and administers more pain medication to Amaya. As a result, Amaya quickly drifts back to sleep. Bree remains by her side. She will reveal the secret she has been silently carrying for the past few years to Amaya once she wakes up. After forty-five minutes, Amaya wakes up from her sleep.

"Bree, you need to go home to your son. I will be fine."

"Girl, I'm not leaving you after all you've been through tonight. How is your hand?"

"Good. I want you to stay, anyway."

"You may not want me to stay after I confess this to you," says Bree while biting her bottom lip.

"You slept with, Q," says Amaya.

"Oh, hell, no! Honestly, as I think about it, I wish that was the secret."

"It's okay. Just tell me."

"There's two more unsolved deaths we need to talk about."

Amaya gives Bree a dazed look. "What are you talking about?"

Bree musters up the courage to tell her secret. "Amaya, I need to tell you something I love you, always have," she says, stammering, her voice quivering. Memories flood her mind as she continues, "Remember your eighteenth birthday? Your grandparents, Mr. and Mrs. Montgomery, wanted it to be unforgettable. They asked me to arrive an hour early and meet them to ensure everything was perfect for you."

As she speaks, the weight of guilt hangs heavy in her heart. Bree's voice cracks, her remorse evident. "I was driving and arguing with Josh on the phone when I ran a stop sign. The screeching of tires and the bone-chilling sound of my car colliding with another, pushing it into a light pole, scared the hell out of me. My car was drivable. Panic took hold of me, and I fled the scene, unaware of the tragic loss of lives." Bree's eyes welled up with tears as she continued, her voice choked with guilt. "It was only later that night that I learned, to my horror, that the car I hit... it belonged to your grandparents, Amaya. I took their lives, and I am deeply sorry."

"You're the one who killed my grandparents?" Amaya exclaims. "How on earth could you have kept that a secret? How have you lived with yourself all these years? I've always been here for you, Josh, and Lil J. Get out!"

"Amaya, please listen to the rest of the story," pleads Bree. "I promise, I will leave." Realizing that Bree would not leave, Amaya presses the nurse's button and calls for help. "I need help to remove a visitor from room 334, please."

Bree continues to share the rest of the story before the nurses arrive to ask her to leave the hospital room. "I didn't find out until later that evening. I couldn't make it to your birthday party because of the accident. My parents dealt with the car situation, but my dad insisted I keep quiet about it. However, my mother and I were determined to go to the police and share our side of the story. My dad wouldn't ..."

The nurse enters the room. "Ma'am, I need to ask you to leave so Mrs. Montgomery can get her rest."

Amaya tells the nurse, "It's okay. She can stay," said Amaya in a reluctant tone.

"Keep going. I have already lost so much tonight. What's one more friend to lose and another lie in my life?"

"Words cannot express how sorry I am that I hurt you. I know you will not believe this. Josh and I were arguing when I figured out Q killed Pamela Hester and he threaten to expose me if I exposed Q. Tonight, I knew it was time for me to turn myself in. I have lived a life of isolation, guilt, and believing I am a bad person because of what I did. I'll be turning myself in tomorrow morning."

"How did you end up at my house tonight?"

"I knew something was wrong as soon as he received that call. He paced the floor, talking to himself in agitation. I've never seen him behave like that, so I discreetly followed him. To my astonishment, my curiosity led me to your house. While standing outside for a few minutes, I heard you screaming. My heart raced with uncertainty, unaware of the events unfolding inside. I panicked and ran to Josh's car, grabbing his gun from the glove compartment. Fear consumed me as I rushed inside, my eyes widening in horror as I saw my husband getting ready to stab you. In that crucial moment, I had no choice but to act, pulling the trigger in defense. Tonight was the first time I've held a gun."

"I'm torn between forgiving you or slapping you with my good hand after hearing all of this."

"I understand. It's time for me to go. Thanks for hearing me out." Bree gets up to leave.

"Wait. I've seen your persistent low mood over the years. You've been living in a safe made prison. I think you have paid penance for the car crash that killed my grandparents. Bree, I forgive you. I can't allow you to be separated from your son. After tonight, I'm choosing to start my journey to healing rather than deal with all this mess. I don't understand how you could keep it a secret, but I'm choosing to forgive you."

"Josh made me keep this terrible secret. I had wanted to leave him a long time ago, but he held me hostage, and the worst part was when I was pregnant and you got us the apartment, I had considered turning myself in, but he convinced me not to and used it against me for years afterwards. That's why I was with him."

"It's time for us to cut away these toxic husbands and enjoy our children," says Amaya as she takes her unharmed hand to rub her baby bump.

"Yes, I'm with you," says Bree in a hopeful tone. "These men are out of our lives and will spend the rest of their 'hoeish' days looking over their shoulder in the shower. It's time to invite fresh energy into both of our lives. After all, we have a precious baby coming soon. I truly believe that joyful opportunities await us."

"Has the obstetrician seen me? I need to know if my baby is alright," says Amaya as she reaches for the nurse call button.

"The doctor came in while you were asleep. She said the baby's just fine. Oh, here." Bree picks up an envelope from the food tray table. "The doctor left this for you. Open it if you want to know the sex of the baby."

"Yes, yes! Give it to me." Amaya rips it open with her one good hand and her teeth gripping the edge of the envelope. "It's a boy!" says Amaya as she shed tears of joy.

"Congratulations! I'm truly happy for you," says Bree as she claps her hands softly grinning from ear to ear.

"I'm going to tell you a secret," says Amaya.

"You have a secret?"

"Yes, I do. This baby isn't Quentin's. I had a drunken tryst in Miami. I was worried I had contracted an STI from him. He didn't give me any diseases. What he gave me is growing in me, my little baby."

"Did you do a paternity test?"

"I was planning to until tonight when he revealed he had a vasectomy before we were married."

"Now, lay back and allow yourself some well-deserved rest. Don't worry, I'll stay by your side until you drift off to sleep."

Bree whispers to herself. *Mr. and Mrs. Montgomery, I finally made it up to you. I saved Amaya's life tonight.*

Chapter Forty-Nine

Amber

Amber's heart is brimming with joy as she arrives at Amaya's house, full of excitement. She is here to invite her daughter to her graduation from the drug court this afternoon. Overwhelmed with joy, Amaya tightly hugs her mother, feeling the warmth of their long overdue reunion. She tells Amber, "I'm proud of you, Mom. Granddad and Grandmother are looking down at you with admiration for what you've overcome in your life."

Amber's eyes widen in surprise as she catches sight of Amaya's growing belly. This is a sight she had only imagined through their phone conversations. "Amaya, I know you've been patiently waiting for this moment. I've been longing to share your pregnancy journey with you. You did the right thing in waiting until after I completed rehab and drug court to tell me."

"Can I touch my grandbaby?"

Amaya takes her hand and gently places it on her stomach. "I'm seven months now, mom. We're having my baby shower tomorrow. I want my mom by my side. Will you come? It will be here tomorrow at 3:00."

"You know I ain't going to miss my baby's baby shower," says Amber as she smiles and strokes Amaya's hair.

"Let's go to the kitchen and have breakfast. The new housekeeper, Paula, lives here and provided breakfast and dinner. She can never replace Sandra, but she has become a trusted confidant to me, and her culinary skills are simply exceptional. Paula's situation is similar to Sandra's when she came to live with Granddad and Grandmother all those years ago. Paula wasn't pregnant, though. Her parents kicked her out at seventeen because she's living her truth. I love her girlfriend. I hope to have a relationship like theirs one day."

"I still can't believe Josh and Quentin did all those terrible the things to you, just to get your money. Yeah, I know it's your money. I couldn't be trusted with all that money." Amber stands up from the kitchen table and yells, "My baby is a badass! She took down two men."

"Not my proudest moment. I was in fight, flight, or freeze mode. My instincts took over, and I fought my butt off to save me and my unborn son."

Amber asks Amaya how she feels about Quentin serving two life sentences and Josh serving twenty-five years in prison. Amaya explains they both pled guilty to reduce some of their time. Quentin is a cook in the kitchen in the prison and she's not sure what Josh is doing. They both are in the same prison. "They both used public defenders because I was not using a dime of my money for them. Bree cleaned out her and Josh's bank account. No dream team for them," says Amaya as she giggles and takes a sip of decaffeinated coffee.

"I can see them pretty boys with a public defender now. If I saw them, I would beat their asses for what they did to you."

Amber and Amaya laugh and talk until it's time to leave for the drug court. Amaya offers for her mother to ride with her. They arrive at the drug court for graduation. Amaya hugs Amber and says, "Finally, having a mother makes me happy." Amaya and Amber find a seat.

The court calls all the graduates to the front of the court. Judge Braswell says. "Graduation is an exciting day for me as well as the graduates. You all have worked hard in this program along with maintaining your part-time jobs. Okay, who's first?"

"Amber Montgomery, can you please come up?" asks the bailiff.

Amber walks up to the front and hugs Judge Braswell. "Thank you for this chance. I would be in prison if you didn't let me be in drug court. Judge, you know you were hard on me. I know that's what I needed. I have my daughter back in my life and I'm going to be a grand diva mama. Amaya, stand up. Let the judge see you."

Amaya stands up, and the judge says, "Your mother was 'something' in the beginning, but she has made 'something' out of her life. I think you are the inspiration for her. Thank you for being here today."

"I'm proud of my mom. Thank you, Judge Braswell, for all you and the court are doing to help people who struggle with substance dependence."

"Amber, I give you this medal as a token of your achievement in rehab and drug court. I don't want to see you back here. Live your life in a healthy and sober manner, and embrace your family."

"I will, Judge. Look everybody, I did it!" says Amber while holding up her medal.

Amber spends the rest of the day with Amaya. They go to a local baby boutique and spend hours browsing through adorable onesies, tiny socks, and cute little hats. Amber and Amaya can't help but squeal with excitement as they imagine the new baby wearing these adorable outfits. They also take their time picking out the perfect maternity outfit for the soon-to-be mom's baby shower.

In between shopping, they treat themselves to a delicious lunch at a cozy cafe, where they chat and laugh, eagerly discussing their favorite baby names and guessing what the baby's personality might be like. As the day draws to a close, they head back to Amaya's house, where they spend the evening decorating the living room with colorful balloons and streamers, ensuring that everything is perfect for the baby shower tomorrow. The anticipation and joy fill the air, and Amber can't wait to celebrate the upcoming arrival of her grandbaby.

Amber wakes up and goes downstairs, where she takes a moment to look around Amaya's home. Her eyes adjust to the room, absorbing the sight of the beautifully arranged furniture and family photos adorning the walls. "I can't mess this up," she whispers to herself, in the house's quietness. "I have to stay clean," she tells herself. With a heavy heart Amber says, "Mom, dad, and Larry, I'm sorry. I don't plan to go back to drugs. I'm a mother, and I refuse to miss out on being with my grandson. Are you all proud of me? Better late than never, right?"

Later, Amber helps Paula make the refreshments for the baby shower. They are in the kitchen, busily preparing a delicious spread of finger foods and beverages for the guests. Amber, with no cooking skills, allows Paula to take charge of the preparation, ensuring that everything is going smoothly.

Amber arranges the platters of appetizers, garnishing each one with a touch of elegance. As Paula feels a bit overwhelmed by her first large gathering, Amber quickly notices and tells Amaya that the housekeeper needs to take a break. Amaya understands and tells Paula to take a break, knowing that Amber has everything under control at this point. With Amber's help and reassuring words, the refreshments are sure to be a hit at the shower.

As people arrive, the first guest is Annie for the shower. Amber is delighted to see Annie and shares her rehab journey and how she's turning her life around. Annie responds, expressing her happiness with Amber's progress and mentioning that her mother would have been pleased.

Everyone is having a wonderful time. Bree talks to Amber about Josh and their divorce. Amber tells Bree this is some Lifetime movie stuff. Then Amber yells across the room, "Amaya!"

Amaya walks over to Amber and Bree. "Yes, mama?"

"You need to write a book."

"No way."

Amber looks at Bree. "Help me out. You know it would be a brilliant book about Quentin's betrayal, deception, and murder."

"Lawd, this is a first," says Bree, her nose wrinkling and her head tilting sideways. "I agree with Amber. I think your experience will provide understanding to ladies who find themselves trapped in the suffocating grip of gaslighting by their men."

"I'll think about it. Now, I'm ready to open my baby's gifts. Mama, come and help me."

Amber's hands tenderly pass each beautifully wrapped gift to her daughter, surrounded by thirty to forty women who are there to celebrate her daughter. The soft chatter of celebration blends with the sweet aroma of freshly baked treats. Amber basks in every aspect of the shower, feeling grateful for being able to share this special moment with Amaya. She gives her the next gift while leaning in to say, "I'm so thankful for doing this with you." Amber pulls her daughter into a warm embrace and whispers, "I love you."

Chapter Fifty

BREE

On this beautiful sunny day, not a cloud in the sky, Bree drops her son off at summer camp. As she drives away from the school, she starts a phone conversation with Amaya about the baby shower yesterday. Bree expresses her admiration for Amber's dedication to maintaining her sobriety.

She mentions that she's on her way to the estate lawyers because they have something for Josh, but since he's in prison, it defaults to her. Amaya remembers its Josh's thirtieth birthday today. Amaya suggests Bree call her after leaving the estate lawyer's office. Bree agrees to call Amaya after leaving the estate lawyer's office.

Bree arrives at the lawyer's office. Mr. Lloyd Crisp greets Bree.

"Please, have a seat," says Mr. Crisp.

"Thank you. I must admit, I was surprised when your partner, Jay Miller, reached out to me last week. I'm really curious to find out the reason for this visit."

Mr. Crisp retrieves the Montgomery's will. He reads aloud. "According to the will, Mrs. Wilson, the Montgomerys, left Joshua Wilson a sum of three million dollars to be received on his thirtieth birthday." The statement further states, "'Joshua, we love you and appreciate the positive influence you had on our granddaughter, Amaya. We are extremely proud of the person you are becoming, especially considering the challenges you have faced with your parents. We have always tried our best to support you, and we hope that this financial help will help you build the bright future you truly deserve.'"

Bree is crying, and through her tears, she shares, "Mrs. Montgomery was Josh's great aunt, but their side of the family was not well off. It was only recently that I learned about how terrible Josh's parents were to them from his brother Jeff. Now, I understand why Jeff continues to support his brother, even after he killed their own mother. The two brothers were estranged for many years; Jeff and his wife are the only ones there for him now. It's heartbreaking to see how someone who was once a good man can change. This is what I can explain to my son - that sometimes, people who haven't healed from their own pain end up hurting others."

Bree calls Amaya to give her the news that her grandparents have shown great generosity. Their kindness didn't shock Amaya. Bree then informs Amaya that she is on her way to the prison to visit Josh. She explains the warden is making a special exception for her to see him today.

Bree has just arrived at the prison. The cleanliness of the facility surprises her. This is her first time visiting her husband, and she's eager to share the news of his inheritance with him. As Josh enters the visitation room, a wide smile lights up his face as he sees his wife, whom he hasn't seen in months. He walks towards her, ready to embrace her, but she leans back in her chair, making it clear she doesn't want to be touched.

"Hey sweetheart. How's our son doing?"

"He's missing you."

"What about you?"

"I'm glad to be rid of you, J."

"It's my birthday and I'm sitting in prison with no support from my wife."

"Let me tell you why I came here today. I was at the Montgomery's lawyers earlier."

"Why were you there?"

"J, they left you three million dollars for you to receive on your thirtieth birthday."

"What?" asked Josh with his raised eyebrows.

"Yes, since you're incarcerated. I'm the executer for the next twenty-five years."

"If only I had known."

"Known what? You were going to get millions on your thirtieth birthday? Then you wouldn't have brutally murdered your mother or hatched that horrendous scheme to gaslight your cousin?"

Josh lowers his head. "Yes, I did this to myself. All for the sake of greed."

"Look where greed got you. You've lost your family, your freedom, and a wonderful best friend/cousin. Think about all of that and the money you lost out on because of your intense desire to be rich."

Bree rises from her chair, her eyes moving up and down at him with pursed lips. She walks towards the exit. Just before stepping out, she glances back, her eyes radiating triumph. "This is my first and last time visiting you. I am filing for divorce," she says in an assertive tone, then departs the visitor's room.

Chapter Fifty-One

Amaya

A year has flown by, and Amaya finds herself surrounded by the joy of motherhood with her ten-month-old son, LB. With a heart full of happiness, she invites her closest friends and her mother, Kathy, Annie, Bree, and Angelica - for a delightful girls' night dinner party on a Friday evening. As they gather around enjoying the soothing sound of soft music playing in the background, the mouthwatering dishes Paula prepared are enticing their senses.

Taking turns, the friends hold the baby, being charmed by LB's light brown eyes sparkling with innocence, his long eyelashes fluttering gently. The ladies run their fingers through his full head of hair. LB giggles and coos, basking in the love and attention from the ladies. Amaya watches them with a contented smile, cherishing this precious moment. The night unfolds with fun games, delectable food, and endless love poured upon the baby, creating an atmosphere of pure joy and affection.

The friends indulge in mouthwatering appetizers, savoring each bite with delight. Laughter fills the room as they reminisce about their shared memories and exchange stories of their own motherhood experiences. They take turns sharing parenting tips and advice, creating a supportive and nurturing environment.

Amber raises her mocktail glass. "Tonight is a beautiful celebration of friendship, motherhood, and the precious bond between my daughter and my grandson. Cheers everyone."

Angelica is curious, so she asks Amaya why the baby's nickname is LB when his actual name is Anthony Larry Montgomery. Amaya replies, "What do you hear me calling him all the time?"

"Little Baby," says Angelica.

Amaya explains, "LB stands for Little Baby. When he grows up, he can choose which name he wants to be called by."

Kathy walks up to Amaya and signals for her to stand up. Amaya sets her plate aside, curious about Kathy's intentions. "Hey ladies, what do you think about meeting here tomorrow morning at 7:00 a.m. for an early run? Is that alright with you, Amaya?"

"I would love to run with my girls. You know running, walking, or going for a jog helps depression, stress, and anxiety," says Amaya.

All the ladies agree and plan to meet there in the morning. Amber is looking sideways at Kathy. "I take offense to three words you said, 'early morning run.' How about we do early morning breakfast and we run to Target?"

Everyone laughs. "Mama, you can stay here tonight and watch LB for me in the morning."

"Now that I can do," says Amber.

"This is totally random, but have you thought about writing a book about your life? The stuff with Q alone could help other women," asks Bree.

"Gosh no. I could never put all my business out there like that."

"Amber, what do you think?" asks Bree.

"Baby girl, that's a good idea. I give you permission to put my past in the book. I'm proud of what I've overcome."

"Let me think about it. Okay, ladies, what's the next game you want to play?"

Chapter Fifty-Two

Amber

It's a Sunday morning. Amber is getting dressed at Amaya's home. LB is now seventeen-months old and sits on the floor looking at his grandma put her makeup on. Kathy has invited Bree, Amber, and Amaya to her church, Oak Creek Community Church. Amber is hesitant about going to any church. But she figures there isn't any harm to visit and get it over with.

Kathy arrives to pick up Amaya and Amber. Paula will watch LB. Amber opens the front door. "Good morning. Are you ready for church?" asks Kathy.

"I don't know. Maybe I should go next time. I don't want people looking at me and talking about me," says Amber as she picks up the baby.

Kathy, being an enthusiastic member of her church, shares more about it with Amber. She wanted to ensure that Amber won't feel judged or looked down upon by anyone in her church community.

Amber, let me tell you about my church. One thing I love about my church is how active the members engage in community service. We preach to children in juvenile detention centers, reach out to the homeless, and organize free community events right at the church.

I admire how the church prioritizes uplifting the youth. During Sunday services, Pastor Adam Cooper showcases the accomplishments of the junior members on the big screen. It's not just that Pastor Adam is a pastor, he is also a dedicated school counselor, which I find truly inspiring.

Oh, my goodness, I love how warm and welcoming Pastor Adam's wife, Ashley Cooper, is. People know Ashley for her warm and heartfelt hugs, which contribute to the welcoming atmosphere of the church.

The church members are incredibly friendly. From the moment you step in, they make you feel like you've known them for years. They truly embody the sense of community.

Another thing I appreciate about our pastor is how he encourages everyone to invite others to join the church. He often asks the question, 'Who's your one?' This is a reminder to reach out to someone and invite them to be a part of the church community. Today, he will ask me, 'Who's your three?' This shows the dedication to expanding their community and spreading the positive message of the church. No one will judge you. If you feel uncomfortable, we will leave.

"You promise?"

"I promise you. Also, I want you and Amaya to meet my friend Linda. Maybe we can sit with her. Linda is in charge of our mission and ministry teams. I love her commitment to our church and community."

As they arrive at the church, friendly greeters welcome them at the door. The atmosphere is warm as people gather around, introducing themselves. Amber immediately feels her spirits lifted, as she experiences a comforting sense of belonging. Soon, Pastor Adams delivers an inspiring message that deeply resonates with Amber. The sermon touches Amber's heart so profoundly that tears stream down her face as she walks down the aisle, ready to dedicate her life to Christ.

Overwhelmed by emotion, she opens up to the congregation, sharing her past struggles and proudly revealing her almost two-year sobriety. Filled with remorse, Amber offers a heartfelt apology to her daughter for the pain she has caused. In a gesture of solace and support, the pastor embraces her tightly. As Amber stands there, the pastor asks several women from the church to come down and pray with her. Amaya doesn't join the church, but she walks to her mother to support her.

Chapter Fifty-Three

Amaya

Amaya has written her story, aiming to shed light on gaslighting and share her journey of overcoming past traumas. As part of this journey, today the ladies are heading to the Cherri Lamb talk show to record an episode. Accompanying Amaya to the studio are her mother, Annie, and Bree.

"I can't believe we're about to meet Cherri Lamb. I know this is petty, but I'm sending a picture of Cherri and me to Quentin," says Amaya as she's adjusting her hair in the limousine's backseat and chuckling.

"I will buy the stamp," says Amber as she snaps her fingers and moves her head side to side.

"Girl, do it. He will be so jealous. He has always been in love with her," says Bree.

"I know, right? Remember, we used to tease him, saying I was his stand-in wife until he married her?" says Amaya.

"I'm so glad we can laugh about this now. It was so hard at first. Even Lil J is thriving. He said he doesn't want to see his father for what he did to Granny. I will let him decide when and if he wants a relationship with his father."

All three ladies hold hands. "We helped each other," says Amaya as she squeezes their hands.

"We here, we here," says Amber, jumping up and down in the backseat.

The driver gets out of the limo and opens the doors for the ladies. Amaya looks up with a gleam in her eyes. "I'm nervous, but I know I can do this. Therapy has helped me overcome so much. I'm finally able to talk in public and not feel like I'm about to pass out."

"Come on, let's get in there," says Bree.

"Give me a minute. I'm trying to take it all in. You know I love Cherri, too," says Amaya.

"You have been comparing yourself to Cherri for so long, wishing you had her outgoing personality and beauty. But I hope you know you are beautiful just the way you are, and you should never try to be someone else. You are just fine, my beautiful friend," said Bree.

As the ladies walk into the studio, they go through security. A staff person leads Amber and Amaya to the dressing room, while Bree takes her seat in the audience. In the dressing room, Cherri greets the ladies. Amber stands in place, unable to say a word, until she suddenly shouts out, "Cherri, me and you favor a little bit," while gesturing to her face. "Can't you see it?" she asks.

Cherri bursts into laughter and responds, "Maybe if I close one eye and squint out the other."

Amaya, trying hard to keep her composure, says, "It's nice to meet you, Ms. Lamb. Thank you for having us on." She can't help but feel the urge to shout even louder than Amber did.

"Call me Cherri, and I will see you two soon."

Amaya and Amber excitedly hold hands, bouncing up and down while silently yelling, "No way, we just met Cherri Lamb!" says Amaya.

"She is so down to earth. I never realized how we favor her so much," says Amber.

"Mama, come sit in the chair. The makeup artists are here to do our make-up."

After forty minutes, a staff person guides Amber and Amaya to the back of the stage, where Cherri is introducing them. The two ladies then walk out onto the stage. Amber takes Cherri's hand and dances with her as they make their way to their seats.

"Amaya and Amber, thank you for being here today," says Cherri.

"Thank you for asking us. This is so surreal," says Amaya.

"I want to congratulate you on your first book. *The Inheritance of Amaya Montgomery*. So tell us what inspired you to write a book about your life?" Cherri has a picture of the book on the teleprompter.

"Well, my mother and my friends encouraged me to write my story. It delves into the painful experiences of emotional abuse, gaslighting, and neglect that I endured as a child and then as a wife. My goal for this book is to bring both a source of hope and support for those who currently find themselves trapped in the same dysfunctional situation that I once experienced. I pray that anyone who reads my book will come to realize that they are not alone, and that there is help available to them."

"Let me tell you, when I read the character of your husband having a crush on me, I cringed. Like this man is the devil incarnate." Cherri looks at the audience and laughs. "If any of you read the book, you know what I'm talking about."

"It was not a good time in my life. I thought he loved me. I'm just glad it's all over," says Amaya.

"Amber, you've overcome living on the streets, substance abuse, and losing her long-term boyfriend. How has your life changed since leaving that life behind?"

Amber sits upright in her chair. "I knew it was time to change my life when me and my man were doing drugs and he overdosed. That was my wake-up call. I had a choice to go to prison or drug court. Drug court helped me rebuild my relationship with my daughter. I have a grandbaby. Oh, and look, I got some new teeth," says Amber as she smiles so big for the camera to see her new teeth.

Amaya gently touches her mother's leg. "Close your mouth, Mama," says Amaya in a low voice.

"Girl, leave Mama alone. She can show off those new pearly whites. Amber, may I ask how you feel about your abusive behavior towards Amaya being written in her book?"

"I told her to put it all in there. I was wrong. Being an addict, you don't realize how you hurt others around you. I'm good with it. It ain't no secret no more."

"I got to ask you. Did you keep the money or donate it to charity?"

"I did not keep the money for myself. Some of the inheritance was given to my mother. I divided the remaining between St. Jude's Hospital and the Trevor Project. Those are organizations my grandparents held dear to their hearts. I have ample resources. Because of their greed, I lost both my cousin and my husband, which is truly heartbreaking."

"How does it feel to be a mother?" asks Cherri, as she put a picture of LB on the screen.

"Oh, Cherri, that is my favorite picture."

"I know. You can thank your friend Bree for sending it to us. Where's Bree? Stand up, Bree." The camera moves to Bree. "Hey Cherri."

"It's amazing," says Amaya. "He came at the right time in my life."

"It was so much fun having you ladies visit us today. Thank you for making yourself vulnerable in order to help others. Good luck with Mama. I bet there's never a dull moment when she's around."

"No ma'am, it's not."

"Audience, please give a hand of applause for Amaya and her mother."

Amaya and Amber leave the stage to a standing ovation. As they make their way backstage, Amaya speaks with confidence. "Mama, this is only the beginning. Quentin and Josh may have tried to break me, but they showed me my resilience. Let's go home now. I can't wait to see what the next chapter holds."

ADDITIONAL CHAPTER

The flickering neon sign outside casts an eerie glow over the room, adding to the sense of unease that permeates the air. The peeling wallpaper and stained carpet only add to the seedy atmosphere, a place where his identity can remain hidden from prying eyes. He checks the locks on the door one more time, ensuring that no unwanted visitors can gain entry.

The man turns off his phone, removes its battery, and avoids using any electronic devices that will track him down. He relies on old-fashioned methods of communication, using burner phones and coded messages to stay in touch with his handler. The tension in the room is palpable as he waits for the crucial documents that will allow him to disappear completely, off the grid and beyond the reach of those who seek to find him.

Restless, he sits in a shabby hotel room, constantly looking out the window to ensure his location is secure. The burner phone rings. He picks it up after the second ring. "When are you giving me my new identity papers? I can't take staying another day in this lousy hotel room."

"I'll have your papers in a couple of days. That hotel is the safest place for you. Make sure you don't go out. Text me what you want me to Door Dash you for today and tomorrow."

The television is on for sound. He is not paying much attention to the tv. Looking up at the television, there's a beautiful baby on the screen. He turns the television sound up. The man on the phone is talking to him, reminding him of the importance of staying low.

"Hush! I'm trying to hear something." The baby on the screen looks just like his baby pictures.

"Change of plans. I'm going to Aurora, Illinois."

"Why in the hell would you want to go there?"

"I see an opportunity and my son."

"Your son?"

"It's a long drunken story for another time."

"They would never think to look for you there."

"I need to keep the first name, Tyler. Change the last name."

"I'm on it. Illinois? I just can't see you there. No more high stakes casino or exclusive clubs for you," the man said, laughing and teasing Tyler.

The men hang up.

Tyler sits on the bed, scratching from the prickly bed cover.

"I'm coming dear. We shall meet again. I think you're going to like it."

ACKNOWLEDGEMENTS

To be honest, I've never really read the acknowledgements at the back of the books. However, as a new author, I feel it's important to express my gratitude and acknowledge the individuals who played a vital role in bringing this book to you.

I want to extend a huge thank you to J. Rene Creative for their incredible work. If any of you were compelled to purchase the book based solely on its captivating cover, then J. Rene Creative did their thang! Not only did they excel in graphic design, but they also went above and beyond by offering valuable advice throughout the process.

I want to express my gratitude to Rosamaund Allen, who did an excellent job of providing valuable suggestions.

Last, but certainly not least, is my sister from another mister, LaTanya Bennett. She not only provided valuable assistance with marketing strategies, but also offered constant words of encouragement. LaTanya is not just a sister and

friend, but someone who truly understands all of
my quirks and loves me unconditionally.

About the Author
Geletta Shavers, LCSW

Geletta, a native of Little Rock, AR, has always been an avid reader with a wide range of interests in different genres; but her ultimate love lies in thrillers. Alongside her passion for reading, Geletta is also a dedicated social worker and licensed mental health therapist. She completed her master's degree in social work from the University of Arkansas at Little Rock in 2017. Being a mother of three children, aged 32, 22, and 11, she has always embraced her role as a caregiver. From a young age, Geletta discovered her passion for writing, even though she initially lacked the skills. However, the joy of crafting imaginative stories kept her motivated.

Geletta's debut novel, "The Inheritance of Amaya Montgomery," was written as a coping skill to help her heal from past traumas and manage current stress levels. As a therapist, she often encourages her clients to write themselves a happy ending to their own stories. Unfortunately, Geletta knows that she will never have the relationship or answers she needs from her mother, who is suffering from advanced vascular dementia. However, through writing her own happy ending, she has found the strength to move forward with her life and forgive her biological mother.

Even though this novel is loosely based on the author's life, Geletta wants to clarify that neither Carolyn Jackson nor Judge Williams had any substance abuse issues, nor did they neglect Geletta as a child.

For updates on events, book signings, new releases, and other information, please follow Geletta on the following social media platforms:

Instagram: author_geletta_123

YouTube: Geletta Shavers, LCSW

Facebook: https://www.facbook.com/profile.php?id=100077708583731

www.gelettashavers.com

If you enjoyed this psychological thriller, please leave a review on Amazon and Goodreads. Your reviews are helpful to authors. Thank you!

CHARITIES

St. Jude Children's Research Hospital and The Trevor Project are two charities that hold a special place in the author's heart. If you're interested in learning more about each charity or perhaps even making a donation, here are their respective website addresses.

https://give.thetrevorproject.org
https//www.stjude.org

Made in the USA
Columbia, SC
24 September 2024